BUHLEY SPARKS, THE GIFT

Bruce Flexer

authorHOUSE®

AuthorHouse™
1663 Liberty Drive, Suite 200
Bloomington, IN 47403
www.authorhouse.com
Phone: 1-800-839-8640

First published by AuthorHouse   4/9/2009

ISBN: 978-1-4389-5019-8 (sc)
ISBN: 978-1-4389-5020-4 (hc)

Printed in the United States of America
Bloomington, Indiana

This book is printed on acid-free paper.

Cover Illustration by Kevin Barry

This book is dedicated to the following people who have enriched my life.

To my wife Terri, who has put up with me and taken care of me for many years.

To my daughter Lindsey and son Jay who have never disappointed me.

To my mom and dad who gave me unconditional love in spite of my grade point average.

To my sister Fran, thank you for all the encouragement.

To my friends Nicky, Stroud, Big Ed, Forest, Moose, and Ben, thank you for all the hours of gut wrenching laughter.

CONTENTS

FOREWORD

Buhley Sparks, The Gift is exactly that to the reader, a gift. Its story is a prism of rich colors vibrant in content, characters and conclusions. Bruce Flexer has stroked a masterful collage of emotions, insights and life confluences that will leave readers enamored to the final chapter.

The Gift is about innocence, wisdom, expectations, disappointments, love, heartache, friendships, oppositions and much more. It is a book that intertwines impossible dreams and enduring commitments. Above all it is a book about the one of life's greatest gifts, the unbreachable love between a father and son regardless of the force or cause.

The Gift is etched in the traditional tapestry of the southern culture and situated in an era where the pace of life was serene and measured the cadence of a stroll up a grassy knoll.

Follow Buhley Sparks as he ventures down life's cluttered path to confront his destiny and ultimately find his purpose, his reason for living.

Nick Doster,
Lifelong friend of Bruce Flexer

Chapter 1

The year was 1957. Buhley Sparks stood with the flat of his back pressed against the warehouse door of Hawkins' grocery store. Every day on his way home from school, Buhley would stop by to see what he could swipe for an afternoon snack.

Buhley cut his eyes toward the back of the warehouse and spied a large, wooden basket filled with ripe, red apples. He thought for a moment as he planned his sneak attack and subsequent escape route. Moving like a stealth night shadow, he crept quickly to the basket of apples. Grabbing the largest one, Buhley turned, bolted out the door and calmly strolled down the back alley, proud of himself and savoring his ill-gotten prize.

Parley Hawkins, an eyewitness to the heist, had smiled as Buhley slyly maneuvered through his store to pluck the apple. Parley had a special affection for Buhley Sparks. Each afternoon, before school adjourned, he would display some sort of fruit or candy in the back of his warehouse in order to give Buhley an easy target for his after school snack. It greatly amused him to watch Buhley slip in and out, all the while thinking he was putting something over on old Mr. Parley.

Hawkins' grocery store was grand central station for the small town of Homerville, Georgia. Everyone gathered there to catch up on the town's gossip. The store was vintage southern. It had wide-planked wood floors, smoothed by years of boot and hard-soled shoe traffic. It was framed with big glass windows, and ceiling fans hung from the rafters. Coca-Cola memorabilia accented the otherwise drab decor. Parley would not allow Pepsi in his store. When questioned, his standard reply was, "I support Coca-Cola. It's a southern product."

Nate Hayes and Ferris Strum sat on the porch of the Hawkins store whenever the weather permitted. They constantly played checkers and talked with anyone who had time to talk. Nobody knew what they did for a living, but whatever it was, it wasn't work. Looking at Ferris, an observer could make two conclusions. Ferris was once a boxer and not a very good one. Not much was known about Nate except that Ferris and he were as inseparable as the red and black squares on the worn checkerboard over which they claimed undisputed squatters' rights.

Parley's store was the first in Homerville to have "piped in" music. A myriad of wires connected eight speakers to the dust laden Victrola record player. Country music legend Roy Acuff was a favorite of Parley's. All of his regular customers knew every word of Roy's hit song "The Wabash Cannonball."

Work was not a necessity for Parley. His family owned thousands of acres of prime timberland and had plenty of cash in the bank. He ran the store only to pass the time and to keep up with folks. Parley made it his business to know how people were doing. If someone was down on his luck and struggling financially, he would have him sign for his groceries. As soon as the fellow was out of sight, he would discretely dispose of the bill. Parley had a heart of gold. He and his wife had never been able to have children, much to their disappointment. To fill his childless void, Parley went about quietly helping those in need, especially Buhley Sparks.

Buhley had only taken a few bites from his apple when Revis Dane, the school bully, and several of his cronies stepped out from the shadows of the alleyway. A model of consistency, Revis was repeating the sixth grade for the second time. He was considerably bigger and stronger than Buhley. Revis and his buddies surrounded Buhley quicker than you could say Little Big Horn. Revis sneered as he spoke. "My sister says you been botherin' her. Is that so?"

Buhley answered with conviction, "I ain't bothered no one."

Revis continued, "She says you keep writing her notes and staring at her."

"I fancy her. She's the prettiest girl in my class," Buhley retorted.

"What do you know about being pretty? You're only in the fifth grade. If you promise me you will leave her be, I won't pound you!" said Revis emphatically.

Buhley craned his neck, and looking eye to eye with Revis, calmly replied, "I can't make that promise."

In one swift, powerful motion, Revis pushed Buhley to the ground. He pounced on the prostrate Buhley like a mountain lion on a lost sheep. Dust flew. Curses and groans punctuated the air as the two boys rolled on the ground in a flurry of punches. Unfortunately for Buhley, it was Revis who landed most of the punches. When Buhley was finally subdued, Revis applied one more punch to Buhley's face before rising to his feet. Buhley lay still. His clothes were tattered, and his face was swelling rapidly. Revis towered over Buhley and barked his final remark. "Bother her again, and you'll get some more of this."

Buhley remained motionless on the sandy dirt. Deep down Revis was hoping there would not be another fight. Although Revis was the victor this time, Buhley had not backed down at all. Revis felt blood trickle from his lower lip where Buhley had landed a quick punch. His face stung from other blows penetrated by the feisty Buhley Sparks. Buhley played dead like a possum as the gang of boys swaggered down the alley. Slowly, he got to his feet and made his way to his half eaten apple. In one fluid motion, he picked it up in his left hand and hurled a perfect strike that hit Revis squarely in the back of his head some twenty paces away.

The apple exploded off Revis' head and splattered onto the face of one of the boys walking beside him. When Revis turned around, Buhley was gone. As Buhley took a short cut home, he contemplated his skirmish with Revis. He had survived and would live to tell the story. Buhley preferred to avoid fights, but when fighting was inevitable, he was a ready participant. His growing liking for girls would probably get him in more trouble over the next few years. He smiled to himself as he recounted the direct hit of the apple on his new nemesis, Revis Dane. Buhley knew he had gotten the worst end of the fracas, but somehow he could not help but think that he had earned the respect of the sixth grade wonder.

August Sparks was tending the field when he caught the eye of Buhley coming up the dirt road. "Go on in the house. Your mamma's not feeling well," he said curtly.

"Yes, sir," replied Buhley.

August Sparks was a man of few words. He was sixty-two years old and hardened by decades of backbreaking work and poor decisions. Buhley was born when he was fifty-two, and needless to say, was a complete surprise. He loved Buhley dearly, but had never told him. August had gone to college to be a pharmacist. His dreams were derailed when his father died, and the money ran out. He farmed a ten-acre tract of land for over forty-five years and had little to show for his arduous efforts. A bad back, sun-baked skin and calloused hands constantly reminded him of his long lost dreams. August, however, was not short of hard work. He rose before sunrise and quit well beyond nightfall. Gambling had plagued him when he was younger and had sent him into a debt spiral from which he had never recovered.

Buhley walked in the house. The screen door slammed behind him, and the sound of wood slapping against wood reverberated throughout the small farmhouse. "Buhley, is that you?" a faint voice called out from the bedroom just off the kitchen.

"Yes, ma'am," Buhley replied.

Ranna Sparks was small in stature but large in spirit. Raised by devout Baptist parents in the backwoods of South Georgia, Ranna's most treasured priorities were her church and her family. After earning a teaching degree from the Women's College of Georgia, she taught for many years in the Homerville elementary school until Buhley was born. She was forty-eight when Buhley Sparks entered the world. He was their only child after several heartbreaking miscarriages.

The delivery had been a difficult one, and Ranna had almost died in the process. A decade later, Ranna still felt the lingering effects of Buhley's birth. Many days she would lie in bed with no energy or appetite. Ranna's iron deficient blood kept her from doing many of the things she loved. But there was one thing that no health condition could prevent her from doing, and that was going to church services. No matter her health and no matter the weather, Ranna Sparks would be in attendance every Sunday morning and night and every Wednesday night as well. Because Ranna never learned to drive, she depended on August to drive her to the services. If August was unavailable, she walked. "We're going to eat Wednesday night supper at the church tonight, Buhley," Ranna called out.

"Yes, Mamma," Buhley replied.

August pulled up to the First Baptist Church of Homerville. His truck had seen its better days. It sputtered and shook as he eased it into the church parking lot. Ranna and Buhley waved goodbye as they got out and made their way to the church fellowship hall. August accelerated, and the truck lurched out onto the highway with a concoction of oily smoke billowing out of the exhaust pipe. He would be back in an hour and a half to take Ranna and Buhley home.

Crawford Jones, a close friend since first grade, yelled, "Hey, Buhley, come eat with me."

Buhley immediately ran to sit next to him. Crawford's nickname was Crawdad. He and Buhley were joined at the hip when it came to most things. Crawdad's father was the preacher of First Baptist, but that did not keep Buhley and Crawdad from routinely skipping prayer meeting to go outside and throw.

"You got a ball?" asked Buhley.

"I sure do!" Crawdad replied with enthusiasm.

"We ain't got much daylight left," Buhley pointed out.

"Yeah, we're gonna have to sneak out earlier if we want to get our throwin' done," Crawdad echoed.

Pastor Jones led in prayer as all reverently bowed their heads. The two boys gave each other the nod, and slipped outside.

"Best out of ten," Crawdad said gleefully.

"You go first," said Buhley as they headed to their favorite spot.

They hopped over the wooden rail fence at the back of the church property. Just behind it stood a makeshift shed where the pastor kept the lawn equipment.

Buhley retrieved the rusted coffee can from the shed that sat next to the faded green John Deere tractor. He placed the empty can on the middle fence post while Crawdad paced off forty-six feet. Crawdad took his windup and let fly. The ball went whizzing by the can and plunked into the shed's back wall.

"0 for one!" shouted Buhley.

Crawdad repeated his windup. Again and again he missed the tin target. On his seventh toss, the ball barely ticked the can. It wobbled to the edge and tumbled to the ground. Three throws and three misses later, Crawdad, exasperated, handed the ball to Buhley who was already focused on the challenge that was before him. "Your turn, Buhley," Crawdad dejectedly mumbled.

Buhley walked out to a bare patch of grass they imagined to be a mound. He took the ball in his left hand and cupped it behind his back. After pretending to get his signal from a catcher, Buhley began what looked like a classic major league windup. He let the ball fly with a perfect fluid motion. The ball sailed through the air and slammed into the middle of the coffee can with such force that both the can and the ball violently ricocheted off the wall of the shed. "One for one," an impressed Crawdad shouted.

With the ease of a fat man taking a nap, Buhley threw the ball nine more times without a miss. Each time the ball obliterated the can. It remained on the ground more flat than round. "Ten for ten! An all time record! I can't believe you did that! How'd you do it?" Crawdad squealed with astonishment.

"I don't know. It just comes easy. I've always been able to throw. It comes as natural as breathin'. I don't know how I do it. I just do it," Buhley softly answered.

CHAPTER 2

Saturday morning brought sunshine and hot, humid weather. Crawdad pressed his nose against the screen door and yelled inside for Buhley. He lingered there as his nostrils filled with the smell of freshly cooked bacon, sausage, and eggs.

"Come on in Crawford," Ranna called out. "Have a seat and eat some breakfast."

"No, thank you. I've already eaten," he said with a pleasant smile. Turning eager eyes on Buhley, he said, "Let's go to the swimmin' hole."

Ranna spun around like a mother hen protecting her chicks. "You wait an hour until you go swimming, or you both will cramp up and drown!" Ranna proclaimed with authority. "Remember Sampson White? He went in the water too soon after eating and sunk like a rock from cramping. They found his body two days later. I won't let that happen to either of you!"

August rarely spoke. When he did, his comments were laced with sarcastic humor. "Sampson White couldn't swim," he smugly declared.

Ranna cut him a look that implied he had said enough on the subject. August shifted his eyes downward and kept eating his breakfast.

Exactly one hour later, around ten o' clock, Ranna allowed the boys to take off to the swimming hole. If either one of them drowned, it would not be because they had broken her time-honored digestive rules. She knew she was right regardless of what August thought.

The swimming hole was formerly a borrow pit that the railroad had dug when they laid the northerly tract that ran parallel to the back of the Sparks' farm. Both boys wore cutoff blue jean shorts. The swimming hole was no place for shirts and shoes. Buhley and Crawdad enjoyed walking in the recently plowed field. The sun burned with greater intensity as it rose in the cloudless sky. The black, moist dirt massaged and refreshed their feet as they walked between the furrowed rows.

Buhley and Crawdad scaled the fence that separated the Sparks' farm from the neighboring farms. They hopped on the well-worn path they had trekked across many times before on the way to the swimming hole. "I'll race ya!" screeched Crawdad.

"You're on," exclaimed Buhley.

And off they went. Crawdad was faster than Buhley and quickly had a big lead. Suddenly, Crawdad stopped dead in his tracks. Buhley came to a halt ten yards behind him and saw why Crawdad was frozen like a statue. Less than three feet up the path from Crawdad, a six-foot diamondback rattlesnake was coiled and poised to strike. Crawdad's eyes were as large as two moon pie sandwiches. What little life he had lived now flashed before him. The menacing noise of the snake's rattles flushed a covey of quail from the nearby brush.

Buhley was close enough to Crawdad to understand the severity of the situation and far enough away to do something about it. In a soft, reassuring whisper, Buhley said, "Don't move Crawdad."

Next to Buhley's foot was a stone the size of a golf ball. Buhley inched his torso toward the rock while keeping one eye on Crawdad and the other on the snake. As soon as he had the stone in his grasp, he locked his eyes on the head of the snake, and with a sharp snap of his wrist, he launched his weapon.

The stone projectile zipped through the air, and in an instant, blasted into the forehead of the imposing reptile. The snake's head snapped to the side, and it fell dead to the ground in a twisted heap. Likewise, Crawdad collapsed in a dead faint. Buhley dragged him away from the slain snake and got Crawdad to regain consciousness by lightly slapping him in the face.

Parley Hawkins swore he had never seen a bigger rattler. Ferris Strum said he had. No one believed him. The diamondback was stretched out in front of Hawkins' grocery, and it measured six feet and one inch from the tip of its nose to the end of its last rattle. Nate Hayes, the reigning village idiot, kept asking, "Is it really dead? Is it really dead?"

Doris Prittchet had her husband, Ihley, in tow as they approached the growing crowd of onlookers. Ihley might as well have been a dog because everywhere Doris went, he followed. Some viewed Doris Prittchet as a high society debutante because she insisted on serving iced tea on doilies whether in her dining room or kitchen. Her sofa and chairs were adorned with the finest linen antimacassars available through the Sears catalogue, giving further evidence of her superior cultural sensitivities.

Everyone felt sorry for Ihley Prittchet. If anyone was henpecked, it was poor Ihley. To make matters worse, Ihley had a wandering eye. His right eye functioned normally, but his left eye moved in an uncontrolled pattern like a space probe spun out of its orbit. His condition made it difficult to determine exactly to whom Ihley was talking. The oscillating peeper, much to his dismay, was a source of constant aggravation to both Doris and him. She frequently accused him of staring at other women. His earnest declarations of innocence fell on deaf ears.

"Ihley, you ever seen a rattler that big?" asked Parley.

Before he could draw a breath to answer, Doris, as was her custom and assumed divine calling, butted in saying, "Of course he hasn't. You know he can't go in the woods because he breaks out in hives. What are you trying to do, Parley, run all your customers off with that disgusting snake?"

Parley did not reply but thought to himself, "No, Doris, just you."

He turned to Buhley and Crawdad and asked, "Now tell me, boys, how this happened."

Crawdad spoke rapidly. "Mr. Parley, you wouldn't believe it. We was racin' on the path to the swimmin' hole. I was out front, and as I come 'round a corner, I ran right up on the rattler, coiled and ready to strike. I stopped 'bout three feet from the snake. Buhley was a ways back. My heart was 'bout to pound out of my chest. Buhley told me to stay put. Then I heard somethin' whiz by me. I saw the snake reel back like it was fixin' to strike. That's when I fell out. When I came to, the rattler was dead, and here we are."

Parley asked with interest, "Who killed the snake?"

"Buhley did! He threw a rock and hit that snake square in the head!" Crawdad said admiringly.

With both eyebrows almost touching his hairline, Parley exclaimed, "You mean to tell me Buhley threw a rock and killed the snake?"

"Yes, sir. Ain't that right, Buhley?" Crawdad proudly stated.

"Yes, sir. That's how it happened," Buhley calmly replied.

"Heck, Mr. Parley, Buhley could knock a fly off a cow's tail at thirty yards!" interjected Crawdad confidently.

"Well, you two have had some kind of morning, haven't you? Why don't you go in the store and have a Coca-Cola on me," Parley volunteered as he patted the boys' heads.

"Yesiree!" they yelped in unison.

"One more thing. I know a taxidermist over in Waycross. I'll have him skin the snake and mount it as a trophy for you boys," Parley offered enthusiastically.

"A-okay by us. Thank you, Mr. Parley!" they called out as they scampered away to indulge in their free sodas.

Parley walked into his store mumbling under his breath, "He threw a rock and killed the snake. If that don't beat all."

Parley made his way to the counter and stood behind it as he watched Doris Prittchet order Ihley to get sundry grocery items as she checked her list and slowly pushed the cart down the aisle. Doris was a good four inches taller than her husband and outweighed him by some sixty pounds. She had been known to slap Ihley hard across the face when she thought he might be looking at another woman. The befuddled Ihley would tamely take her abuse while silently cursing his twirling orb.

"You need any help finding anything, Ihley?" Parley shouted,

As Ihley looked up to answer, Doris interrupted as if on cue, saying, "Parley Hawkins! You know Ihley's been comin' in this store for over twenty years. If he don't know where something is by now, then he's a bigger fool than I thought."

Parley peered at Ihley as he placed a five-pound bag of Dixie Crystals sugar in the cart with his back turned to Doris. Parley broke into a broad grin as he deciphered Ihley's private conversation with himself. "One of these days, Doris. One of these days," muttered the beleaguered man.

Like many others in Homerville, Parley hoped he would be present when Doris Prittchet's day of reckoning came. Perhaps he would refer Ihley to the taxidermist in Waycross. Watching her as she walked out of the store with Ihley right on her heels, Parley chuckled at the thought of a permanently stuffed Doris.

Buhley walked up the dirt road to his plain white, framed house. It had a tin roof and a front porch with uneven floorboards that were painted dark green. The railing of the porch was virtually hidden by the sweet smelling honeysuckle vine that intertwined it. August had finished his work for the day and was enjoying the relaxing sway of a rocker as well as a big chaw of Beechnut chewing tobacco. His brown-stained teeth confirmed that he was a frequent and long-time Beechnut user. August had cut a sizeable hole in the porch deck to accommodate the disposal of his tobacco juice. The boards framing the hole were splattered from drips and misses.

Buhley pulled a chair up and began rocking in sequence with his father. After a few moments of silence, Buhley's head began to nod. "I heard you killed a rattlesnake today," commented August.

"Yes, sir," a startled Buhley replied.

"Best not let your mamma know, or you won't see that swimmin' hole for a time," advised August.

"Yes, sir," answered Buhley.

August and Buhley closed their eyes and continued to rock in rhythm as the late afternoon breeze blew softly across the porch. Soon they were both asleep.

Wilma Jones hugged her son, Crawford, as she never had before. She was grateful he was alive after hearing the tale of his harrowing snake encounter. "Mamma, he was that close to me," Crawdad said as he stretched his arms.

Pastor Jones lifted a fervent prayer of gratitude for Crawdad's rescue from "that evil serpent," during grace before supper. "Daddy, Buhley threw a rock and killed the snake," said Crawford.

"Buhley Sparks threw a rock and killed the snake?" replied Pastor Jones in amazement.

"Yes, sir." said Crawford, "If'n he had'na hit it, he'd a bitten me for sure," said Crawford.

Pastor Jones thought for a moment how hard it must have been for Buhley to hit the snake in the precise spot with a rock. He shook his head and said, "That's amazing. Pass the biscuits, please."

Ranna opened the screen door as far as it could go and stretched the spring to the breaking point and then let go. The door flew around and slammed into the door jam. It sounded like a bomb exploding. Both August and Buhley were startled from their sleep and jumped out of their rockers. Ranna laughed until her stomach hurt. August and Buhley were steaming mad until they got a whiff of the creamed corn simmering on the stove and the fried chicken already on the table. "Ya'll gonna sleep or eat? Supper's getting cold," said Ranna as she walked back in the house.

Both August and Buhley hurried in and washed up. As they sat around the table, Ranna asked August to ask blessing over the food. With one eye closed and the other on a drumstick, August bowed his head and said, "Lord, thank you for this food, and we could use a little rain. Amen."

Sunday morning found Ranna in her regular pew. Buhley and Crawdad sat on the back row. The church was full because Pastor Jones could sure preach a sermon. This Sunday he was preaching on temptation. Amens were flying all over the place, and everyone was listening except for Buhley and Wadeus Wadkins.

Buhley had his own battle with temptation. Cheryl Dane was sitting in eyeshot of him, and he was fixed on her. She had on his favorite dress. Buhley was trying to figure out a way to kiss her without getting slapped or once again being beaten up by her brother Revis. Wadeus Wadkins was asleep. Every church has a church sleeper. Wadeus Wadkins was Homerville First Baptist Church's sleeper. He was the best church sleeper anyone had ever seen. He was a portly man and didn't have much of a neck. He could rest his chin directly on his chest, so his head never moved. He didn't snore, and he always woke up in time for the last hymn. Pastor Jones didn't mind because he knew Wadeus worked the graveyard shift at the saw mill. He was just glad to see him in church. Doris Pritchett was in her usual seat. She was listening to the sermon but every now and then would cut her eyes on Ihley to make sure he wasn't eyeing another woman.

Outside after the service, Parley cornered Ranna Sparks and Wilma Jones. "Ladies, I've got some tickets to the Jacksonville minor league baseball team, and I know two boys who would love to go," said Parley.

They agreed. Both Buhley and Crawdad were excited to be going to their first real baseball game. Homerville was so small that it didn't offer organized baseball. Nearby Travisville did, but Buhley and Crawdad never signed up. Although they played a lot, they had never participated in or seen an organized baseball game. Parley honked the horn, and out of the house bolted Buhley with Ranna close behind.

"Parley, what time will you be back?" asked Ranna.

"Now, Ranna, don't you worry about a thing. We'll be back when we get here."

He eased the car into reverse and slowly backed up. Crawdad was already in the back seat, and both boys waved as they started on to the highway headed towards Jacksonville. Ranna walked back into the house, wondering if she had made a good decision.

Parley Hawkins had plenty of money but never flaunted it. One thing he did enjoy was a nice car. Every year he would trade for a brand new Cadillac. Both Buhley and Crawdad were used to older model vehicles that found and accentuated every bump in the road. They hadn't gotten down the road very far when Crawdad said, "Mr. Parley, this car's nicer than our living room."

Buhley agreed. The highway from Homerville to Jacksonville was a winding two-lane road with lots of oak trees that hung over both sides forming a canopy. Buhley and Crawdad hung their heads out of the windows like dogs and let the cool air provided by the shade of the oaks run over their faces and through their hair. Parley pulled off the road at State Line Cafe and asked, "Who wants an ice cream?"

Three car doors opened and closed and Parley and the boys entered the restaurant. Up to the counter and on three stools, they sat. "Three of the biggest vanilla ice cream cones you got, nice lady," Parley said.

The boys couldn't take their eyes off of the waitress's arms. They were huge, and they waddled all around every time she made a move. They wondered to themselves how she got her uniform on and especially how she got it off. She delivered the ice cream cones with flab a-flailing. Parley thanked her, and thinking about his brand new Cadillac, said, "Boys, let's eat 'um right here."

Back in the car and on down the road they drove. They arrived at Jacksonville Stadium about thirty minutes before game time. The Jacksonville Tidal Wave was playing the Birmingham Hammers. With a series win, the Jacksonville Tidal Wave had a chance to become the division leader. The parking lot was full. The stadium held about six thousand, and on this night, every seat would be filled. As soon as they exited the car, their noses were filled with the smell of freshly popped popcorn. They could hear the faint sound of "cold drinks" become louder as every fast-paced step brought them closer to the ballpark. The ticket taker tore the three tickets in half, and Parley, Buhley and Crawdad made their way through the oil-deprived turnstile. Buhley Sparks was filled with excitement, and his senses told him that he was about to experience something magnificent. It was all he could do to not break out into a run. He had listened to ball games on the radio hosted by great play-by-play men who painted wonderful pictures.

In Buhley's mind, the smell of the ballpark made the whole trip worthwhile. With great anticipation, they ascended the ramp way leading to the opening of the stadium. When they reached sight of the field, Buhley stopped. Never in his years on earth had he seen a more beautiful sight than the brown clay of the infield against the green grass, the white chalk lines that showed the perfect symmetry of the field, and the pitcher's mound out there all by itself, calling the combatants to battle. The fence was decorated with signs of businesses that supported the Tidal Wave. Then he heard a sudden pop. He looked to his left to see the Tidal Wave's starting pitcher warming up in the bullpen. With effortless ease, the right-hander popped the catcher's mitt -- the ball seemingly a magnet to wherever the catcher set his target. Some of the opposing team players were playing pepper down the right field line. The crack of the ball against the bat assured Buhley that he was in the right place at the right time.

Parley ushered them to their seats, and directly the two managers and umpires went over the ground rules at home plate. As the managers headed back to the dugouts, a loud voice came over the PA system. "Ladies and gentlemen, the Jacksonville Tidal Wave."

With that, the players bolted from the dugout and ran to their positions, the stands erupting in applause. The pitcher walked out of the dugout, crossed a well-manicured infield, and took his place on the mound to begin his warm up tosses. Soon the umpire yelled, "Play ball!"

Buhley Sparks had not blinked his eyes yet. He drank in every ball the infielders fielded, the way the outfielders gracefully ran down every fly ball. Even the minute aspects of the game caught Buhley's attention. He was intrigued with the signs given by the third base coach, with the way the managers paced back and forth in the dugouts, with the way the umpire called balls and strikes in deliberate fashion.

The game was a pitcher's duel. The score was nothing-to-nothing in the bottom of the ninth when Armstrong Kay belted an inside fastball over the 320-foot sign in left field. The home run sent the fans into a standing ovation that did not end until Armstrong came back out of the dugout and tipped his cap. The fans slowly started towards the exits, and Parley herded the boys in the direction of the car. Crawdad immediately went to sleep. Buhley just sat in the car going over every detail of what he had just seen. Parley noticed Buhley was wide-eyed and asked, "How'd you like the game, Buhley?"

"Mr. Parley, that's the most fun I've ever had," replied Buhley.

Parley recognized Buhley was deep in thought and said softly, "I'm glad, son. I'm real glad."

Ranna sat out on the front porch in a rocking chair, swaying back and forth. Every time she saw headlights, she would bow up out of the rocker in hopes that the car would slow down and turn into her driveway. August was sound asleep in bed. The rooster crowed early for him, and he figured if Ranna needed him, she knew where he was. Parley pulled into the driveway at about 11:30 p.m. Ranna made a fast walk off the porch to the car. She hugged Buhley as if he had been off to war and was home on furlough. She thanked Parley for carrying Buhley to the game and returning him safely. After a quick bath, Buhley went straight to bed. July nights in Homerville were like an oven, and he lay in bed sweating profusely. He had an oscillating fan fixed where it rotated exactly the length of his body. The air would blow up from his toes to the top of his head and back down. He lay there thinking about the game. Soon the blowing air and the hum of the motor eased him into a deep slumber.

CHAPTER 3

56 Johnson stood behind the bar in Clips, a beer joint on the county line. It was a typical South Georgia beer joint a white block building with no windows, a red door and the words "Free Beer Tomorrow" painted in bold letters on one side of the building. 56 wore a waist apron designed to hide his gut accumulated from a life of consuming peanuts and cold beer. His clientele consisted mostly of sawmill workers from all shifts. There were no clocks on the wall. You never knew if it was one o'clock in the afternoon or one o'clock in the morning. Friday night fights were never scheduled but almost always occurred. Clips had a few tables scattered around a pool table in the corner. It wasn't much, but it was enough to draw a crowd on most nights.

56 got his name from his dad. His dad sired him when he was fifty-six years old, and he was proud. He named his son 56 Johnson to remind him and everyone else that at fifty-six years of age, he still had it. 56's dad had been a moon shiner and whiskey runner in the prohibition days. He had a still in the woods and ran the moonshine at night. He spent most of his days staying one step ahead of the revenuers. Making lots of money, he buried shoeboxes full of it all over the county. Only 56 knew where the money was buried. When business was slow or a need came up, 56 would creep out at night and dig up a shoebox and get himself "well" for a while.

Benny Armstrong glared at the man who had just told him he would pay him next payday. "If you can't pay, don't play," said Benny.

Benny Armstrong was a twenty-five-year-old saw mill worker who padded his income playing pool. He was mid height with Popeye-like forearms and a quick temper. He was a baseball-catching prospect who had signed a scholarship to play at the University of Georgia but got kicked off the team for fighting. He let everybody know he liked three things: cold beer, fistfights and big-breasted women.

"Hey, 56, get a load of that guy. I oughta take him out back and get my money's worth," said Benny.

"He ain't from around here," 56 replied. "I seen his eyes when you were talking to him. I 'spect he'll be back with your money shortly."

Buhley finished his breakfast and headed out to the barn. He searched through all the stuff August had collected and stored there. He looked around old plows, bags of feed and other such things until he found an old bucket of red paint his daddy used to repair the rust on his tractor. Walking to the broad side of the barn, he stood next to the wall and marked off a knee to belt high strike zone. He painted a small red square in the middle of his measured strike zone. After stepping off the required measurement for the pitching mound, he dug his heel into the dirt to mark the spot. Not waiting for the paint to dry, he began throwing pitch after pitch. The ball, dotted with red paint, bounced off the wall, and Buhley acted as an infielder and fielded each grounder. August made a slow walk in from the field to get a cool drink of water. He stopped to watch Buhley. "What's that game gonna get you?" asked August.

"What do you mean, Daddy?" asked Buhley.

"I mean, son, sooner or later you're gonna have to decide what you're gonna do with your life, and it's gotta be something that will put food on your table. Chunking a ball ain't exactly what most people do for a living." August was still bitter at the opportunities he had let slip by, and he occasionally took his frustrations out on others. "One folk then another been telling me how you can chunk. Let me see for myself."

Buhley dug in, wound up and let fly with a fast ball that hit dead center in the middle of the board and left an impression even August could see. He threw another that hit the exact spot. August's eyebrows rose just a little bit.

"Buhley, maybe we ought to sign you up for baseball over in Travisville. It's too late this summer but maybe next year."

August walked over to the water spigot and turned it on. He kept watching Buhley throw as he waited for the warm water to turn cool. He knelt down and took a sip. Throwing his hat off, he stuck his head under the faucet and let the water run over his head and down his neck. Grabbing his hat, he turned off the faucet and started a slow walk back to the field, occasionally cutting his eyes over to his boy. Buhley continued to throw, only now with a smile because his dad had shown an interest.

Benny Armstrong walked into Clips and headed straight for the bar. "56, give me the coldest Pabst Blue Ribbon you got," said Benny.

56 reached down in his apron and threw a tightly wound wad of money to Benny. "That fella came back in here and paid you. He said you was the best pool player he'd ever saw. I told him you could fight better than you could play pool. He got on outta here pretty quick."

Benny sucked down half that beer, and 56 asked, "What happened at Georgia with you and that baseball scholarship?"

"I got kicked out for fighting," replied Benny.

"I know," said 56, "but tell me the story."

"Give me another beer on the house, and I'll tell you."

56 popped the top of another Pabst Blue Ribbon and leaned on the bar in such a way as to take the weight of his gut off of his legs for just a little while.

Benny started. "I got a baseball scholarship to the University of Georgia to play catcher. There was another boy up there from Macon whose daddy had money, and he threw a lot of it at the school. He couldn't do nothing better than me. Hit, catch, throw, nothing. He knew I was better than him, but he played a lot because of his dad's money. He resented me, and one night, he called me a hayseed plowboy, and I whipped his ass. They told me, 'One more time, and you're gone.'"

"So what happened?" asked 56.

Benny continued. "So there we was playing South Carolina, and the first time up, I hit a gapper in the left center for a double. The next time up, the catcher says to me, 'Hey, Stubby, you ain't shit. The first time you saw a fastball. This time you're gonna feel one.' The next pitch hit me right in the rib cage. I got mad as a hornet. I was so mad I didn't even go down. I just stood there. I heard the catcher laugh, and without even looking, I mule-kicked him in the right shoulder with my steel cleats, and he went down. I took off after the pitcher and jumped him and hit him as many times as I could in the face and arm before they could pull me off. The next thing I know, I'm on the side of the road hitchhiking back home. Then I heard the saw mill was hiring in Homerville, and here I am."

56 said, " I bet that pitcher never threw at anybody again."

"I know he didn't," said Benny. "I broke his arm, and he never pitched again."

"Do you ever miss the game?" asked 56.

"Only every day, 56," replied Benny. "Sometimes I'll be somewhere, and I'll get a whiff of a certain smell, and it will remind me of baseball, and all the memories will come flooding back. It's a great game, 56, a great game." He gulped down the last of his beer and walked over to the pool table to check out the action.

Buhley pulled up a rocking chair beside August where he rocked every evening before supper. Just then Buhley saw Cheryl Dane walk by out on the road. "Hey, Cheryl," yelled Buhley.

"Hey, Buhley," Cheryl yelled back.

August leaned over his chair and spat his Beechnut chewing tobacco juice through the hole in the porch. "You sweet on her, Buhley?" asked August.

"She's the prettiest girl in my class," replied Buhley. "I spend half my time just staring at her."

August started. "Let me tell you something about women, son. We can't live with 'em, and we can't live without 'em. They'll chew you up and spit you out, and you'll come back looking for more. Now I got lucky with your mamma, Buhley, but I know lots of men who go from one woman to the next and ain't got nothing to show for it except they've shrunk down to nothing. You understand, son?"

"Yes sir, but I'm hooked," replied Buhley.

August had not put that many words together in a long time. He had sweated a lot that day, and the chewing tobacco had given him a high. They began to rock in their chairs in a slow unison, and soon they were both asleep.

Parley Hawkins sat behind the cash register at Hawkins grocery store listening to Johnny Cash's "Ring of Fire" waffle out of his phonograph. In walked Wadeus Watkins and his wife Sweetiepie.

"What's say, Wadeus?" said Parley.

"Not much, Parley," replied Wadeus.

"And how are you today, Miss Sweetiepie?" asked Parley.

"I'm fine, but nothin' extra," said Sweetiepie.

"What can I help you find?" asked Parley.

Sweetie replied, "I need some mixings for pound cakes."

Sweetiepie Wadkins was a big woman. She had attractive features that were diminished by her size. She wore large flowing moo moos and was known as a caring person who had a heart for the needy. Sweetiepie was famous for making pound cakes and taking them to people. The only problem was the pound cakes were lousy. They were bland, and if they sat overnight, they became rock hard. When Pastor Jones first came to town, Sweetiepie repeatedly took him pound cakes. They tried to eat the first one but had to throw it out along with all the others she brought.

Sweetiepie once asked Pastor Jones, "How'd you like my pound cakes?"

Pastor Jones was quick on his feet and answered, "Sweetiepie, pound cakes like those don't last long in our house."

Parley always liked it when Sweetiepie came in his store because she had the softest, most tranquilizing voice of anyone he had ever heard. He asked her a lot of questions just to hear her talk. Her voice was so soothing that after the third or fourth syllable hit his eardrum, he became relaxed all over. "Sweetiepie, who you cooking cakes for?" asked Parley.

He turned down the music so he could hear her real well. "Mrs. Hatcher and the Clemsons. All them been sick," replied Sweetiepie.

"What's going on with them?" asked Parley.

Sweetiepie went on to explain. Parley followed them out of the store as they left. He looked at Feris Strum and said, "Feris, I believe I'd pay that woman to just sit in a chair and talk to me. I'd pay her big."

Feris, flat face and all, just looked at Parley and didn't say a word. Nate Hayes, who wasn't all there, said, "There goes a lot of woman."

Early Moon stood in his pasture counting his head of cattle. He called himself a cattle rancher. Most folks knew you couldn't make a living with twenty-three head of cattle, and the rumor was that Early made whiskey in the woods behind his place. The rumors were correct. Early Moon made and sold white lightning whiskey by the jar. He had perfected his recipe to the point where his whiskey was as smooth as drinking water. He was proud of his white lightning and insisted on sampling every batch.

Early was a bad drinker - a mean drunk. His personality went from bad to worse when he drank. He had a son named Edsel. Edsel Moon was quick as a cat. Much of his quickness was attributed to avoiding the business end of a cattle prod wielded by his dad when Early would come back from the woods drunk.

Edsel was a natural athlete who stayed outside all the time. A natural born tree climber, he could jump from one tree to another like a squirrel. Edsel could do front flips or back flips on the run or standing still. His skin was golden bronze from hours spent outside. Except for the business end of a cattle prod, he wasn't scared of anything. When something mischievous happened in town, most folks would think of Edsel Moon.

Buhley sopped up the last bit of gravy on his plate with a piece of biscuit and put it in his mouth. Before he finished chewing it well, he asked Ranna if he could go out for a while. "Not if you don't have better manners than that, Buhley Sparks. I didn't raise you to talk with your mouth full. You know better than that. I declare. I think sometimes I need to send you and your dad off to manners school."

August defended himself. "Now, darling, I didn't do nothin. I hadn't talked with my mouth full one time tonight."

"That's because you haven't said anything. Where do you think Buhley learned that? He certainly hasn't seen me do it," replied Ranna.

"You get home before worrying time. You hear me, son?" said Ranna.

"Yes, Ma'am," replied Buhley.

Buhley hurried out the front door and down the road toward Cheryl Dane's home. Across the street from her house stood a massive oak tree with large limbs perfect for climbing and sitting. Buhley snuck his way up to the tree and made a slow climb to a limb that gave him the best view of the Dane house. Cheryl's room was on the front right, and her window was in plain view. Buhley was in luck this night. Cheryl's drapes were open, and she was lying on her bed reading. He sat in the tree gazing at her and dreaming of one day making her Mrs. Buhley Sparks. It was the dusk of evening, and he hadn't been sitting there long when a big flock of birds came flying into the tree. They flew all around him, making a racket. He threw up his arms to knock them away, lost his balance, and fell out of the tree.

"Woo!" yelled Buhley. He hit the ground with a thud.

Mr. Dane ran out into the front yard and yelled, "Who's there? Who is that?"

Buhley had barely hit the ground before he was up and in a full run back to his house. Cheryl, hearing the commotion, stuck her head out of the window in time to see a silhouette run off into the night. She lay back down on her bed and began to read again, only this time with a smile. Buhley ran into the house, soaking wet with sweat and panting as if he'd just finished a marathon.

"Buhley, what in the world? You look like you just busted out of prison," said Ranna.

"No, ma'am, I just wanted to get home before worrying time."

August figured what Buhley was up to and walked by, patted him on the head and smiled. Buhley ran himself a hot tub and climbed in to soak his bruised ribs. The next morning Ranna sent Buhley to town to buy some sugar. As he walked down the street towards Hawkins grocery store, he noticed a crowd gathered in front of the barbershop. When he got closer to the store, he saw the people gazing at the top of the building. He stopped and looked up to see Edsel Moon standing on the edge of the roof and looking down.

"What you doing?" Buhley yelled.

"I'm fixing to jump off this roof onto the pavement," hollered Edsel.

"What for?" yelled Buhley.

"I'm hungry and ain't got no money."

The crowd that gathered had thrown some coins into a pile on the sidewalk to get him to jump.

"Hey, Buhley, how much money is down there?" called Edsel.

Buhley walked over to the coins and counted the money.

"About $1.45," yelled Buhley.

"That's enough," said Edsel.

With that he did a quick bend down, leaped into the air and not only did a jump but tucked his head, grabbed his knees and turned a double flip, landing perfectly on his bare feet. The ten or eleven people standing around applauded in awe. Edsel scraped up the money and put it in his pocket. He took a bow and said, "It's a pleasure doing business with ya'll." He left and swaggered directly to the drug store and ordered a slaw dog and a vanilla ice cream cone.

Buhley walked into Hawkins grocery store still shaking his head in amazement. "Hello, Buhley," Parley said from behind the cash register.

"Howdy, Mr. Parley," replied Buhley. "You should have seen what Edsel Moon just did."

"There ain't no telling what that boy did. I ain't sure I want to know, but tell me anyway," said Parley.

"He climbed up on the roof of the barber shop and for $1.45 did a double flip down to the pavement, barefoot and all."

"Nothin' you could tell me about Edsel Moon would surprise me. He's stuck on stupid most of the time. I'll be surprised if he makes his fifteenth birthday."

"Sometimes in class he'll just start mooing like a cow, and the teacher will whip him good, and it don't seem to bother him none."

"He's got a screw loose. That's what he's got," said Parley.

Buhley paid for the sugar and headed for the door. "Tell your mamma and daddy hello," said Parley.

"Yes, sir."

Ranna was out on the porch snapping beans. "Here's your sugar, Mamma," said Buhley.

"Thank you. Crawford's looking for you. He's around back. I told him you'd be home shortly."

"Thank you, Mamma. I'll see you later."

Buhley walked around to the back of the house. Crawford was sitting on a big stump, chewing a piece of sour grass. Buhley walked over to him, still with a slight limp from falling out of the tree.

"What you limping for?" asked Crawdad.

Buhley looked around both ways to make sure nobody was looking or could hear. "I fell out of a tree last night."

"Fell out of a tree!" said Crawdad with astonishment. "What were you doing up in a tree last night?"

"You know that tree across from Cheryl Dane's house? That big oak with all those limbs?"

"Yep," said Crawdad.

"That's the one," said Buhley.

"I know what you were doing. You was looking in on Cheryl, weren't you?"

"Don't tell no one, Crawdad, but she's got me twisted all around."

"Did anybody see you?"

"Her dad came out the house from the noise and everything, but it was dark, and I don't think he knew who I was."

Unbeknownst to Buhley, August was just around the corner of the house, hand sharpening an axe. He heard every word. All August could do was smile for he, too, had once fallen out of a tree in search of the hand of a lady. Buhley and Crawdad walked out towards the field to mess around.

Ranna continued to snap beans on the porch. She heard a car turn into the driveway and looked up to see Sweetiepie Wadkins getting out. Ranna was kind as could be, but the thought ran through her mind that she was glad she did not see a pound cake in Sweetiepie's arms.

Miss Ranna, can you use some company?" asked Sweetiepie.

"Yes, Lordy, come on up," replied Ranna.

Sweetiepie negotiated the few steps up to the porch very carefully. She put one leg on a step, and then as quickly as she could, the other followed one step at a time until she was on the porch. The porch creaked as she walked to the rocking chair beside Ranna. To sit down, she started easing backwards and then kind of fell into the chair. As big as she was, she hung out of that rocker on all sides. There was not a sweeter lady around, and Ranna was glad she came by to visit. "Miss Ranna, can I help you snap some beans?" asked Sweetiepie.

"No, thank you, I'm about done," said Ranna.

"I've been out delivering cakes today, and I saw you on the porch and decided to visit for a spell," said Sweetiepie.

"I'm glad you stopped by."

Ranna thought for a moment about those rock-hard pound cakes Sweetiepie made. She also thought about all the work that went into making and delivering them to people who were having a hard time.

Ranna started, "Sweetiepie, I tell you, what you do with making and taking all those cakes, it's a ministry. That's what it is all right. Every time you take a cake to someone, they know that you have been thinking of them, that you care for them and that you took the time to bake for them and visit them. Yep, it's a ministry all right. And I'll tell you this. If everybody had the heart that you have, Homerville and this world would be a better place."

Sweetiepie grinned from ear to ear. "Pastor Jones could preach a sermon on your life," Ranna continued. "Too many people do too much talking and not enough doing. You are a doer, and we could all learn a lesson from you."

Sweetiepie began to tear up, and they rocked in silence while Sweetiepie reclaimed her composure. Ranna had wanted to say all those things for a long time and was glad she had the opportunity. They talked a while longer, and Sweetiepie wedged her way out of the rocking chair. She started to waddle her way to the steps, then stopped and turned to Ranna. "Thank you for those kind words, Miss Ranna," said Sweetiepie.

"I'm glad we had this time to visit," said Ranna.

"I'll see you Sunday," said Sweetiepie.

She waddled her way back to her car and drove away. Buhley and Crawdad came in from the field. "Mamma, can we make some mayonnaise sandwiches?" asked Buhley.

"There's a brand new jar of Blueplate in the pantry. It hasn't even been opened," said Ranna.

"Hey, Buhley, I'll arm wrestle you for the opening," said Crawdad.

The boys liked to open a fresh jar from the store. It made a popping sound and sucked air quickly into the jar and vibrated the arm for just a second. Buhley had been throwing a lot and had built up his arm. He made quick work of Crawdad.

"Ah, that feels good," said Buhley, popping open the mayonnaise jar.

The mayonnaise lay perfectly undisturbed in the jar like the surface of a lake on a windless day. "Let me dip the first dab," said Crawdad.

"All right," answered Buhley.

Crawdad eased the knife into the mayonnaise like a surgeon beginning an operation. He pulled out a large amount and dabbed it on the bread. He made his sandwich and began eating. "Hey, Buhley, is there anything better than a mayonnaise sandwich?" asked Crawdad, mayonnaise running out the corner of his mouth.

"Not in this world," said Buhley as he bit into his sandwich.

"You looking forward to starting back to school next week?" asked Crawdad.

Buhley and Crawdad would be going into the sixth grade. "Heck, no," replied Buhley. "What I want to do that for? I like messing around too much."

"Me, too," said Crawdad.

Deep down Buhley was excited about school because he would get to see Cheryl Dane every day.

CHAPTER 4

Doris Pritchett stood out on the sidewalk in front of Hawkins grocery and bossed Ihley to hurry and bring the car around. Ihley quickly shuffled down the way and got in the car. When he pulled up in front of the store, he edged too close to the sidewalk and one tire went up on the curb. Doris yelled, "Ihley, what's wrong with you? Can't you do anything right? Move over! I'm driving. What are you? Blind or half drunk?"

Ihley moved over and sank down in the seat. Parley walked out front, shaking his head and said, "He'd have to be blind or half drunk to marry her, ain't that right, Ferris?"

Ferris Strum, flat face and all, looked up at Parley and said, "Amen, brother."

Early Moon had sampled a new batch of his moonshine. He was driving to the hardware store to pick up some things for his whiskey-making business. There wasn't much traffic from his house to town, and that was good because he was using every inch of road going from side to side. Buhley and Crawdad had walked up town to do some messing around. As they ambled along the sidewalk and approached the hardware store, Early turned the corner and headed their direction, weaving through the heart of town. This was not the first time Early had driven in this condition. His truck had lost its muffler a while back, and he never bothered to have it fixed. As Buhley and

Crawdad reached the front of the hardware store, Early turned in to park. His foot never found the brake, and the truck jumped the curb and onto the sidewalk. Crawdad looked up just in time to push Buhley and himself out of the way. The truck vaulted right through the plate glass window of Matty Lee's hardware store. Matty Lee was a respected businessman in Homerville. He had been there all his life and now was running the store his daddy had started. He was a God-fearing Christian man with always a kind word for everyone. Matty Lee was in the back of the store when the truck drove in. To him, it sounded like an explosion. He rushed out front to see Early Moon slumped over the steering wheel of his truck, which was still idling. He gave a quick glance to assess the damage and then turned his anger towards Early.

"Early Moon, I can't believe you can get in your truck and think you can drive when you're in this condition. You could have killed those two boys out there and someone else. Look what you've done to my store not to mention yourself! Look at you! You're no account," yelled Matty Lee.

Early Moon slowly raised his head from the steering wheel and looked around. He had not heard a word Matty Lee said. "Well, I'll be damned. How did the hardware store get inside my truck?"

The surroundings quickly sobered up Early, and he apologized to Matty. "Matty Lee, I'm sorry. I'll make it up to you. I promise."

With that he put his truck in reverse and headed it up onto the street and back towards home. Buhley and Crawdad could not believe what they had seen. Matty Lee shook his head and began to clean up.

Buhley and Crawdad headed home. August was rocking on the porch when Buhley walked up. Buhley pulled up a rocking chair beside August. "Daddy, you won't believe what I just saw," said Buhley.

He waited on August to ask him what, and when he didn't, Buhley started. "Edsel's daddy drove his truck clean through Mr. Matty Lee's hardware store. I mean clean through, Daddy. And then he sat there for a time while Mr. Matty Lee yelled at him. And then he backed his truck out of the store and drove away."

August knew that Early drank and thought this would be a good lesson for Buhley. He leaned over the side of his rocker, spit tobacco juice and then started. "Buhley, there ain't but one thing I can tell you about alcohol, and that is it's bad. It's like an angry mule. It will kick you to the ground and stomp on you while you're down. It will grab hold of you and never let go. It will take you farther than you want to go, cost more than you want to spend, and keep you longer than you want to stay. It will hurt you and those around you. It might make you feel good for a spell, but then its spell is on you. And it makes you do stupid things like driving a truck through a hardware store. You understand, son?"

"Yes, sir," replied Buhley.

They began to rock in unison, and soon they were both asleep.

Just before dark, Early Moon drove up to the hardware store and handed Matty Lee a big wad of cash. They shook hands, and Early Moon drove away.

Buhley woke up early Monday morning and ate his breakfast faster than usual. On his way out, he dipped into the bathroom and checked his hair. He arrived at school early so he could scope out the room and find the desk that would give him the best eyeshot of Cheryl Dane. When class started he had moved three times and settled in on the perfect desk placement.

The morning went quickly, and soon it was time for recess. Buhley was slow to get outside. When he reached the playground, he saw a crowd gathered in a circle. In the middle of the circle stood Edsel Moon and a new kid. The new kid had picked up a sticker and thrown it in Edsel's face. Without thinking, Edsel punched that new kid right in the stomach. The new kid went down to the ground, gasping for air. When he was able to get up, he walked off crying towards the principal's office. Buhley and Crawdad laughed to themselves. Edsel said, "That'll teach him to mess with me."

The door of the principal's office burst open and out walked Ida Mae Jewel. Ida Mae Jewel was principal of the Homerville School. She had never married and was a lifetime educator. Now in her mid fifties, the school was her life. She ran the school with the care of a pastor and the discipline of a warden. She had solid white hair and always wore a string of pearls, high heels and a nicely pressed dress. Ida Mae Jewel tromped her way out to the playground through the dirt, lifting one leg in front of the other. Her neatly pressed dress flowed out from the waist, and it turned with every step. She made her way to the crowd with the new kid following behind. "Now which one of these boys punched you?" asked Ida Mae.

The new kid pointed to Edsel Moon. Ida Mae walked up to Edsel. "Did you punch that boy in the stomach?"

"Yes ma'am," said Edsel.

"How do you think it feels?" asked Ida Mae.

"I don't know," said Edsel.

The last syllable of the word "know" had not completely left Edsel's mouth before Ida Mae Jewel reared back, and with a roundhouse, punched Edsel Moon directly in the stomach. He sank to the ground gasping for air and embarrassed that he had been dropped by a fifty-five-year-old woman. "That's how it feels, Edsel. Now you know," said Ida Mae.

She dusted off her hands, straightened her hair, and tromped back to her office.

Every kid present just stood in awe of Miss Ida Mae Jewel. They did not dare laugh at Edsel for fear of reprisal. She was the only one in the county who could handle Edsel Moon.

"That was a jaw dropper," said Crawdad.

"I ain't never gonna cross her," said Buhley. They were always respectful and scared of Miss Ida Mae, but what they had just seen took it to a new level.

56 Johnson snuck out the back of Clips and headed down a darkened dirt road. The moon was bright, and he made sure no one was watching. He hung a right and made his way one hundred or so yards into the woods. 56 had a small spade in his hand and began to dig. It didn't take long before he shined his light in the hole and pulled out a box full of cash. He took a quick glance around and made his way out of the woods and back up the dirt road to the

rear of Clips. 56 put half of the cash in the safe and half in the register. He let out a loud whistle, and all the eyes in Clips were on him. "OK, boys, the drinks are on the house."

Those who were fixing to leave decided to stay. Benny Armstrong made his way to the bar and ordered Pabst Blue Ribbon beer. "56, you're a good man. How in the hell did you know I was thirsty and down to my last dollar?" said Benny.

"I could see the way you was walkin'. You looked kind of slumped and dejected like you were thirsty and down to your last dollar," said 56.

"That's real funny. What are you? A bar-tending comedian or something? You get that sense of humor from your daddy?" Benny asked with a tone of sarcasm.

"Not hardly," replied 56. "The only thing my daddy left me was alone. He wasn't hardly ever home. Between making shine, delivering it, and avoiding the law, he didn't have much time for us. He'd drive by occasionally and drop off a batch of money for my mamma. My mamma was the one who raised us."

"What was your mamma like?" asked Benny.

"She was a fine God-fearing woman who loved us very much. She was too ashamed about my daddy to go to church, but she made sure we had plenty of scripture learning. My daddy must have made a lot money cause we never wanted for nothing, that is except for my daddy himself. My mamma did her best to make up for his absence, and in many ways, she did. But a boy needs a dad. You know what I'm saying, Benny?"

"I sure do, 56."

56 wasn't about to tell Benny about the note his daddy gave him on his death bed, explaining to him about the money he had hidden all over the county.

Ida Mae Jewel motioned for Buhley and Edsel Moon to come into the hallway outside the classroom. Buhley's stomach went into his throat. He thought to himself, "Oh, my goodness, what have I done?"

He was relieved when Miss Ida Mae said, "I want you two boys to go out into the school yard and lower the flag. Now run on and bring the flag back to my office."

"Yes, ma'am," they both said.

"And boys, don't let the flag hit the ground."

"Yes, ma'am," replied the boys.

They walked out to the flagpole. Buhley reached to untie the rope from the clasp to lower the flag. Before he could get it untied, Edsel started shimmying up the flagpole like a monkey up a tree.

"What are you doing?" hollered Buhley.

"I'm getting the flag," Edsel yelled back. In no time, Edsel was up at the top of the pole. He had unhooked both top and bottom of the flag and slid down the pole like a fireman answering a call.

"Here you go," said Edsel as he gave the flag to Buhley.

"Dadgumit, Edsel, you could have dropped that flag, and Miss Ida Mae would have whipped us good. You beat every thing! You know that!"

Edsel strutted away and proudly said, "Nobody will ever forget Edsel Moon."

56 Johnson walked into Hawkins grocery store. Parley was in the back, checking in stock. He had his stereo system off so he could hear customers come in. "I'll be right there," Parley yelled from the back.

"Take your time," shouted 56.

Parley hustled up to the front of the store, and before he could see who it was, yelled, "Is that you, 56 Johnson?"

"Yes, sir."

Parley greeted him. "You old rascal, how are things on the other side of the track?"

"'Bout the same as you. We all got the same problems; only you can pay for yours, and we can't," said 56.

Parley and 56 grew up together and were in the same class from first grade through graduation. Their lives had taken them different directions, but they still remained friends and had great respect for each other. "Don't give me that stuff. I can see from the size of your stomach you've eaten pretty good. Don't let that thing get the best of you. Sit down and drink a Co' Cola with me and visit a while," said Parley. "What can I do for you today?"

"I just came to get some groceries for the house and some nuts for the bar."

Parley pulled up a chair for 56 and handed him a Coca Cola. He went behind the register, pulled his chair out and set it next to 56. "How's your business?" asked Parley.

"Sometimes I have to beat'em with a stick to get 'em in, and sometimes I have to beat'em with a stick to get 'em out," replied 56.

"I know that feeling."

"I see Feris Strum and Nate Hayes still sit out in front of your store."

"Yep, they're part of the furniture now. That's what you call ambiance."

"Ambiance? What's that?"

"Let's just say I can't ask them to leave," said Parley.

"I gotcha."

"Anybody out your way doin' any hard luck livin' right now?"

56 thought for a moment. "Clois Brown. You remember him. He was a grade or two behind us. He lost his job over in Travisville, and he's got them children to feed."

Parley answered, "I'll throw a few groceries in a box, and you take it to him on your way back and just tell him we wish him well."

"Thank you, Parley, he'll appreciate that," said 56.

After talking awhile longer, 56 got up to leave. "I'll see you next time Parley."

"Ok," said Parley.

Parley noticed his friend's stomach again and couldn't resist adding, "Hey, 56, let me know next time you're coming, and I'll have the door widened."

56 replied, "I can't get my fill of that beer and those nuts."

"It's always good to see you old friend. Don't be so long between visits."

"I'll do it," said 56 as he walked out the door and to his car.

Jubel Odom walked slowly with his mule in tow up to August Sparks' house. Ranna was on the porch sweeping. "Miss Ranna, how's you today?" asked Jubel.

"Fine, thank you, Jubel," said Ranna.

"Is Mr. August here?"

"He's around back working on his tractor. Go on back there."

"Thank you, ma'am," said Jubel.

He yanked the reign on the mule and headed around the corner towards the barn. Jubel Odom was an older black man who did plowing or any other kind of work he could get. Even though he was past fifty-five, his physique was still chiseled in stone. Not one time in his life had he missed a hard day's work except on Sundays, the Lord's day. He raised three fine boys, all college educated, and was well respected in both the black and white communities. He always carried his plow mule, Buckswamp, with him. Buckswamp tended to be lazy sometimes and would rouse the ire of Jubel every now and then.

Jubel walked over to where August was working. "Mr. August, how's you today?"

"Doin' fine, Jubel. An' you?" responded August.

"I'm fine, suh, real fine, suh. Thank you for asking, suh. How's ol' Buhley boy? I ain't seen him for a time."

"He's just fine."

"Mr. August, you gots any plowin' needin' doin'? Me and ol' Buckswamp got a little time right now, and it's just about plantin' time."

August thought for a minute. He was having trouble with his tractor and needed to plant his corn as soon as he could. Although he really couldn't afford to pay to have it plowed, he liked and admired Jubel Odom and would help him any way he could. "I tell you what, Jubel. Go ahead and work the five acres over there for the cornrows. How long you reckon that'll take?"

Jubel looked it over and thought for a moment. "'Bout day and a half; yes, suh, 'bout day and a half."

"The hand plow's right over there," said August, pointing to it.

"Come on, Buckswamp."

Jubel started in the direction of the plow. As soon as Buckswamp saw the plow, he just sat down on his hind legs. Jubel yelled, "Get up, Buckswamp!"

Buckswamp just sat there. Jubel grabbed the reigns tightly and pulled as hard as he could. The veins and muscles in his arms and chest rippled as he pulled against the mule. Buckswamp pulled hard the other way. Jubel was a wise man and had encountered this problem before. He eased up on the reigns and said, "Okay, Buckswamp, let's go home."

He led the mule in the direction they had come. He stopped at the oak tree right beside the house and tied Buckswamp to the tree. "Mr. August, can I borrow a branch?"

August had been watching and was interested in what Jubel was going to do. "Help yourself," replied August.

Jubel pulled down a limb and tore off a branch. He walked around to the backside of Buckswamp as if nothing was going to happen and then began to whip that mule. "Now I told Mr. August we was gonna be through by noon time tomorrow. And one way or another we is," Jubel said as he continued to whip Buckswamp.

You could hear hee-haws all over the county as that mule quickly changed its mind. Jubel stopped the whipping and walked to the front of Buckswamp. "Now you gonna do right?" he asked as he and the mule stared at each other.

Jubel untied Buckswamp, and the mule took off running directly to the plow, got his front legs into the harness and waited for Jubel to hook him up the rest of the way. Ranna stuck her head out the kitchen window and yelled to August, "What's all the racket about?"

"Jubel and Buckswamp had to have a prayer meeting," said August.

"Oh," said Ranna as she pulled her head back through the window. She understood.

Buhley and Crawdad took their lunch out under the big oak tree at the Homerville School. "What you got today, Buhley?" asked Crawdad.

"Two ham sandwiches. I don't know why my mamma always wastes a perfectly good mayonnaise sandwich by putting ham in there," said Buhley as he took the ham off the bread and made sure all the mayonnaise was left in the sandwich. "How 'bout you, Crawdad?"

"I got peanut butter and banana sandwiches."

"Peanut butter and banana!" exclaimed Buhley. "Your mamma got you on a diet or some'um? That ain't fit for human eating."

Crawdad was hungry and replied, "Well, today it'll have to do."

Just then a big black crow came down out of the tree and scooped up the ham Buhley had thrown out of his sandwiches and flew back up to the top of the tree. Buhley finished his lunch and took his watch off, laying it on the ground beside him so he could comfortably tuck his hands behind his head and lean back on the tree to rest. The sun shown off the silver watchband with the glare getting the attention of the crow. Buhley hadn't closed his eyes very long when he heard the fluttering of wings right by his ear. He opened his eyes just in time to see the crow grab his watch and fly up to the top of the tree. Crawdad yelled, "Did you see that, Buhley? That crow has your watch!"

Buhley was mad and worried at the same time. "My daddy will kill me if I lose that watch."

The crow sat in the top of the tree with the watch in his mouth. He began cawing nonstop. "He's laughing at you, Buhley. Listen to him," said Crawdad.

"Keep your eye on him, Crawdad. Don't let him get away."

He found a rock that was round in shape and felt good in his hand. Because of the way the crow perched in the top of the tree, Buhley couldn't get a good throw at him. "Crawdad, get a rock and throw it up into the tree and spook that crow," said Buhley.

"What are you gonna do, Buhley?" asked Crawdad.

"When you spook him and he flies off, I'm gonna knock him down with this rock."

"No way."

Buhley was now more mad than worried. "Dadgumit, Crawdad, just hurry up and spook him."

Crawdad picked up a rock and chunked it up into the tree near the crow. The crow immediately flew off directly over the two boys. Buhley watched the crow fly over and sighted him in like a skeet shooter. He let fly with the rock, and it met the bird with a precise hit. The watch fell out of the bird's mouth and dropped directly into Buhley's hands. The bird fell a few yards farther in front of Buhley.

Crawdad's mouth dropped to his knees. "You're a legend, Buhley Sparks, and I'm just proud to know you."

Buhley walked over to the crow that was stunned and trying to regain flying ability. "Mr. Crow, let that be a lesson to you," said Buhley.

He put his watch back on his arm, picked up his lunch bag and walked back to class. Crawdad, still in awe, walked a couple of paces behind Buhley Sparks, the legend.

CHAPTER 5

Several years passed, and nothing changed much in Homerville. Now fifteen years old, Buhley had hit a growth spurt and was six feet two inches tall. His voice had changed, but he hadn't begun to fill out. August, a step or two slower, was still working all the time. Ranna's health had gotten worse, and the only thing that remained regular in her life was her worship. Even though she had never smoked a day in her life, the doctors diagnosed her with emphysema. She had a difficult time breathing and was growing more and more tired.

Parley walked in and sat in the chair of Hooty Lou's Barber Shop. Hooty Lou was the town barber. He was a slight man who had a laugh like a hyena - a real high-pitched laugh that caught your attention. People loved to hear Hooty tell a story. In fact, he was a terrible barber, but a great storyteller. Hooty had a sign hung in his shop that read, "Don't worry. It'll grow back."

Some of the stories he told were true. Some were not, but folks didn't care. It didn't seem to bother his customers that their haircuts were uneven, not as long as he entertained them with his tales. Nobody dared let Hooty Lou give him a shave because he was spastic when he laughed, and he laughed all the time.

Parley sat down in the chair. "Hooty, what you been up to?" he asked.

"Not much, Parley, but me an' old Elbert Files went fishin' the other day," said Hooty.

"Y'all do anything?" asked Parley.

"We did a few. I don't think Elbert remembers much about it 'cause he stopped off at Early Moon's on the way to the river and got him a couple of jars. But I'll tell you what happened."

Parley closed his eyes to relax. "By the time we got to the river, Elbert had finished one jar and was working on the second. He was singing "Amazing Grace" at the top of his lungs and missing every third syllable. I got him quieted down, and we got the boat in the water after he backed the trailer off the side of the ramp. He was so snookered I made him put on a life jacket. Wouldn't you know it! We got down the river a ways and stop, and he throws his bait out. That bait hadn't even gotten wet good, and blam! Sump'in big hit it. I yelled for Elbert to set the hook. He stood up and yanked on that rod like no tomorrow. He must've aggravated that fish 'cause when he yanked the line, that fish yanked back. Ol' Elbert being in the condition he was had no business standing up in the boat fighting a bigun. Well, it didn't take long, and he fell over the side of the boat," said Hooty as he let out a loud and long hyena laugh.

"That life jacket was only half floatin' him," Hooty continued, "and he was bobbin' up and down like a drunk up cork. Soon as I quit laughing, he was a good two hundred yards down the river. I cranked up the motor and went after him. He had gotten his overalls snagged on a stump in the river and was stuck. That fish had taken his fishing pole way down the river. We never got it back. You know, Parley, ol' Elbert's a pretty big fella. I couldn't get him back in the boat by myself, and he wasn't able to help. So I had to tie a rope around him and drag him behind the boat back to the ramp. He was pulling more wake than the boat itself. When we got back to the ramp, he staggered up and got back in the boat, soaking wet and all, and we went to our favorite hole and caught us a few fish."

Parley had long since opened his eyes, enjoying the story. "Wha'd y'all do after that?" he asked.

"We came back to the ramp but had to leave the boat there on account of when Elbert backed the trailer off the ramp, the axel broke in two."

By this time, both he and Parley were laughing. Hooty had finished cutting Parley's hair and spun him around to the mirror. "How's that?" asked Hooty.

Parley noticed one side was longer than the other and replied, "Same as always, Hooty. Let me know when you and Elbert go fishing again, and I'll come back and get a haircut."

Parley walked toward the door. "I'll see ya, Hooty."

Fourth of July in Homerville was a big deal. The whole town came out for a street party with downtown's main street blocked off. The stores always put patriotic displays in their windows with a trophy given to the best display. The contest usually was between Matty Lee and Hooty Lou. Matty Lee proudly showcased the trophy in his window until it was run over by Early Moon's truck. All of the women would bring their best fixings for a huge dinner on the grounds. There were different booths set up with games of chance and various entertainments. Parley and 56 Johnson had planned the evening. They threw some money together for the fireworks that would end the celebration, and Parley added a couple of big washtubs full of iced down Coca-Colas. The big draw of the evening was a dunking booth that Parley borrowed from the Lions Club over in Travisville.

Around five o'clock, folks started coming to town. All the women took their dishes to two long tables set up for food. Wilma Jones helped organize the salads, breads, vegetables, meats, and desserts so the line would move in an orderly fashion. Edsel Moon rode his cow, Slump, to town. Slump thought he was a horse, so Edsel rode him like one. Edsel tied Slump up to a tree on the edge of town and tried to find something to do that would bring himself attention. Parley looked around, saw the crowd was full and let out a couple of loud whistles. Getting everybody's attention, he said, "Thank you all for coming as we celebrate our country's birthday. 56 Johnson and I are glad you are here, and at this time, I'll ask Pastor Jones to say a blessing before we eat. Pastor Jones!"

Parley nodded towards the pastor. Pastor Jones began, "May we pray. Our gracious heavenly Father, we humble ourselves before you this day. Grateful we are to live in such a bountiful country as America. As we celebrate her birthday, let us be ever mindful of the blessings you have showered upon us and our country. Bless today this food to our bodies and our bodies to your service. In the name of Jesus Christ, we pray."

"Thank you, Pastor," said Parley. He pointed to the food. "Yonder's the eatins. Let's get at it."

People in Homerville weren't shy about eating. Plates were grabbed up quick and fast, and soon the line was moving to the approval of Wilma Jones. Doris and Ihley Pritchett were midway in line. When they got to the food, Ihley would hold a heaping of something over his plate and wait for Doris' approval or disapproval before adding to his plate. Sweetiepie Wadkins brought a pound cake and placed it front and center in the dessert section. Parley had to figure out how to dispose of it. He spotted Buhley and Crawdad. "Buhley! Crawdad! Come here for a minute. Listen here. Ms. Sweetiepie brought a pound cake, and we need to get rid of it without her knowing. She's a wonderful person, but on the Fourth of July, nobody should suffer her pound cake. Crawford, go around there and talk to her and get her back facing the table. Buhley, you go grab the cake off the table. Take it to the back of my store, and dump it in the trash. And Buhley, don't drop it on my floor. It'll break into a thousand pieces."

"Yes, sir," they both replied as they walked off.

Edsel Moon had gathered some of the younger children together and was trying to burp "The Star-Spangled Banner." Parley noticed everybody was eating and thought it a good time to announce the winner of the patriotic store display. He let out a loud whistle. "Folks, can I have your attention just a minute? I know everyone's enjoying all these ladies' fine cooking and rightly so," said Parley.

Just then Sweetiepie Wadkins turned and glanced at her cake plate. Noticing it was empty, she turned back and looked at Parley with a smile on her face. Parley continued. "It's now time to give the award for the best store display. Take a second look around at some of the hard work people put in. Don't they look good?" Parley asked, as he started the applause. "All of us should be thankful to live in this country and this town of Homerville, and it's my pleasure to once again give this award to Matty Lee."

Matty Lee had a flag draped in his store window and on either side hung his daddy's and granddaddy's army uniforms. At the bottom of the flag was a sign that read, "All gave some. Some gave all." Everyone broke out in applause, and Matty Lee rose and walked towards Parley who handed him the trophy. The cup on the top of the trophy was pinched shut. Parley said, "Most of you folks know this trophy was displayed in Matty's store window and was runned over by a truck tire. We just ain't had time to get it fixed. But that don't dampen the spirit in which it's given. Soon as y'all get finished eating, start meandering around, and we'll start up the dunking booth."

Parley walked over to a washtub and grabbed a Coca-Cola. 56 Johnson went over to Pastor Jones and struck up a conversation. "Reverend, that was a nice blessing. I know I'm not in church very often. I usually have a late night on Saturday. My mamma gave us lots of scripture learning, and I ain't never forgot it."

Pastor Jones put his arm around 56 and said, "I'm glad you told me about your mamma. I could tell by the kind of man you are that Jesus has a place in your heart. You're welcome to worship with us whenever time allows, and don't let the fact that you're not in church keep you from worshipping."

"I won't, Pastor. I won't," said 56.

Parley climbed up on the dunking booth. He and 56 had filled it with water earlier in the day. The dunking booth had a board for someone to sit on over the water. A ball was to be thrown from about twenty-five feet through a twelve-inch diameter hole. The ball would then strike a piece of wood mounted onto a rod that would trigger the latch holding up the board over the water. For fifty cents, a person got three balls to throw. Sitting on the board over the water, Parley began to yell at people. "Hey, is there anybody man enough to lay down some money?"

Matty Lee stepped up, and a small crowd watched in anticipation. He gave his money to 56 and took aim. Matty was a nice fella, but people could see from his first toss that Parley was in no danger. As Matty walked away, Parley yelled, "Hey, Matty, keep your day job."

Next up was Wadeus Wadkins. Wadeus had no neck at all. His head came right off his shoulders. His whole body lurched as he threw, and the balls went everywhere. Parley was lucky he didn't get hit. As Wadeus walked off, Parley yelled, "Wadeus, if you're gonna throw again, let me know 'cause I'll need some insurance."

Several other people stepped up, and none threatened the hole. Parley had a parting shot for each one. Just about everyone had finished eating and had gathered around the dunking booth. Ihley Pritchett sheepishly made his way up to the booth to try his luck. He had separated himself from Doris and wanted to have some fun. Everybody knew Ihley wasn't a ball player. He proved that when his first ball bounced to the backstop. His second ball sailed completely over the backstop. The third throw hit the backstop well to the right of the target. He turned to leave, and Doris was standing right behind him looking down on him. She barked, "What do you mean coming over here and embarrassing yourself like that? You're no ball player. Move along, and let someone up here who knows what he's doing. Do I have to look after you all the time?"

Ihley shuffled away in shame. Parley had no parting shot for Ihley. He knew Ihley suffered enough. Everyone heard a thud. Benny Armstrong had slammed a one-dollar bill on the table. "Give me six," he said confidently.

Parley straightened up a little bit and hung onto the board. He knew Benny had played a lot of ball. "Hey, Parley, you ready to take a bath?" yelled Benny.

"No, I usually wait till Saturday," Parley fired back.

Benny let go, and you could hear the ball hiss as it hit the backstop close to the hole. The next ball was in the same location, and each one left a mark on the backstop. His last throw hit the edge of the hole and went straight down. All around the hole were indentions where Benny Armstrong's balls had hit. As he walked off, Parley relaxed and yelled, "Hey, Benny, maybe I'll wait till Saturday for that bath. Wha'd you think?"

Benny pushed his way through the crowd. He went over and got a Coca-Cola to cool himself down. More people tried and failed. Parley was having fun taking pot shots at everyone. He saw Buhley in the crowd. He put his hands over his eyebrows like he was looking far off. "Hey," he yelled, "is that you, Buhley Sparks?"

Buhley had not planned on throwing. He only had one quarter in his pocket. Everyone shoved him up to the front. "I ain't got enough money, Mr. Parley. I only got a quarter," Buhley said.

"Somebody help this poor boy out," yelled Parley.

Crawdad reached in his pocket and slapped another quarter on the table. "There you go, Buhley. Now you got no excuses, and by the way, you couldn't hit the broadside of your daddy's barn," said Parley.

Parley started to laugh. When Parley laughed his head tilted back and his mouth opened wide. This was a deep belly laugh. He was in the middle of a laugh when Buhley picked up his first ball and let fly with a perfect motion. The ball sailed through the air, went perfectly through the target and slammed into the board behind the hole. The latch triggered, and Parley was sent hurtling down. It all happened so fast that Parley was still laughing when he hit the water. Down into the cylinder he went, inhaling a mouthful of water. He was stunned and coughing when he came up for air. Everyone in the crowd was applauding. Parley fixed the board back in place and climbed on top. Regaining his breath, he yelled at Buhley. "Even a blind hog finds an acorn now and then. Let see what you got now."

Parley started another belly laugh with his head tilted back. Buhley fired again and POW! The sound of the ball darting through the hole and slamming against the board exploded through the crowd. Parley fell like a sack of potatoes into the water and once more inhaled a mouthful. Again the crowd applauded. Parley bobbed up from the water and hung onto the side of the cylinder. He was much slower getting the board set up and climbing back on top than he was before. He didn't say a word as Buhley threw his third ball for a perfect strike. The water was still sloshing around as Parley hit it again. He came up from under the water, clinging to the side of the cylinder until he could catch his breath. Someone slapped a dollar down on the table and yelled, "Keep on throwing."

Buhley picked up another ball and let fly. It went perfectly through the middle of the hole. Parley just clung there, watching him throw. He was too tired to climb back on top. The crowd had begun to count with every throw. Each was a perfect strike. Four, five, six, seven, eight, nine, ten. Buhley stopped. "That's enough," he said.

The crowd was silent. They parted for him to walk through and patted him on the back. Somebody said, "Atta boy, Buhley."

Others were just amazed. Someone started to applaud, and everybody joined in. Parley climbed out of the water and stood soaking wet by the booth as Buhley walked away. He leaned over to 56 and whispered, "What have we got here?!"

Buhley walked over to a washtub and grabbed a Coca-Cola. It was almost dark, and he felt someone grab his arm. When he looked up, he saw Cheryl Dane. "Where did you learn to do that, Buhley?" she asked.

He was caught off guard and stumbled for words. "I don't know. I could always throw, I guess," he said shyly.

Just then a loud boom exploded, and the sky was lit up with fireworks. Buhley stood by Cheryl, pretending to look up in the sky. He couldn't take his eyes off her. The light from the fireworks gave her face a radiant glow. To him, she was more beautiful than ever. As the fireworks continued, Buhley thought to himself, "The Fourth of July in Homerville.... What a perfect night."

Bobby Fleet parked his weathered, black sedan in front of Hawkins grocery store. He got out and looked at Ferris Strum and Nate Hayes. "How are you fine gentlemen this morning?" he asked.

Hearing no response, he said, "Good, good. Could either of you fine gentlemen tell me where I might find Mr. Parley Hawkins?"

Ferris looked at him and gave him a head nod towards the inside of the store. "Thank you very much. I enjoyed visiting with you. We'll have to do this again real soon," Bobby said as he walked into the store.

The store was empty except for Parley. He was playing Patsy Cline on the rigged up stereo system and was sitting in his chair behind the cash register with his feet propped up on the counter. His eyes were shut and heavy from the soothing sound of the music. Bobby Fleet skegged his way in, dragging his shoes and looking around like he owned the place. In his late twenties, Bobby Fleet had jet-black hair and wore it slicked back except for several strands that fell over his forehead and bobbed around when he walked and talked. He chewed gum out of both sides of his mouth and wore city-type clothes --the likes of which folks in Homerville had never seen. He was a fast talker and a good one. He could charm his way past the devil himself.

"Mr. Hawkins!" Bobby said a little loudly to get Parley's attention.

Parley's head bolted up from his half nap. Parley turned down the music and answered, "Yes, sir, what can I do for you?"

Bobby reached out to shake his hand and handed him a business card. "Mr. Hawkins, my name is Bobby Fleet, and I represent Mr. Satch Moak's traveling all-star baseball team. We're gonna be in your area in about a month and wondered if you would like to get a team together and play us."

Parley's eyes were still a little puffy from his nap. "Look around here," he replied. "This is a one-horse town. I'll bet you I couldn't even get ten guys from here that have ever played a game of catch. All we do is farm and cut trees. That's it. We don't even have a ball field. I'm afraid you're just wasting your time with us."

Bobby Fleet never gave up that easily. "I've already been through Travisville. They have a ballpark over there that's perfect. They say they have a couple of players, too. Maybe y'all could combine and make a team. What ya say?"

Looking down at Bobby's business card to remember his name, Parley said, "Bobby, to be honest with you, I still think you're wasting your time. It ain't gonna happen here."

Bobby stuck out his hand and shook Parley's. He turned to leave and said, "That's too bad, Mr. Hawkins. Satch Moak has plenty of major league connections. If you had any real ballplayers, it would be a great way to showcase them."

Parley perked up and said, "Wait a minute! Say that again."

"Satch is well-connected in the big leagues and is always scouting for different teams."

Parley was flooded with the memory of Buhley and the Fourth of July. He remembered how Buhley, with effortless ease, had thrown that night. "Bobby, come on back in. Sit down, drink a Coca-Cola with me, and tell me how this thing works."

He pulled up a chair for Bobby and handed him a drink. Bobby started,

"Mr. Hawkins."

Parley stopped him. "Call me Parley."

"Okay, Parley," said Bobby, "this is how it works. We do the promotion with your help, of course. We'll put signs in storefronts, ads on telephone poles and everything. We come to town with our team and play your team. We'll play a nine-inning regulation baseball game with major league rules. It won't cost you a dime. We get all the gate and concession receipts. That's how we make our money. But here's the gravy. We pay five thousand dollars to any team that beats us. That's the incentive you have to play the game -- besides having a great fun event for your whole town to enjoy. So what ya think?"

"Sounds like it might work. Let me make some calls and see what I can do. I've got your card, and I'll be in touch. What date next month did you have in mind?"

Bobby whipped out a small calendar book and said, "Any day between the seventeenth and the twenty-fourth."

They shook hands, and Bobby turned and skegged his way towards the door. Opening the door, he turned back to Parley and said, "One more thing, Parley, we ain't never been beat."

He closed the door before Parley could reply and turned to Ferris Strum and Nate Hayes. Tipping an imaginary hat to them, he said, "Gentlemen, it's been a pleasure."

Bobby hustled to his sedan and drove away. Parley got on the phone and called 56 Johnson, telling him the story. "That Benny Armstrong, he can play ball, can't he?" asked Parley.

"He sure can, and he'd love to play again," replied 56.

"You know anybody else we might get?"

"I know one or two, and I'll talk to Benny and ask him. I'll call you in a day or so."

"Okay," said Parley as he hung up.

Stepping outside to tell Ferris and Nate about the possible game, he spotted Buhley walking in front of Matty Lee's hardware store. "Buhley. Buhley Sparks," Parley yelled. "Come over here. I want to tell you something."

Buhley crossed the street and went into Hawkins. "Sit down. You won't believe who just came in," said Parley.

He told Buhley the whole story. "I want you to pitch for us. What do you think?"

Buhley just sat there, trying to absorb everything. "You want me to pitch to an all-star team in front of the town?" he asked.

"Of course," replied Parley. "I seen you throw at the Fourth of July. You almost drowned me. I ain't never seen nobody throw like that. 56 Johnson is going to ask Benny Armstrong to play. He was a great catcher, and he can help you. What do you say, Buhley?"

"Mr. Parley, all I've ever wanted to do is pitch. But I ain't never thrown to a live batter, just the side of a barn mostly."

"I seen you, Buhley. I know you can do it. I heard how you could throw, and then I seen it for myself. Tell me you'll do it, and let's get this show on the road."

Buhley sat in silence for a good while, then asked, "Will it be almost like that game we went and saw in Jacksonville?"

"Almost."

"I'll do it."

Buhley hurried home. It was late afternoon, and August was rocking on the porch in his usual chair. Buhley pulled up a rocker next to him and said, "Daddy, guess what?"

August remained silent. Buhley waited long enough and then said, "Mr. Parley told me he's gettin' up a baseball team to play this traveling all-star team next month, and he wants me to pitch."

August leaned over and spit his tobacco juice through the hole in the floor. "You gonna throw against an all-star team?" asked August.

"Yes, sir."

"You ready?"

"I don't know."

"Better find out," said August as he closed his eyes and began to rock.

Buhley joined him and soon they were both asleep.

CHAPTER 6

"Hell yeah, I'll play," said Benny Armstrong as he slammed a half empty Pabst Blue Ribbon down on the bar at Clips. "You tell me when and where, and I'll be there. I know a couple of guys at the saw mill who might be interested in playing, too. I've heard of that team. They have some ex-major league players, former minor league players, and some college players. They're real good."

56 Johnson leaned against the bar and took some of the weight of his gut off his legs. "Have we got a snowball's chance in hell of beating them?" asked 56.

"No," answered Benny before 56 had gotten the last syllable out of his mouth. "They'll kill us. But I'll suffer the humiliation just to be able to put on the catching gear one more time and feel the pop of the ball against my mitt."

"You know, they pay five thousand dollars to any team that beats them," said 56.

"I'll guarantee you if they are playing teams like us, old Satch Moak ain't paid that out, not one time. I remember when I was getting looked at, I played on an all-star team for the south against the north. The north beat us and then turned around and played Satch Moak's all-star team. Satch Moak turned them every which way but loose. That's the way it will be with us, only a lot worse," said Benny.

Buhley lay on his bed, staring at the ceiling. All he could think about was Parley saying, "We want you to pitch."

Over and over the words went through his mind. Not even the hum of the motor from his oscillating fan could ease him to sleep. He didn't remember closing his eyes when he heard Ranna yell, "Breakfast is ready."

Buhley scarfed down his breakfast and headed out to find Crawdad. He met up with Crawdad in town at the drugstore and told him about the game. Sitting at the counter drinking a Coca-Cola, they discussed the matter. "Maybe I better go tell Mr. Parley it ain't such a good idea me pitching against the all-star team," said Buhley.

"What for?" asked Crawdad. "What you got to lose? Nobody expects you to do good. Nobody expect us to win. It's a win-win situation for you. This is what you've been wanting to do all your life. Heck, Buhley, I seen you do things with your arm nobody else anywhere could do. Remember when you killed the snake? Remember when you knocked the crow out of the air? Remember the Fourth of July? You got a gift, Buhley. You just could always throw, and this is a great opportunity for you to use your talent."

"I guess you're right."

"Of course, I'm right. I'll help you practice. I'll catch, and you can pretend we're pitching to batters. We better start today; we only have a few weeks left."

"Okay," said Buhley as they slurped the last of their Coca-Colas.

Their straws went around every inch of the glasses in search of the last drop of soda. Job completed, they put the glasses on the counter and walked out.

Parley called 56 Johnson. "Did you get Benny Armstrong?" asked Parley. "He'd of played last night."

"He said he'd ask a couple of boys from the sawmill. From what he told me, this team don't take no prisoners. I figure our town folk will support this game, but I hope they realize it might get ugly, quick and fast. You need me to do anything else?" asked 56.

"I appreciate you talking to Benny. Talk it up to the folks at Clips and anybody you see. We ain't got much time to put it together, but it sure could be interesting. I'm going to call Bobby Fleet and tell him we're in. I'll call you later."

Buhley and Crawdad walked up the road towards Buhley's house. August was pulling out of the driveway when they arrived. His truck was smoking worse than ever. He rolled the window down, motioning for Buhley and Crawdad to come over. They got as close to the truck as they could and still breathe. August reached in his glove compartment and pulled out two Milky Way candy bars and threw one to each boy.

"Thank you, Mr. Sparks," said Crawdad.

"Thank you, Daddy," said Buhley.

"Buhley, I got to go to town. Look in on your mamma for me. She ain't feeling too well this afternoon."

"Yes, sir," replied Buhley.

The boys went inside the house. Walking into Ranna's room, Buhley saw her lying on the bed. For the first time, Buhley noticed her breathing was especially labored. Buhley knelt down and took Ranna's hand. "Mamma, you all right?" asked Buhley.

"I'm just a little tired. That's all. You go on about your business. I'll be fine," she answered.

"I'll be outside throwing with Crawdad if you need me."

"Okay," said Ranna.

Buhley started to get up and pull away. Ranna held his hand with both of hers and looked him dead in the eye. "I love you, Buhley," said Ranna.

"I love you, too, Mamma."

She gently let go of his hand and closed her eyes. He turned and quietly left the room. Crawdad had gone outside, and Buhley met him there. They threw the ball back and forth until Buhley was warmed up. Crawdad got in a catcher's position, and Buhley let fire with a fastball. "Dadgumit, that hurts!" yelled Crawdad as he threw his glove down and began shaking his hand in the air. "I can't catch you anymore with this tired old glove. I might as well just be using a dishrag or something. It would feel the same."

Buhley was trying to hold back from laughing too hard. "Wait just a minute. I'll be right back," said Buhley. He went inside to his mamma's couch where she had several decorative pillows on either side. He took the one he thought she would miss the least. Grabbing the scissors from her sewing machine, he cut open the pillow and ripped out part of the inside foam. When Buhley walked back outside, Crawdad was running his hand under the water spigot, trying to stop the stinging. "You all right?" Buhley asked with a laugh.

"Does it look like I'm all right?" answered Crawdad, comparing his swollen hand to his normal one.

"Put this foam in your glove and see if that helps," said Buhley.

"Anything's better than bare-handed," said Crawdad as they began to throw again.

Parley called Bobby Fleet. "Looks like we're good to go."

"Great," replied Bobby.

"We need to set a firm date so we can gather a crowd," said Parley.

There was silence on the line for a time. "What about the twentieth, Saturday, August twentieth? How's that sound? Twelve noon. Satch likes to play at noon, so he can get people to eat lunch at the game."

"That sounds perfect. I'll have some signs made up fast, and we can post them quickly. That'll give us about three weeks to promote the game."

"Thanks for your help, Parley. I'll see you in a few days."

"We're looking forward to the game. Everybody I've talked to is excited."

"You're gonna see a great baseball team, and just remember one thing."

"What's that?" asked Parley.

"We ain't never been beat."

Bobby hung up before Parley could respond.

Hooty wrapped the tissue paper around 56 Johnson's neck. He then placed the barber sheet over him and sat him comfortably in the chair. Grabbing the scissors, Hooty approached his head and then stepped back. "You want the usual, 56?" asked Hooty.

"No, I want a good hair cut this time," replied 56.

"I'll tell you what's the truth. You got about the best head of hair to cut of any customer I know. It's flat in the back and round on the top. Some of my customers have an odd number hair, and it's impossible to get a straight part. But you, you got an even number hair and the straightest part I ever saw."

"I bet you say that to all the customers," said 56.

"You're right, I do," said Hooty as he let out a loud hyena laugh. "Now just relax, and I'll make this as painless as possible."

He began to snip 56's hair. "What's this baseball game I keep hearing about?" asked Hooty.

"We got us a down right barnburner of a game come Saturday the twentieth. That's what we got. Satch Moak's all-star team is coming to town to play some of our boys and some boys from Travisville. It ought to be something else. You gonna go see it?" asked 56.

"What time's the game?" asked Hooty.

"Twelve noon."

"That's my busiest time of the week It'll be a sacrifice, but I'll be there."

"Ain't nobody gonna come in for a haircut that day. Everybody in Homerville's going to the game. Besides, the whole town will be a lot safer if for one Saturday afternoon you ain't got no scissors in your hand."

Just then, Hooty got a little too close to 56's ear lobe. "Ow!" yelled 56.

"Sorry about that! Your head moved."

"Watch what you're doin', will ya?"

"Oh, I did! I did! I saw the whole thing," said Hooty as he let out another hyena laugh and wiped off the cut.

He put a small band-aid on 56's ear lobe and finished the hair cut. He spun 56 around to the mirror. "How's that?" asked Hooty.

"Same as always. I'll see you next time," said 56 as he paid Hooty and walked out the door.

56 walked down to Hawkins grocery. It was Saturday, and the store was busy. Parley was behind the counter ringing up groceries. He glanced up to see 56 and the band-aid on his ear lobe. "Looks like you visited with Hooty Lou," said Parley.

"He's dangerous. That's what he is." Replied 56.

"He's got a license to maim," said Parley.

56 turned towards the door. "You look busy. Everything for the game is shaping up nicely on my end. How about yours?" asked 56.

"Same."

"I'll call you later."

Bobby Fleet parked in front of Hawkins Grocery Store later that afternoon. He got out with a stack of signs under his arm and made his way into the store. The mad rush was over, and the store was empty. Parley was in his usual spot, relaxing behind the counter to the silky voice of Jim Reeves.

"Hello, Bobby Fleet. How you doing? What you got there?" asked Parley.

Bobby held up one of the signs. "This oughta wet their whistle," said Bobby as he held it up proudly.

Parley slowly read it aloud. "Satch Moak's traveling all-star baseball team vs. Homerville/Travisville. Saturday, August 20th at 12:00 noon. Travisville Baseball Field. Admission $3.00. Full concession stand available. Come see some of the best baseball players in the Southeast."

"What ya think?" asked Bobby.

"That oughta do it."

"Where can we put 'em?"

"You can put them in every store window in town. I've already talked to the owners. You can start by putting one right there," said Parley as he pointed to a spot close to his door.

Bobby hung the sign and grabbed the others and headed for the door. "One more thing, Parley."

"I know. I know. Y'all ain't never been beat," replied Parley sarcastically.

"You got that right," said Bobby as he left with the signs.

At dusk, Bobby Fleet motored out of Homerville in his black battered car. There were signs everywhere. They were on the telephone poles, on the trees, and in the store windows. The folks in Homerville were beginning to get excited.

August pulled up to the Baptist church Sunday morning and let Ranna and Buhley out of the truck. He waited until they were far enough away before he drove off, keeping them from being overcome with smoke from the tailpipe. Like always, the church was full. Everyone was in his normal seat. The title of Pastor Jones' sermon was "Opportunities God Gives Us." Pastor Jones always preached with a strong, confident voice. He began his sermon. "There may be some of you in the congregation this very day who are facing an unknown in your life."

Buhley perked up as he thought about the baseball game that loomed less than a week away. Pastor Jones continued, "God wants you to turn this unknown into an opportunity. No matter where you are, or what the circumstances, you can be a witness. A witness for the Lord Jesus Christ who said 'I will never leave you nor forsake you.'" Buhley listened intently. He became more at ease with every sentence and point preached by the pastor. By the time Pastor Jones finished, Buhley was looking forward to the game. After church let out, Parley grilled Buhley on how he had been practicing, how he was feeling and if he was ready to play.

On Sunday afternoon in Homerville, folks went visiting. Ranna was rocking on her porch as a car pulled up in the front yard. Wilma Jones and Sweetiepie Wadkins got out. In their arms, they carried casseroles and vegetables. They had enough food to feed a small army. After they took all of it in the kitchen, they walked out onto the porch. Sweetiepie was breathing hard from going up and down the steps. She waddled her way over to a rocking chair and fell back into it. Wilma Jones sat on the other side of Ranna. "Miss Ranna, we noticed you ain't been feeling too well lately, and we wanted to lift a burden off of you with this food. The ladies of the church want you to know that this is just the start and that we will help you every way we can," said Sweetiepie in her soft, soothing voice.

Ranna continued to rock as she responded. "Thank you very much. It wasn't necessary, but greatly appreciated."

Her sentences were shortened because of the absence of breath. "We just want you to know how much everyone at the church loves you. We thank you for all you have done for our church and the work of the Lord all these years, and we'll make sure that everything will be taken care of," said Wilma.

Ranna closed her eyes tight, fighting back the tears. There was a long pause of silence as she tried to regain her composure. Wilma caressed her hand in support. Sweetiepie began to softly hum "What a Friend We Have in Jesus." The hymn eased into the air, soothing Ranna's anxiousness. They rocked in silence as Sweetiepie's medicinal voice comforted and healed the situation. After visiting for a long while, they left Ranna with a feeling that everything would be all right.

Buhley lay awake staring at the ceiling. The words of comfort from Pastor Jones' sermon had long since passed. He was soaking wet with sweat, not as much from the heat as from nervousness over the upcoming game. All the folks he ran into told him they were coming. Running away, faking sickness, or just not going - all of those thoughts raced through his mind. Just then Ranna came into the room. Slowly she walked to his bedside and sat down. She ran her hand gently through his hair. "Is something bothering you, Buhley?" asked Ranna. "You don't seem like your normal self the last week or so."

Buhley was as honest as the day was long, and he saw no other way around it, but to tell Ranna the truth. "Mamma, my stomach is tied up in knots over this baseball game. I ain't been able to eat in two days. I feel like runnin' away. I don't know why I ever told Mr. Parley I'd pitch in that game. I feel like folks is coming in from all over. What if I don't do good, Mamma? What if everybody is disappointed in me?"

Ranna continued to gently stroke his hair. She let him completely finish and then talked to him in her reassuring voice. "Buhley, I don't know much about baseball, but I know a lot about you. And I have every confidence that you'll do just fine Saturday. No matter what happens, remember this. Your daddy and I love you. You could never do anything good or bad to take our love away from you. I know how important this game is to you. You may not have noticed, but I've been watching you throw for years. People tell me you have a gift. The whole town will be proud of you no matter what the outcome. Now just close your eyes, and everything will be fine."

Buhley closed his eyes. Ranna continued to gently stroke his hair until her only child was asleep.

CHAPTER 7

Satch Moak stepped off the bus and looked around. "Okay, boys, get dressed and get loose," he said.

At six-foot-five and very little flab, Satch Moak was an imposing man by anyone's standards. In his day, he was a powerful hitter who hit massive homeruns though he never learned to hit a curve ball and his major league career was short. An old football injury left him with a slight limp. At sixty-five, Satch had forgotten more about baseball than most major league managers ever knew. Walking around the park, he surveyed the capacity of the stands and the condition of the field. Bobby Fleet arrived in his well traveled sedan. "What's the gate look like today, Bobby?" asked Satch.

"The whole town's comin'," said Bobby.

"This could be a big payday," replied Satch.

"It's headed that way."

"This team any good?"

"I don't think so. They got one player, a catcher named Benny Armstrong. He played a little," said Bobby.

"I remember him. What about pitching?" asked Satch.

"As far as I know they got nothin'."

Satch walked over to the dugout and sat down and watched his team start throwing. Parley drove up to the field with Crawdad, Buhley and a couple of more players. Bobby Fleet motioned for Parley to come over to the dugout.

"Parley, I want you to meet Satch Moak. Satch, this is Parley Hawkins," said Bobby.

Satch remained seated as they shook hands. "Thank you for letting us come to your town," he said. Always concerned about the gate, he then asked Parley, "We gonna have a crowd today?"

"There won't be a seat in the place," answered Parley. Remembering what 56 had said about the team, he added, "You gonna take it easy on us?"

"I ain't never throttled these boys. You can't pull the reigns on thoroughbreds," Satch replied confidently. "Good luck to you, Parley."

As Satch walked out of the dugout to talk to his players, 56 drove up with Benny Armstrong and a couple of other players. Edsel Moon rode Slump to the game, tied him to a telephone pole and then joined his team.

Before long, folks started to arrive. Bobby Fleet took up the money, staying busy as people kept coming. About eleven thirty, the stands were almost full. Satch glanced over at the seats, noting the number of people eating hot dogs and cotton candy and drinking Coca-Colas. "This is going to be a haul," he thought to himself with great satisfaction.

Parley took his team out for a round of infield. Ground balls went through legs, and throws went everywhere. Shaking his head, he said, "That's enough."

The sound of the ball off Satch Moak's fungo traveled all through the stands. Every eye was on the field. Leaning over the fence in the dugout, the Homerville team watched as every ball was fielded cleanly. Their jaws dropped at the crispness of the throws. They were awed by the perfect round of infield. Nudging 56 Johnson, Parley said, "This is gonna be like David and Goliath, and David ain't got no stones."

56 nodded in agreement.

Benny Armstrong took Buhley down to the bullpen. "What kind of pitches you got?" asked Benny.

"I got a hard ball, a slower hard ball, a mover and a dipsy-doodle," replied Buhley.

"What's a dipsy-doodle?"

"I hold the ball a certain way, and I don't know what it's gonna do."

Benny walked down behind the plate in the bullpen. "We ain't got very long to warm up. Just try and hit my mitt wherever I put it. Throw your fastball to start with," said Benny.

"Okay." Buhley wound up and let go. Benny's mitt remained frozen as the ball landed perfectly in the middle.

"Damn, that was a good pitch. Do that again," said Benny.

He moved his glove high and inside. Buhley fired and again hit Benny's catcher's mitt without it moving. Benny stood up and took off his mask. "You throw like this today, and who knows."

"I ain't never pitched to a live batter," said Buhley.

"All you gotta do is keep your eye on the glove, pretend the batter ain't even there, and just play catch with me," instructed Benny. He squatted down. "Throw me your other pitches, and we'll make up some signals. Whatever pitch I call and wherever I put my glove, you just throw it right there, and you'll do fine."

They threw a few more pitches and walked back to the dugout. Buhley looked up at the stands and saw they were packed. His stomach turned. He hadn't eaten in two days, so there was nothing to get sick on.

Ranna came to the game with Pastor and Wilma Jones. She waved to Buhley as they made eye contact. Early Moon and Elbert Files sat up in the top corner of the stands and shared a jar of moonshine. Wadeus and Sweetiepie Wadkins sat in the middle. Wadeus had just gotten off the graveyard shift at the saw mill and had one eye closed and the other one on the way. Miss Ida Mae Jewel sat on the edge of an aisle in her neatly pressed dress and string of pearls. She looked around, noticing some of her former pupils with pride and others with shame. Feris Strum and Nate Hayes sat on the front row much like they did each day in front of Hawkins Grocery. Nate Hayes, who wasn't all there, kept asking, "What's the score?"

Flat face and all, Feris just looked at him. In the corner of the stands, Buhley looked up to see Cheryl Dane take a bite out of some cotton candy. He was glad their eyes didn't meet. His stomach couldn't take one more ounce of nervousness. Matty Lee and Hooty Lou had closed their stores early and ridden together to the game. Buhley noticed the two of them, Hooty making small motions with his hands and Matty, as usual, laughing at one of his stories.

Jubel Odom brought his three boys to the game. "You boys just watch ol' Buhley boy throw. I ain't seen nothin' like it. Y'all just watch and see what I told you. I seen him hit the same knot in the same board ten times in a row. He didn't know I was watching. I seen him do it. Ol' Buhley boy, he's sump'in. That's what he is."

Doris bossed Ihley Pritchett all the way to the game. After blaming him for their being late, she blamed him for the bad parking spot and for getting a bad seat. She complained to him about the cost of the game. Ihley just shuffled along behind her as they walked to their seat. Listening to her, people shook their heads and once again felt sorry for Ihley.

Hovis Briggs called Satch and Parley to home plate. Hovis Briggs was a well-known umpire in South Georgia. He was a no-nonsense man who loved baseball and loved to umpire. Although he didn't think this would be a very competitive game, he welcomed the chance to see some good players. "Gentlemen, we're gonna play nine innings today. The ground rules are the same here as they are everywhere. I'm gonna call a wide strike zone to move this thing along, so let your boys know. Are there any questions?" asked Hovis.

"No, sir," replied Satch and Parley.

"Gentlemen, we're gonna flip a coin to see who is home team and visitor. Satch, call it in the air," directed Hovis. He flipped the coin.

"Heads," said Satch.

"Heads it is," confirmed Hovis.

"We'll be home," said Satch.

"Gentlemen, let's have a clean game, so we can leave here with our heads held high."

Satch and Parley shook hands and walked back to their teams. Gathering his team together, Satch said, "Okay, boys, let's get this one over early."

Parley told his team, "Just do the best you can, play hard and have fun."

Bobby Fleet had moved from collecting money and assumed his other duty as the game's official PA announcer. He leaned in close to a slightly rusted microphone and boomed, "Ladies and gentlemen, Satch Moak's traveling all-star team!"

The players ran to their positions, and the pitcher warmed up. Hovis watched him throw a few and said, "Throw it down, and let's play."

The catcher threw it to second, and the players threw it around. "Play ball!" yelled Hovis.

Along with everyone in the stands, the Homerville team was in awe of the all-star team's uniforms. They were perfectly outfitted. The only way you could tell the players apart was by the numbers on their backs. Edsel Moon stepped to the plate wearing a pair of overalls, no shirt and an old pair of shoes. Finished with one jar of moonshine, Early Moon and Elbert Files were working on a second. In unison they yelled, "Atta boy, Edsel!"

He swung at three pitches and walked back to the dugout. The next two batters did the same. Benny Armstrong grabbed Buhley as they walked out of the dugout. "Remember to throw the pitch I call, and put it where I place my mitt. We're gonna mix it up on these boys," said Benny.

Buhley nodded. He was too nervous to speak. Walking out to the mound, he stood on the rubber. With a glance at the stands, he saw Cheryl Dane watching him. Buhley looked away quickly. He picked the ball up and began to get loose. His pitches were wild. Hovis stood behind Benny to get a look and then moved off to the side. One or two of the balls went all the way to the backstop. Benny went out to talk to Buhley. "What's wrong? You ain't throwin' nothin' like you did in the bullpen," said Benny.

"I'm scared, Benny. I ain't never pitched to a batter, much less in front of the whole town," replied Buhley.

"What are you used to?"

"Out behind my house on the side of the barn, there's this knot in a board. That's what I throw at."

"Then just put yourself out there and wherever I put the glove, that's the knot. Don't even look at the batter. Just get the signal. Then throw to the knot."

"Okay."

"Batter up!" yelled Hovis.

The first batter stepped in. Benny signed a fastball and put his glove over the heart of the plate. Buhley saw the knot and fired a fastball that sailed perfectly into the middle of Benny's glove.

"Str-ike!" yelled Hovis.

The crowd erupted in applause. Benny stood up and pointed at Buhley in affirmation before throwing back the ball. Buhley felt a sudden rush of warmth and adrenaline pump through his body. A weight lifted off his shoulders. With nerves calmed, he wanted the ball. Benny moved to the outside part of the plate for the second pitch, and again the ball found the middle of the catcher's mitt. "Str-ike two!" yelled Hovis as he shot his right arm out signaling a strike.

Benny called for a change up for the third pitch. Buhley let go, and the batter swung way too early before the ball crossed the plate. Watching the batter head for the dugout, Hovis turned and asked Benny, "Where'd y'all get this kid? Where's he been playing? What's his name? I ain't never seen him, and I've seen 'em all."

"Believe it or not, that's the first live batter he's ever faced," answered Benny.

"Don't lie to me on a Saturday," said Hovis.

"I ain't lyin'. He's thrown against a barn all his life, an' that's it."

With applause from the strike out dying down, the next batter stepped up. Buhley struck him out in four pitches, and again the crowd went wild. The third batter was a left-handed fellow named Porty Hughes. Porty had ninety-six major league home runs to his credit. Although an injury cut his career short, he still possessed a big league eye and swing. Buhley jammed him on his first pitch, and he pulled it foul. The next pitch was a touch off the outside corner, and Porty slapped it over third base where it curled foul before hitting the ground. Stepping out of the batter's box, he looked at Satch down at third. Satch clapped his hands. "Let's go, Port," he called out. "Let's get this thing started."

Porty stepped back in the box. Benny called for a breaking ball. Buhley wound up and let go. The ball came right at Porty's chest, and he leaned back to avoid the pitch. Just as the ball neared the plate, it darted down and in, catching the inside corner. "Str-ike three!" yelled Hovis.

Porty walked off shaking his head. Catching up with him, Satch asked, "What's going on?"

"That guy can throw," said Porty. "I ain't never been thrown a breaking ball like that before."

He got his glove and went to the field. Satch looked up at Bobby Fleet who held out his arms in disbelief.

Benny led off the top of the second inning. It had been a long time since he had faced live pitching, but somehow he felt at home. He grounded out to the second baseman. The next two batters struck out. Buhley walked out to the mound and threw a few warm-up pitches, and Hovis yelled, "Batter up!"

The first pitch was tapped lightly to Crawdad at second base. He used his chest to knock the ball down and throw it to first base in time for out number one. The second batter hit a lazy fly ball to centerfield where Edsel Moon unorthodoxly caught out number two. When the third batter popped up behind home plate, Benny caught it for out number three. The game moved along quickly. The score was zero to zero in the middle of the seventh when Buhley walked out to the mound. At Benny's instruction, he had moved the ball in and out, slow and fast, frustrating Satch Moak's batters.

It was a hot day. Doris Pritchett told Ihley that she was parched and to hurry down to get her a Coca-Cola. "Don't you be long, Ihley. I'm not about to thirst to death. Now do something right for a change and hurry up."

Ihley shuffled his way down to the concession stand. With the long line, it took a while for him to make his purchase. His wandering eye was particularly active and rolling all around as he made his way back to the seat.

As the players were warming up for the bottom of the seventh, he approached Doris with the drink. "Where have you been, Ihley?" she demanded loudly. "I could have driven to Atlanta, bought a Coca-Cola d'rectly from the company in less time than it took you to bring this to me. I'll bet you were down there carousing with a woman. That's what I think. You're gonna get yours. I'll not put up with a letch such as you."

Everybody in the stands and on the field noticed what was happening. Parley paid special attention. Doris reached back to slap Ihley. Catching her hand in front of his face, he held it firmly but gently, forcing her to sit down. He stood over her as she sat. All eyes were on Ihley Pritchett. "Doris, I've had enough of you," he said in the strongest voice folks had ever heard him use. "All I've ever done is what you've asked. I've provided for you. I've loved you. I've stuck by you all these years, and what have I gotten in return? All you ever do is belittle me and talk down to me in front of everyone. You treat me like I'm some mangy, rat-trap dog that you're stuck with. If I'm so bad, why'd you marry me in the first place? I know I'm not the catch of the town, but you ain't neither. If you can do better, go ahead on, 'cause I've had it."

Doris sat in stunned silence. "And one more thing," said Ihley, "here's your Coca-Cola."

He held the drink over her head, dumping the whole thing on top of her. The crowd and the Homerville players began to cheer and applaud. Getting up with Coca-Cola dripping off of her, Doris ran down the stands and out of the stadium in complete humiliation. Ihley sat down in his seat. He was mobbed with well wishes. "Atta boy, Ihley."

"'Bout time, Ihley."

People patted him on the back. Down on the field, Parley let out a loud whistle and caught Ihley's eye, giving him a thumbs up.

Hovis looked at Benny and asked, "What's that all about?"

"That's about a man un-henpecking himself," said Benny as he put his mask on.

"Batter up!" yelled Hovis.

After six complete innings, Buhley's arm still felt pretty strong. He retired the side in order. The seventh and eighth were repeats of the first six. By the start of the ninth inning, neither team had scored. Satch gathered his team together. "Maybe that kid's getting tired. Let's hold 'em here, and we'll scratch out a run when we get up to bat, get on the bus and get the hell outta here. Ducky, close this thing for us."

Satch pointed to Billy Duckworth, a stumpy lefthander who threw gas. Up at bat was Edsel Moon. He'd struck out his first three times, but now he dug in. On their third jar of moonshine, Early and Elbert yelled in not so perfect unison, "Atta boy, Edsel!"

Ducky quickly got two strikes on Edsel. The third pitch delivered a breaking ball. In desperation, Edsel hit a swinging bunt down to the third baseline. It got by Ducky and teetered on the foul line. Ducky yelled to the third baseman, "Let it go! Let it go!"

The ball rolled on the chalk, then kicked back into fair ground. By the time the third baseman picked it up, Edsel Moon stood on second. After the next two batters struck out, Benny Armstrong came to the plate. With Edsel Moon on second, two out, and a scoreless game, Satch yelled out to Ducky, "Don't give him nothin'!"

Ducky was proud and thought to himself, "I ain't backing down from nobody."

The first pitch was outside for ball one. The next pitch brought a strike. The third pitch was outside for ball two. Two and one was the count. Satch yelled from the dugout, "Don't give in, Duck. You got a base open. Don't give in!"

Benny could see by Ducky's eyes that he was not going to walk him. Benny looked for something to hit. The two and one pitch was on the outer half of the plate. Swinging, Benny met it solidly, sending a line drive over the second baseman's head. Edsel Moon was rounding third when the center fielder cut the ball off and made a perfect one hop throw to the plate. In the stands, everyone was on his feet. Edsel slid hard into home plate, kicking up a dust storm Ty Cobb would be proud of. About the same time, the catcher caught the ball on the hop and applied the tag. Hovis crouched low to get the best angle on the play. When the dust settled, Hovis was right on top of the plate. All eyes were on him, and it seemed an eternity before he made the call. Pointing at one of Edsel's tattered shoes, which barely touched the plate, he yelled out, "No, no, no! He got in there. No, no, he's safe!"

Hovis turned to the crowd and threw his arms wide, indicating that Edsel got in under the tag. The place went berserk. Cokes, popcorn and everything else went flying. Jumping up, Edsel Moon did a standing back flip and headed to the dugout where he was greeted with hugs and backslaps. Early and Elbert attempted to shake hands, but missed. Hanging his head, Satch shook it back and forth.

Ducky got the next batter. It was the bottom of the ninth, one to nothing. Satch Moak had the number nine-hitter leading off. Gathering his team together, he told them, "We're gonna play the percentages. If we get a runner on, we're gonna sacrifice him to second and play for a tie, and maybe we'll get lucky."

Benny noticed Buhley's warm up pitches weren't as crisp as before. Heading over to talk with him, he asked, "You gettin' tired?"

"Just a little," replied Buhley.

"Listen," said Benny, "we ain't got but three more outs, and the great Satch Moak goes down. You got it in you?"

Buhley nodded.

Giving Buhley the ball, Benny trotted back to home plate.

"Batter up!" yelled Hovis.

Dallas Ford stepped to the plate. He previously had struck out at bat. Framing a fastball on the outside corner, Buhley kicked and fired. The ball went right down the middle of the plate with less pace and no movement like before. Dallas swung and hit a line drive gapper into left center. Fast as lightning, Edsel Moon somehow cut off the ball, holding Dallas to a single. The next batter laid down a perfect sacrifice bunt and moved Dallas to second. Satch called his next hitter over. "He's gettin' tired. You'll get a pitch to hit. Be patient," he said.

Hobson Smith stepped in the batter's box. He also had struck out his previous times at the plate. Impatiently, Hobson swung at the first pitch and hit a lazy grounder to second. Crawdad fielded the ball and threw to first as Dallas Ford ran to third. With two outs and a man in scoring position, up steps Porty Hughes. Porty was the only player on the team to have struck out but once. He looked at Satch. "Let's go, Port. There he is," said Satch, referring to Dallas on third.

Benny called time out. "Let's walk him," he suggested.

"No way," said Buhley.

"He either beats us, or we beat him. Just don't give him nothin' to hit."

Benny strolled back to home plate, buying Buhley a few precious moments to rest his arm. The count went quickly. Two balls. No strikes. Satch yelled down to Porty, "Pick yours now! Pick yours!"

Benny called for a breaking ball on the outside part of the plate. Buhley let go. It had no snap and just floated over the plate. Porty picked up the spin right away. Waiting on the ball, he then let out a massive swing. Crack came the sound of ball meeting bat -- a loud crack unlike any heard thus far in the game. The neck and head of everyone in the stands immediately snapped forward at the sound. With the ball sailing high and deep to right center field, Dallas Ford headed for home plate. Satch watched the ball for a moment and then looked at Porty Hughes. Porty was in a home run trot. He'd hit many a ball over the fence in his day, and in his mind, he'd just hit another. Satch looked back at the white orb quickly growing smaller in the midday sun. Without a doubt, it was gone.

Buhley turned and saw Edsel Moon in a full run. Edsel leaped, landed both feet on the top of the fence, and like a monkey on a limb, just perched there. Every eye watched as the ball smacked into the outstretched glove of Edsel Moon. He stood atop the fence with the ball, waiting for the umpire to give the out signal. When the ump held his right thumb high, Edsel did a front flip onto the warning track. He whooped and hollered all the way to the infield where he was mobbed. Taking off his hat, Satch threw it to the ground in disbelief. Early Moon jumped out of his seat on the back row of the stands and yelled, "Atta boy, Edsel!"

When he did, Early fell straight back off the stands, tumbling twenty feet down and landing on his backside in the rear of a flatbed truck full of hay. Leaning over the railing, Elbert Files looked down and slurred, "What'd you do that for?"

Early lifted up his head. "Well, I'll be damned," he said. "How did this hay get in the middle of me?"

After the game, Satch gathered his team together. "Men, we just got beat. That young man can pitch, and you'll never see a catch like that again. Let's get cleaned up, get on the bus and get outta here."

Parley grabbed Buhley. "Unbelievable!" he said. "That's what you are. I ain't never seen nothin' like this, and as long as I live, I never will again. You just shut down the best of the best."

"Yes, sir," replied Buhley, smiling as big as his mouth would allow.

Calling Parley and the winning team over, Satch said, "Mr. Hawkins, congratulations to you and your team. This is the first time we've been beat."

He reached into his back pocket and pulled out a roll of one hundred dollar bills, counting fifty of them slow and hard into Parley's hand. Tipping his hat, he turned to walk away. He took a few steps and turned around. "Hey, pitcher!" he yelled.

Buhley looked up. "Come over here," said Satch.

"Yes, sir," said Buhley as he walked over to Satch.

Satch put his arm over Buhley's shoulders. "What's your name, son?" asked Satch.

"Buhley Sparks."

"Buhley, I've been in baseball almost fifty years and seen a lot of good pitching, but I'm not sure I've ever seen anything like you. How old are you, son?"

"Sixteen."

"What school do you play for?"

"We ain't got a team at our school."

"Then where do you play?"

"I don't, Mr. Moak. I ain't never pitched a game until today."

Satch's knees went weak. Holding himself up with Buhley's shoulders, he asked, "You tellin' me this was your first time?"

"Yes, sir."

"Let's go sit down," said Satch. They walked into the dugout and sat down by themselves. Satch asked him question after question about how he had learned to pitch. "I know lots of baseball people. It's my hunch some of them will want to look at you. Do you mind giving me your phone number?" asked Satch.

"We ain't got no phone. You can call Mr. Parley. He knows how to find me."

Satch got up and patted Buhley on the shoulder. "You're a hell of a pitcher, Buhley Sparks."

As Satch Moak turned and walked away, Buhley sat on the bench and watched, still absorbed in every word he'd uttered. The ballpark was almost empty when Buhley walked to the parking lot and got into Parley's car. As they started to drive away, Parley noticed Bobby Fleet getting into his car. Driving his car over near Bobby, he rolled down his window and yelled, "Hey, Bobby, remember one thing!"

"What's that, Parley?" asked Bobby.

"We ain't never been beat."

With that said, Parley hurriedly rolled up his window and drove away. Bobby just stood, taking in a dose of his own medicine.

From the front seat, Crawdad turned to talk to Buhley. "Mr. Parley divided the winnings between all the players. We each got five hundred dollars. Here's yours," said Crawdad as he reached back over the seat and handed Buhley five crisp one hundred dollar bills.

"I ain't never seen, much less held, five hundred dollars. Thank you, Mr. Parley."

Buhley grew quiet, staring out the window on the way home. The conversation he'd had with Satch replayed itself over and over in his mind. It was late afternoon when they pulled into Buhley's driveway. August was on the porch in his rocking chair chewing his afternoon tobacco. Pulling up a rocker beside August, Buhley sat down. "We won, Daddy," he said. His father just stared straight ahead. "I did good, too."

August leaned over and spit his tobacco juice. "So, you gave them boys what for, did you?" said August.

"Yes, sir. I wish you coulda come."

"This farm never stops. If you ain't riding it all the time, it'll leave you."

"Yes, sir, I understand," replied Buhley.

August reached over and patted Buhley on the arm. That was his way of telling Buhley that he was proud of him. Before long, the evening breeze had eased them both to sleep.

CHAPTER 8

Benny Armstrong slammed his winnings down on the bar at Clips and held a Pabst Blue Ribbon beer high in the air. Letting out a loud whistle, he shouted, "Drinks are on me!"

56 Johnson was in his usual spot leaning against the bar. "I'll never forget today, never. Who'd a thunk it? We beat Satch Moak. How did it feel, Benny?" asked 56.

"Better than a one punch fight," replied Benny.

He sucked down the last half of his beer and asked for another. "Man, oh, man! We beat the great Satch Moak. I can't believe it. Did you see him throw his hat when Edsel caught that ball?" asked Benny.

"Yeah," replied 56.

Everyone crowded around Benny, peppering him with questions about the game. He sat on a bar stool like a king and his court, drinking in the moment and answering every question with pride.

Buhley lay on his bed, the sweat on his body evaporating in the air of his oscillating fan. He stared at the ceiling, savoring the events of the day. His stomach was full from a supper of fried chicken, fresh garden tomatoes, field peas and mashed potatoes. Ranna tiptoed into the room and sat down on the side of his bed. Her emphysema now affected her breathing to the point that her sentences were broken from shortness of breath. "We're so proud of you, Buhley," said Ranna.

"Thank you, Mamma," replied Buhley. "Why didn't Daddy come to the game?"

Ranna gently stroked Buhley's hair. "You daddy loves you very much. He's very proud of you. He had some failings earlier in his life that still haunt him. Your dad thinks if he's not working, he's going to lose the farm. That's not true at all, but he doesn't see it that way. But let me assure you, he's real proud of you."

Buhley turned his head, looking Ranna in the eyes as a sign he understood.

"Thank you for supper, Mamma. I was starving."

"You're welcome, son. You just go ahead and relax now 'cause you did good today. You did real good."

Ranna got up and walked towards the door.

"Turn the light off, please, Mamma."

"Sleep good, sugar. I love you," she softly replied, turning off the light.

He lay in bed, staring at the ceiling. Vivid memories of the day rushed through his mind. The conversation with Satch Moak again replayed in his thoughts. Then pretty Cheryl Dane. Buhley remembered glancing at her in the stands and wondered what she thought of his performance.

Edsel Moon's catch came to mind, and he laughed at the centerfielder's antics. With flash recollections, he relived the thrill of striking out all of those ex-major league, minor league and ex-college players. Soon Buhley's eyes grew heavy, and the air and hum from the oscillating fan eased him to sleep.

August dropped Ranna and Buhley at church the next morning. As usual, he let them get away from the truck before pulling off, so they wouldn't be overcome by exhaust fumes. The sanctuary was filled as always. Buhley and Crawdad sat with Ranna. One row over sat Doris and Ihley Pritchett. For the first time anyone could remember, Ihley sat tall in the pew. Although Doris was a good three to four inches taller than Ihley, this day no one seemed to notice. He sang the hymns loudly, greeted people with confidence, and most of all, seemed to be wearing the pants in the family. Pastor Jones got up to preach. "As I look out on the congregation this morning, I see all familiar faces. No doubt, all of you either heard about or saw the baseball game yesterday. I want to take a quick moment and congratulate those in our flock who participated in the joyous win. Parley, would you stand? Parley helped organize the game. Buhley and Crawdad, please stand. Now is there anyone I'm overlooking?"

Pastor Jones looked around. "Let's give these participants a big round of applause."

The church was filled with the sound of clapping and adulation. Buhley looked down at Ranna who was smiling from ear-to-ear. Looking around at all of the people, he felt ten feet tall. After the service, he was deluged with many questions about the game.

Parley walked into Hooty Lou's Barber Shop and took a seat. "What's shakin', Hooty?"

"Not much. How 'bout you?"

"Business must be slow. I don't see no blood on the floor."

"Well, sit right down, and we'll take care of that," answered Hooty as he let out a loud hyena laugh.

He put the barber sheet over Parley after wrapping his neck in tissue paper. "You want the usual?"

"Do I have to?"

Hooty eased the chair back, and Parley settled in for another bad haircut.

"You know somethin', Parley?"

"What's that?"

"Buhley Sparks has been gettin' his hair cut in here all of his life. We've talked a lot of baseball together, especially pitching. You know, I taught him all he knows about pitching."

Parley rolled his eyes. "Oh, yeah."

Hooty continued. "As a matter of fact, I called his pitches last Saturday. I bet you didn't know that, did you Parley?"

Parley didn't respond. "Well, neither did Buhley," said Hooty as he staggered backwards with a loud laugh. "Did you hear that? Neither did Buhley!"

He laughed so hard he had to take a seat. Parley was glad because Hooty was still holding a razor. Just seeing Hooty break up made Parley burst out laughing himself. Rising up, Parley looked in the mirror, checking his hair on both sides. Hooty calmed down, finished the haircut and spun him around to view the results. "How's that?" asked Hooty.

Parley noticed his hair was now uneven. "You ain't lost your touch."

August sent Buhley up to Matty Lee's hardware store to get some parts for his tractor. From behind his counter where he was helping another customer, Matty spied Buhley and gave him the thumbs up sign. "Great game the other day, Buhley. Way to mow 'em down."

"Thank you, Mr. Lee," replied Buhley. "Where are your three-eighth inch bolts?"

Matty signaled the correct aisle. "Thank you," said Buhley as he walked back towards the shelf.

"Let me know if you need some help," called out Matty as Buhley took off around a corner and went out of sight. Looking his customer in the eye, Matty stated, "That boy can pitch."

Buhley found what he needed and headed to the counter to pay. Rounding the corner of the aisle without looking up, he ran into Cheryl Dane. He instinctively reached out and grabbed her arm. The touch of her silky smooth skin made his stomach jump up into his throat and his knees weaken. She, like Buhley, would be a senior in high school. Cheryl had blossomed into a beautiful young woman.

"Oh, excuse me, Buhley!"

"No, no, Cheryl, that was my fault. I wasn't paying attention."

"I'm glad we ran into each other. I wanted to tell you what a wonderful game you pitched the other day. My dad loves baseball and knows a lot about it. He said he's never seen anyone pitch like that. Not ever."

While she talked, Buhley just stared, taking in how pretty she was. He longed to kiss her right then and there in Matty Lee's hardware store.

"Thank you, Cheryl. I saw you at the game eating cotton candy."

Cheryl's eyes lit up. "You saw me?"

"Yeah, but I was so nervous. I didn't know what I was doing."

Buhley sensed her sparkle of interest when he told her he'd noticed her at the game. He wondered if she possibly had feelings for him. "I was so proud of all of ya'll. It was a great day," she added.

Buhley gazed at her a moment longer in silence. With a shake of his head, he remembered August and the bolts. "Well, I gotta get these parts back to my daddy."

"I'm glad I got to see you."

"Me, too," said Buhley. "See you later."

After paying for the merchandise, Buhley headed for home. En route, he ran into Jubel Odom and Buckswamp who'd just finished up a day of plowing. "Buhley Sparks, how you is?" asked Jubel.

"I'm fine, Mr. Jubel."

"I seen you chunk that ball the other day. I seen ya. You chunked that other team right outta town. That's what you did. I seen it. I had my boys with me. My boy Amos goes to school. They plays ball where he go. He say he seen 'em play and ain't seen nobody do what you can do. You got a gift. That's what you got. Use it wisely, ol' Buhley boy. Use it wisely."

"Yes, sir."

"Come on, Buckswamp. Let's get to the house."

Jubel and Buckswamp continued their slow walk home.

When Buhley arrived, he gave August the parts and went into the house. Some ladies from church were helping with cooking and housework while Ranna rested in a living room chair. Buhley pulled up a seat beside her. "Mamma, can I talk to you?"

"Of course, Buhley."

"I got this girl I can't quit thinkin' about. She's got me covered up, Mamma. I mean covered up through and through. I think about her in the morning when I wake up and at night when I go to bed."

"Who is it?"

Buhley paused for a moment. "Well, it's… it's… um… it's Cheryl Dane," he shyly stammered.

Ranna nodded approvingly. "Oh, she's a beautiful girl and nice, too. You'd do proud by her."

"I been fixed on her since kindergarten. I just saw her at Matty Lee's, and my stomach shrunk all up, and my knees went weak. How do you know when you're in love, Mamma?"

"Sounds like if you're not yet, you're missing a good opportunity," Ranna said in a broken sentence between breaths. "You're probably just infatuated with her. Some people start out with infatuation, and it grows into love."

"How did you know when you were in love with Daddy?"

Ranna smiled to herself. "He was a tough nut to crack. He wasn't easy to get to know, but once I did, I slowly fell in love with him. Your daddy's been real good to me, and I love him dearly. He's had some bad things happen to him, and his exterior may be a little rough, but inside, he's a lovable, dear person, and that's the man I married."

She put her head back on the chair to catch her breath. After pausing for a moment, she took Buhley's hand. "When you're truly in love with someone, you'll think, 'I want to spend the rest of my life with this person.' That's how you'll know."

Buhley answered, "Yes, Mamma." To himself, he thought, "I'm already there."

"Will you take me to my room? I want to lie down."

"Yes, ma'am."

Buhley helped his mother walk slowly to the bedroom, her slight frame leaning against him. As Ranna lay on the bed, she held one of his hands with both of hers. "Bless your heart, Buhley! I'm so proud of the way you've turned out. I believe God has big plans for you, and I love you with all my heart."

"I love you, too, Mamma," he answered quietly as he leaned over and kissed her on the forehead. "Now, you just rest and don't worry about a thing."

She looked at him and smiled and slowly closed her eyes.

That night Buhley lay in bed thinking about what his mamma had told him. He couldn't quit thinking about Cheryl and how beautiful she looked. He wanted to spend the rest of his life with her. School was starting soon, and he would be sure to get a seat next to her. In his mind, Buhley went over the conversation Cheryl and he had had at Matty Lee's. He was sure he detected excitement in her voice when he told her he saw her at the game. Buhley was looking for something to keep his hopes up, something to build on. He lay awake planning their future together until his eyes could no longer remain open.

The next day when Buhley awoke, he looked at the clock, noticing it was later in the morning than he usually slept. The usual breakfast smells weren't in the air. Buhley heard people milling around the house. Getting out of bed, he dressed and walked into the kitchen. August sat at the kitchen table with his face in his hands. "Daddy, what's going on?" he asked. Slowly, August lifted his head, redness and puffiness surrounding his eyes.

"She's gone, Buhley," said August.

"Who's gone? What do you mean?"

His voice cracking, August answered, "Your mamma. She passed on early this morning."

Hitting him like a sledgehammer, Buhley realized that the conversation he had with Mamma the day before was their last. Light headed, his knees buckled. Wilma Jones rushed over, grabbed Buhley and held him up. Buhley looked at his daddy and saw a heartbroken man. He saw a man who had just lost his soul mate and the love of his life - a man needing comfort. Suddenly, a calm came over Buhley, and he regained his strength. It was as if Ranna was speaking directly to Buhley, telling him, "Don't worry about me. I'm fine. Go to your daddy and take care of him. He needs you."

Buhley walked over to August and sat down beside him. As August put his face back down in his hands, Buhley began to rub his back and search for the right words to say. Nothing came. He just leaned over to August's ear. "I love you, Daddy," he whispered.

August kept his face in his hands and moved his head back and forth to affirm Buhley's words. For a long while, Buhley just sat and rubbed and held his dad. Every now and then, he would tell August not to worry -- that everything would be fine.

After a time, August lifted his head out of his hands, looked at Buhley and asked, "What am I going to do?"

Buhley didn't hesitate at all. "I'll take care of you, Daddy. Everything will be all right."

August rested his head on Buhley's shoulder and kept it there for a while. Then he rose and went into his room, closed the door and lay on the bed. Wilma Jones assured Buhley that all the arrangements were made, and she would stay as long as she was needed.

The news of Ranna's passing spread quickly, and folks came from all over to pay their respects. Story after story was told of how positively Ranna had affected the lives of many. Keeping a close eye on August, Buhley shared with him the encouraging words. More withdrawn more than ever, August sat on the porch in his rocker, acknowledging visitors yet barely hearing a word that was spoken. He stared straight away like he was in a trance. Hundreds of people visited the small farmhouse, and enough food poured in to feed a large army. Crawdad faithfully stayed near Buhley.

On the afternoon before the funeral, while August took a nap, Buhley and Crawdad walked out into the field. "You doin' all right, Buhley?" asked Crawdad.

"I almost passed out when I was told the news yesterday morning. Your mamma had to hold me up. And then the strangest feeling came over me. This peace, this strength… It was like my mamma was tellin' me she was fine and to go help my dad. He's broke up pretty good." Tears came to his eyes. "He looks so broken, so lonely, and there's nothing I can do to help him."

The emotions overcame him, and he cried uncontrollably. Crawdad kept close by, but didn't say a word. Buhley cried till he was exhausted. "Sorry, Crawdad. I don't want to let Daddy know I cried. I gotta be strong for him."

Putting his arm around his best friend, Crawdad nodded. "I understand. Just rinse your face off at the faucet before you go back in, and he'll never know."

The First Baptist Church was as crowded as it had ever been. People spilled out into the churchyard. On each side of the church, the three large stained-glass windows were opened, and folks gathered around them to hear the service. Everyone stood as August and Buhley entered. Sweetiepie Wadkins stood in the front corner of the church and sang a cappella, "What a Friend We Have in Jesus." Her soft, soothing voice wafted through every nook and cranny of the sanctuary, giving relief to aching hearts.

As they made their way down to the front pew, Buhley kept his arm around his father. Parley sat on the seat next to August's left, and Crawdad sat by Buhley on his right. August kept his head down through most of the service except when he tilted it back to look up at the ceiling, all the while just staring blankly.

The congregation sang all the stanzas of "Amazing Grace" and "The Old Rugged Cross" before Pastor Jones joined the pulpit. Slowly opening his Bible, he looked out at those in attendance and then down at his Bible again. Upon opening his mouth to begin his talk, he was overcome with emotion and paused for a short time. Pastor Jones lifted his head once more and began to speak. "We come here today to celebrate the life of Mrs. Ranna Sparks. She was small in stature, but large in spirit. Ranna had three loves in her life, her Lord and Savior Jesus Christ, her family and her students. She was a schoolteacher by trade, but an inspiration in life. Over the past few days, I have met many of her former students who expressed to me the gratitude and love they have for her in their hearts. The time she shared with them and the concern she showed them helped direct them on the paths to the successful lives they are living today."

Many in the congregation nodded their heads in agreement. The minister continued. "Ranna's pride and joy was her family, August and Buhley. She loved y'all very much," he said, gazing down at the two of them. "Often we would talk after a service, and she would relate to me the goings on in her family. She always spoke with adoration and affection when speaking of you. Ranna had great maternal instincts, and she took care of her family. I know personally that she was a great cook and spent many hours in the kitchen making sure her boys were well fed. I've tasted no better fried chicken or creamed corn than I've had at the table of Ranna Sparks. She went to great lengths to make her family's life as comfortable as possible. While Ranna may not have been blessed with an abundance of material things, she gave her family the greatest blessing of all, her love. Not one time did you go to school, Buhley, and not one time did you leave the house, August, that you didn't know in your heart that she loved you. Ranna wasn't shy about showing her love to her family. They were the foundation upon which she lived. It was the foundation upon which she was most happy. I can remember coming here as a first year pastor and visiting the Sparks' farm house. We would sit out on the porch and rock, and with joy in her voice, she would tell me how she and August had met and how Buhley was a late gift from God. You could look at her in that setting, on that porch of her house, and know that's where she belonged." Pastor Jones looked at Buhley and August once more. "Both of you gave her great pleasure, and she loved you with all her heart."

He paused and looked over the congregation. "Perhaps what we'll remember most about Ranna Sparks was her great love for her Lord and Savior Jesus Christ. It was that love that created all the other acts of love that benefited most of us here. In the fifteen years I've pastored this church, I don't recall a service or a church event where I didn't see Ranna in attendance. If you didn't see her arrive, most times you could hear her come up in the old Chevy truck that August still drives today. Many of us strive to live Christ-like lives. Ranna Sparks succeeded. She never had the opportunity to preach a sermon, so she lived one. We should be comforted in the fact that as we abide in this sanctuary this very hour, so Ranna Sparks abides with her Lord and Savior Jesus Christ."

Later that afternoon, August and Buhley sat out on the porch in their rocking chairs. The ladies of the church were milling around in the kitchen, making and planning meals for weeks to come. Buhley thanked everyone for coming, as August looked blankly ahead. As the sun began to set, the crowd of people who had come to the funeral and then to the house began to depart. The ladies gave Buhley all the food instructions, and he thanked them for their efforts as they left. Night overtook day, and Buhley found himself alone with August on the porch. This was the first time they'd been on their own since Ranna's passing. Buhley thought. He knew they needed to get back to normal as quickly as possible or at least get started going through the normal motions. Touching August's arm, Buhley took the first step. "Daddy, maybe we better go in and get some supper."

August didn't say a word as he slowly raised himself out of the rocker and headed inside.

CHAPTER 9

A year and a half passed by. Buhley graduated from high school and began to help August around the farm. Parley Hawkins also was using Buhley to harvest his timber property. Throwing himself into his work more than ever, August's age was becoming more and more apparent. Some of the regular chores August had always done now required Buhley's help. Jubel Odom came by more often and helped August with the farm's upkeep. The ladies from church still checked in regularly to see what they could do.

The phone rang at Hawkins's grocery store. Listening to Jim Reeves on the patched-up stereo system, Parley turned the music down and answered the phone. "I'm trying to reach Mr. Parley Hawkins," the voice said.

"You got 'im reached," replied Parley.

"Mr. Hawkins, my name is Buzzy Preacher. I'm calling representing the Atlanta Peaches concerning Buhley Sparks. We'd like to have him come down to spring training for a tryout," explained Buzzy.

Parley was stunned and stammered into the phone. "Huh? What? Wha'd you say? Is this a joke or sumpthin'?"

"This is not a joke, Mr. Hawkins. On the recommendation of Satch Moak, we'd like Buhley Sparks to try out for the Peaches."

Parley thought for a quick moment. "Tell me how this works."

He sat by the phone and took down all the information, asking all the questions he could think of. "Thank you, Mr. Preacher. I'll call you tomorrow."

Hanging up the phone, Parley jumped from behind the counter and threw down his apron. Nose-diving out the door and towards his car, he briefly turned to Ferris Strum who was busy warming a porch chair. "If anybody comes in the store, tell him to help himself."

He jumped in his car, not waiting for a response. Ferris looked at Nate Hayes, with a puzzled look on his face. Making a quick exit out of town, Parley headed for some of his timberland where Buhley was working. He had just traded for a brand new Cadillac, but didn't spare the horses. Though the car drove more smoothly than any other vehicle available, it threw Parley around like a bad carnival ride when he turned from the highway onto a dirt road filled with bumps, crevices and puddles. He rode hard until he reached the location where the men were working. Parley stopped the car, got out and stood beside the road until the ringing of chain saws quieted down. Letting out a loud whistle, he turned every eye upon him. "Buhley! Buhley Sparks, come over here!" he yelled at the top of his lungs.

Thinking something was gravely wrong, Buhley threw down his gloves and ran towards the car. "What's wrong, Mr. Parley?" he asked out of breath as he reached the Cadillac.

"Nothing, son. Nothing. I got some good news to tell you. Sit down in the car, and let's talk."

Buhley was filthy from working and knew how Parley felt about his Cadillac. "Mr. Parley, maybe I better not sit in your car. I'll mess it up."

Parley signaled for him to get in. "I don't care, Buhley. This is big. Real big!"

As Buhley sat down on the luxurious front seat of that brand new car, it sank down with him. Tired from the day's work, his whole body relaxed. Buhley thought how much nicer the seat felt than any chair at home. Parley sat down behind the steering wheel and adjusted the seat as far back as it would go to give them room. "Buhley, I got a call from a Buzzy Preacher of the Atlanta Peaches. They want you to come down to spring training for a tryout."

Buhley just stared at Parley in silence. His stomach went up into his throat. He stammered his reply. "They want me to come try out for the Peaches? That's the big leagues. How'd they know about me?"

"Satch Moak told Buzzy Preacher about you, and they want a look."

The old memory of that conversation with Satch Moak came flooding back to Buhley. He remembered Satch saying, "I know some people who might be interested in you."

Seeing Buhley was lost in thought, Parley interrupted. "You gotta go in two weeks, and it's only a tryout. Might nothin' come of it."

Buhley stared off in the distance. "I understand."

"You need to talk to your daddy and make some arrangements. If you want to do it, I'll call 56 Johnson to get Benny Armstrong to throw with you before you go."

"Yes, sir."

After letting him sit a little longer to absorb the news, Parley nudged him. "Get on back to work, and I'll speak with you tomorrow."

"Yes, sir."

Buhley got out of the car and went back to where the men were working. Walking slowly and thinking, he stumbled. "Something wrong, Buhley?" asked Sporty Schuster.

Sporty Schuster was a man's man. He was forty-five years old and looked like he had been cut out of a block of granite. When he was seventeen, Sporty started to work for Parley. Since then, he had worked his way up to foreman. Parley paid him well, and he earned every dime. A legend in Homerville, Sporty was strong as an ox, but gentle as a lamb -- unless he was riled. The story was told that when he was downtown with his wife one night, a stranger made a pass at her in a not so gentlemanly way. Sporty squared off with him and let him throw the first punch. Catching the man's fist with his hand, he bent it back until the man knelt down on the ground. When he let the man up, the stranger took off running and was never seen again. Even Benny

Armstrong respected Sporty Schuster. "No, sir," Buhley slowly answered. "Mr. Parley just told me that the Atlanta Peaches want me to come down to spring training for a tryout."

Sporty rushed over to shake Buhley's hand. "Congratulations!"

Buhley gave Sporty a weak-handed shake. Sporty stopped him. "Listen to me, Buhley. When a man gives you a handshake, you give him one back. Don't give him a dishrag, or he'll not think two cents of you. When you go down there with those ball players, you give them a handshake that says, 'Buhley Sparks is in town.' You understand?"

"Yes, sir!" replied Buhley as he gave Sporty a firm grip.

"It's the little things in life that make a difference. You only get one chance to make a first impression." That said, he reached down with one arm, cranked the chain saw with a single pull and went back to work.

Late that afternoon, Sporty dropped Buhley off at his house and drove away. August sat on the porch chewing his afternoon tobacco. Pulling a rocking chair next to August, Buhley cleared his throat. "Daddy, can I talk to you a minute?"

August nodded his consent. "Mr. Parley got a call from the Atlanta Peaches today, and they want me to come down to spring training for a tryout."

Not saying a word, August raised his eyebrows as far up his forehead as they could go. "What do you think, Daddy?"

August leaned over his chair and spit a stream of tobacco juice before answering. "I've watched you chunk for a long time. I never thought anything would come of it, and I done told you so. Maybe I'm wrong. Somebody thinks you can, or they wouldn't bother with you. I don't want you to regret not doing something on my account."

"Thank you, Daddy. I have to leave in two weeks."

August stared straight ahead and nodded in the affirmative.

"I'm going in and fix supper. You want butter or gravy on your mashed potatoes?" asked Buhley.

"Gravy," replied August with his eyes closed.

The next morning Buhley climbed in the truck beside Sporty. "You talk to your dad last night?" asked Sporty.

"Yes, sir."

"What'd he say?"

"He don't say much of nothing most of the time, but he let me know it was all right with him if I go down there."

"How 'bout that! Parley told me he was going to come find you and talk with you today to see what you're gonna do. I think he's as excited as you are."

"I'll bet he ain't as worried. I might go down there and make a fool of myself. What if they laugh at me or something?"

Sporty shifted gears in the truck and gave Buhley a sidelong glance. "I ain't never seen you throw, but people tell me you're a sight for sore eyes when it comes to pitchin'. The one thing I always tell people is just do your best. That's all you can do. If that ain't good enough, then at least you can come back and look me in the eye and say, 'Sporty, I did my best. I gave it every ounce of effort I had.' If you do that, Buhley, you'll have no regrets. And if you have to come back here, it ain't so bad. Parley's a great man to work for, and your dad's got the farm and all. Sounds to me like you got a win-win situation. If they keep you, you'll be doing something you love. If they cut you, you'll be living with people that you love. You can't lose."

Buhley grinned. "Thanks for telling me. I ain't thought of it that way."

Parley drove up about mid-morning, bouncing his shiny new Cadillac on the rutted dirt roads. Buhley saw him stop his car and started walking towards him. "You talk to your daddy?" asked Parley.

"Yes, sir."

"What'll it be, Buhley Sparks?"

"I'm going."

"Hot dang!" said Parley as he danced a little jig.

Watching from a distance, Sporty Schuster laughed. "Boss is more excited than Buhley."

An arm across Buhley's shoulders, Parley started planning. "I'll call Buzzy Preacher and tell him. Then I'll get Benny Armstrong to throw with you a couple of times before you go. We ain't got much time."

With a parting slap to Buhley's back, Parley walked towards his car. He took a few steps and turned back. "Congratulations, Buhley. This is quite an honor. No matter what, you can be proud of it the rest of your life."

"Thank you, Mr. Parley."

As Parley drove away, Buhley walked back to where the men were working and began strapping a harness around a big log, getting ready to hoist it up on the truck bed. Sporty studied him for a moment and then spoke. "Listen, anything you gotta do to get ready for this tryout, just do it. They ain't gonna bother with you but one time, and if you don't cut the mustard, it's adios amigo. They won't send no Christmas card neither. So if you need some time off, take it. We'll make do."

"I appreciate that, Mr. Schuster."

Back in town, Parley found a couple of customers waiting in the store. He rang up their purchases, delaying until they left to pick up the phone to call Buzzy Preacher. Parley bit his lower lip and said a quick prayer. "Lord, don't let me mess this up." His hands shook as he dialed. "Buzzy Preacher, is that you? Hey, this is Parley Hawkins," he said, trying to sound casual. "You called me about Buhley Sparks. I spoke to Buhley, and he'd be right honored to come down there to y'all's place and throw for you."

"That's good, Parley, but let me remind you this is just a tryout. If he's not what we're looking for, he'll probably be back right away. Unfortunately, a lot of boys come down here with big dreams and leave with broken hearts. We take what Satch Moaks says seriously. Of course, I've never seen him pitch, but if he's what Satch says he is, then we want a look," said Buzzy.

"I understand. Buzzy, have you got just a minute to let me tell you a little bit about Buhley, so when he comes down there, you'll understand what's comin'?"

"Of course."

"Buhley grew up in Homerville -- a one-horse town, but the darn horse died. He ain't never been north of Macon nor south of Jacksonville. Your place will be as far as he's ever been from home. He lost his mamma about a year and a half ago, and it's just him and his dad. He was born late in their marriage, and his dad is a little old now and more dependent on Buhley than he used to be. It's hard to believe, but he ain't never played organized baseball. I'm not even sure he knows all the rules. But what I am sure of is he can flat pitch. I know that. He's got a natural born gift. That's what he's got. I'm telling you all this, Buzzy, so you'll know that he ain't a man of the world or nothing. I care very deeply for him, and I don't want to see him hurt. I'm not talking about him not being able to pitch for y'all. I understand this is the big league, and it's a business. If he ain't good enough, so be it. I'm talking about somebody taking advantage of him or making fun of him. It sure would rest my mind to know you might look in on him a good bit and make sure he's being treated proper and all."

"Don't you worry about a thing, Parley. I'll make sure he's all right. I'll be excited to meet him and will pick him up personally from the bus station."

"You're a good man, Buzzy."

"If you have any more questions, give me a call; otherwise, I'll expect Buhley to be here on the twentieth."

"That sounds good."

Hanging up the phone, Parley sat back behind the counter, put on a Pasty Kline album, propped his feet up and began to relax. He cut his eyes out the window and saw Benny Armstrong walking on the other side of the street. Jumping up, Parley ran outside and called, "Benny! Benny, come over here! You got a second?"

"Be there in a minute," Benny yelled back, walking into Matty Lee's hardware store. When Benny ambled into Hawkins, Parley already had a spare chair pulled up near the counter and an opened bottle of icy cold Coca-Cola waiting. "Sit down for awhile and drink a soda with me," invited Parley.

"What's up?" asked Benny as he took a big slug from his bottle.

"Buhley Sparks has been invited to come down to spring training and try out with the Atlanta Peaches."

Mid-swallow, Benny lurched forward in his chair, spitting most of the soda on the wooden grocery floor. Between choking coughs, he blurted, "Are you kidding me?"

"No, sir."

"Well, I'll be damned." He paused and thought for a moment. "You want me to practice with him before he goes down there?"

Parley grinned. "Benny, you read my mind. I sure would be grateful if you could help him."

Downing the last of his Coke, Benny nodded. "Be my pleasure."

He shook Parley's hand as he turned to leave. As he walked out of the door, Parley heard him say, "Well, I'll be damned. Buhley Sparks got him a tryout."

Climbing out of Sporty's truck, Buhley said, "Thanks for the ride."

"See you tomorrow," said Sporty.

"Yes, sir."

August sat on the porch in the late afternoon light. Settling into the rocking chair beside his dad, Buhley gave him the news. "I told Mr. Parley I'm goin'."

August didn't speak -- just nodded. His eyes took in Buhley's filthy, tired-looking appearance. "Seems you ran into some work today."

"Yes, sir."

"Never saw that hurt nobody."

With that said, August closed his eyes. Buhley, eyes already closed, did not respond. They began to rock in unison and soon both were asleep.

Benny Armstrong put his arm around Buhley and said, "You still got it, son."

They had just finished throwing at the Travisville ballpark where they had played against Satch Moak's all-star team.

"Let's sit in the stands and talk for a minute," Benny continued. "I ain't never had any major league experience, personal or nothing. But I've talked to enough people who have, and they all say the same thing. It's a business. Think of it as a piece of meat on the grill. When one side's done, they flip it over and cook the other side till it's done. When the whole steak's cooked, they throw it away and put another on the grill, and the whole process starts again. You see what I'm saying?"

"I think so."

"Lots of these guys who go to spring training, they got stuff behind them. They've played in college or the minors or their daddy knows a scout or they got an uncle in the organization or something like that. You -- you got nothing behind you. You ain't even played one game of organized baseball." Benny shook his head in disbelief that Buhley was even getting a tryout. "I have a lot of respect for you, Buhley, and I ain't never seen nobody throw like you, but to them, you're just another piece of meat to throw on the grill. They may not even give you a chance to get cooked on one side before they throw you away. Understand?"

"I understand. Sporty Schuster told me the same thing. He told me I'm in a win-win situation. I go down there, and if I make the organization, that's great. If I don't, I come home and continue my life here, and that's great, too."

"Hell, sounds to me you got it figured out. I told you those things because I didn't want you going down there looking for a picture that wasn't there."

Walking back to Benny's car for the drive back to Homerville, Buhley smacked the baseball in the palm of his hand. "Thanks for everything, Benny."

Buhley sat waiting on the porch when Parley drove up the dirt drive to the Sparks' farm. "Buhley, we gotta head out. The bus will be here in ten minutes," said Parley.

Picking up his daddy's old tattered suitcase, Buhley stepped off the porch, heading towards the field. "I'll be right back, Mr. Parley." He walked to the edge of the field and stopped. August was out working in the middle of the garden. "Daddy, I gotta go!" yelled Buhley.

His daddy stopped and looked up just long enough to give a half wave. "I won't be long, Daddy!"

Once more, August looked up briefly, this time giving a slight nod. Worn out suitcase in hand, Buhley walked to Parley's car. He remembered what Ranna had told him about August; her words echoed from that evening after he'd pitched against the all-star team. In the car, Buhley sat in silence.

Parley knew Buhley was troubled over leaving August. Putting a hand on Buhley's shoulder, he said, "Don't worry about your dad. I've known him since before you were born. He's a good man. He's just hurting a little, but not from what you're doing. I promise I'll look in on him every day, and the ladies of the church will feed him like a prize hog."

"Thank you, Mr. Parley."

As they backed out of the driveway, August propped himself on the hoe, saying softly, "Go get 'em, boy!"

The bus pulled up right on time. It was almost empty, and Buhley was the only one boarding in Homerville. "Well, I guess it's time," said Parley.

"Yes, sir," replied Buhley as he stuck his hand out to shake Parley's. "Thank you for everything, Mr. Parley. And thank you for looking in on Daddy."

"No problem. You got both of my phone numbers, don't you, Buhley?"

"Yes, sir."

"You don't hesitate to call me day or night, no matter what, you hear?"

"I will, Mr. Parley."

Shaking hands for the last time, Buhley climbed aboard the bus and chose a seat near the front. The bus doors closed, and with brakes letting out a blast of air, the bus slowly pulled away from the corner. As the Greyhound accelerated down Main Street, Parley looked towards the sky and said, "Lord, be with him."

Buhley looked out the window as storefronts began to pass by faster and faster. Reaching the last block of town, he spied Cheryl Dane who waved as the bus drove past. Not believing his eyes, Buhley jumped out of his seat and ran to the back window. He waved, both of them staring at each other until the bus turned a corner and drove out of sight. Wide-eyed, Buhley returned to his seat, excited that Cheryl had seen him off. His excitement was interrupted by a voice asking, "Where you headed, son?"

Startled by the question, Buhley looked up in the rearview mirror to see two eyes watching him. "I said, 'Where you headed?'"

"Bradenton, Florida," replied Buhley.

"What you gonna do there?" asked the voice.

Buhley inhaled to answer. The man said quickly, "No, no, don't tell me. You're going to see an uncle."

"No, sir."

"You're going down there to work," said the man.

"No, sir."

"You're going down there to find your long lost love?" he asked.

"No, sir."

"Then why you going?" asked the man.

"I'm going to try out for the Atlanta Peaches," replied Buhley.

"Come on up and sit by me," said the eyes from the rear view mirror.

Buhley moved up to the front seat across from the driver. "My name's Harold E. Munn." He pointed to an engraved sign that read, "This vehicle is operated by Harold E. Munn."

Sticking out his hand, he asked, "What's your name, son?"

Giving Harold's hand a shake, he answered, "Buhley Sparks."

"You a ballplayer?" asked Harold.

"Kind of."

"Kind of? I doubt the Atlanta Peaches invite kind of ball players to their tryouts. You must cut the mustard pretty good."

Buhley sat and didn't respond. He didn't need to say much. Harold talked a lot. Harold E. Munn had driven a Greyhound bus for twenty-five years. Besides talking and visiting with his passengers, Harold also liked to eat. He kept a large bag full of sandwiches next to his seat and always had one that he was working on. "You ever been to Bradenton?" asked Harold.

"No, sir, I ain't never been past Jacksonville."

"I've been all over the southeastern United States. Know it like the back of my hand. Biloxi, Birmingham, Chattanooga, Atlanta, Memphis. You name it. I've been there. I can tell you where the best hamburgers and bathrooms are in all those places," stated Harold as he took a bite out of his half-eaten ham sandwich.

Buhley just sat and listened while Harold continued to talk on and on. The driver paused only to take bites out of his sandwiches. "You meet all kinds in the line of work I'm in. Most people are good people. Take you, for instance. You ain't never been south of Jacksonville. I'm taking you on your first real trip, and it gives me pleasure to know that. How in the world did you get a tryout with the Atlanta Peaches anyway?"

"I really don't know for sure. I pitched a while back, and I guess I did pretty good. After the game, Satch Moak said there might be some people interested in me, and sure enough, a year or so later, the Peaches called, and here I am."

"Three years ago I saw Satch Moak's team play a college all-star team in Birmingham. Satch's team walloped them good. I don't remember the score, but it was a whippin'. How'd y'all do against them?"

"We beat them one to nothing."

"Y'all beat them?" Harold said in a disbelieving voice.

"Yes, sir."

"What position did you play?"

"I pitched."

"And you held those guys scoreless?!"

"Yes, sir."

"No wonder the Atlanta Peaches want to look at you. Must be one sumpthin else pitcher."

As Harold continued to talk and eat sandwiches, the time flew by, and soon the bus pulled into the Bradenton terminal. "This is it, Buhley. It's been a pleasure visiting with you. Good luck with your tryout. Maybe some day soon, I'll turn on the radio and hear, 'Now pitching for the Atlanta Peaches, Buhley Sparks.'"

"Thank you, Mr. Munn."

After shaking Harold's hand, Buhley took his suitcase, stepped off the bus and entered the terminal. As he stood looking around, a voice said, "Buhley Sparks, is that you?"

Buhley turned around to see a gray-haired man staring at him. "Yes, sir," he answered.

"Buhley, my name is Buzzy Preacher."

Buzzy Preacher, a middle-aged man whose hair had grayed prematurely, had a slight build and a fidgety way about him. He was the dugout coach for the Atlanta Peaches and a yes-man for Slug Matthews, the manager of the team. Buzzy knew more about people than he did about baseball. Many times he was the go-between for the players and the brash manager of the Atlanta Peaches. His baseball-playing career consisted of a dismal season in rookie ball where he was not asked back. That year he'd made friends with Slugg Matthews and had been with him ever since. Together they were starting their fifteenth season with the Atlanta Peaches. Remembering what Sporty Schuster had told him, Buhley stuck out his hand and gave Buzzy a firm handshake. "Nice to meet you, Mr. Preacher."

"Call me Buzzy."

"Yes, sir, Mr. Preacher."

"There's about a half an hour left in today's workout, so we're going to the field. Slug may want you to throw a little to see what you can do. Ol'

Satch sure spoke highly of you, and we appreciate you coming down here to throw for us."

"My pleasure, Mr. Preacher."

"Call me Buzzy."

"Yes, sir, Mr. Preacher," replied Buhley as they got in the car and headed for the spring training complex.

When they arrived at the field, Slug Matthews was standing on the sidelines watching his team take a round of infield. Buzzy and Buhley walked over to where he stood. "Slug, I'd like you to meet Buhley Sparks. He's the young man I told you about."

Barely looking up, Slug said, "Good to meet you, kid."

A short, plump no-nonsense man with a flat top haircut, Slug Matthews called everybody kid. Whenever he called out that name, everyone stopped and looked to double-check who he was talking to. Slug had pitched a few innings of big league ball. Because his curve ball didn't curve and his fastball wasn't fast, his career had been short. But he knew a lot about baseball and always guided his team to the top of the standings. He'd made the playoffs a number of times, but had yet to make it to the World Series. Watching his team for another minute, Slug then turned to Buhley and asked, "You play in college?"

"No, sir," replied Buhley.

"What high school did you play for?"

"Our high school didn't have a team."

"You play American Legion Ball or somethin'?" Slug asked a little louder.

"No, sir."

"Well, where the hell did you play, kid?" Slug asked with exasperation.

"I really ain't never played organized baseball," came the sheepish reply.

Slug grabbed Buzzy by the shirt and dragged him a couple of yards away. He got right in Buzzy's ear and in a mean whisper hissed, "What do you mean bringing me a green horn down here that ain't never wore a pair of baseball pants? What do you think this is, Kindergarten or something?"

Buzzy interrupted and said, "Satch said he could pitch."

"Satch Moak's brain's gone soft. He's been around that traveling all-star crap too long. He wouldn't know a pitcher from a plowboy, and from the looks of things, he sent us a plowboy."

Releasing Buzzy's shirt, Slug yelled, "Hey, kid!"

Everybody stopped and looked. "Elser, come over here!" yelled Slug.

Elser Riggs, a thirty-five-year-old grizzled veteran catcher, had been with Slug Matthews and the Atlanta Peaches his whole career. Catching had worn his knees down to nothing. He was still a great defense catcher and called the best game in the majors. Elser trotted over to Slug. "Yes, sir, Slug," said Elser.

"Take this boy down to the bull pen and let him throw twenty or thirty pitches. Then come back to me and tell me if he's got something or got nothing. Either way, I want to know. You understand?"

"Yes, sir, Coach."

As Elser and Buhley started walking down to the bullpen, Slug turned to Buzzy. "If that boy ain't got nothing, take him right on back to the bus station, put him on a bus and get him the hell home!"

Buzzy nodded in the affirmative.

Elser looked at Buhley and stuck out his hand. "I'm Elser Riggs," he said.

"Buhley Sparks. Glad to meet you."

"Don't worry about Slug. His bark is worse than his bite."

"I'm glad about that 'cause his bark has a lot of bite."

They began to toss the ball back and forth and continued their conversation. After a few minutes, Buhley said, "I'm loose."

"Okay," replied Elser as he moved to position and squatted behind the plate. "All right, Buhley, I'm gonna move the target around a little bit. Just try and hit the catcher's mitt."

Buhley nodded. He took the ball in his glove and looked square at the target. Winding up, he threw the pitch. It whisked through the air and landed perfectly in Elser's unmoved glove. The sound of the ball popping the leather glove reverberated throughout the ball park. Watching his players, Slug was standing a fair distance from the bullpen when he heard the noise. "What was that?" Slug asked as he looked around.

"I don't know," answered Buzzy.

"Good pitch," yelled Elser, throwing the ball back to Buhley.

He moved over to the other side of the plate and set his target a little lower. Buhley kicked and fired another perfect strike into the stationary catcher's mitt. "Great pitch!" said Elser as he returned the ball to Buhley. Moving to the opposite side of the plate, Elser moved the target high in the strike zone. Once again Buhley threw a perfect strike. "Damn, that was good. Throw a breaking ball!"

Buhley nodded. He let fire, and the ball started off the plate, darted sharply down and into the target set by Elser. "Unbelievable!" said Elser.

Standing up, he took off his catcher's mask. "Where'd you learn to throw like this?"

"I don't know. I could just always throw."

They threw a few more pitches, all with the same results.

"I'll be right back," said Elser as he ran to find Slug as fast as a thirty-five-year-old catcher with bad knees could.

"You need to come watch this boy throw!" Elser told Slug.

Walking to the bullpen, Slug called out, "Let me see what you got, kid."

Buhley wound up, throwing strike after strike. Up, down, inside, out. It didn't matter. Wherever Elser put his glove, that's where the ball went. "Watch this, Slug," said Elser.

He stood straight up and held his mitt as high as it would go over his head and closed his eyes. "Let it fly, Buhley."

Buhley wound up and threw the ball. Smacking perfectly into the catcher's mitt, the ball hit with a force that closed the glove behind it. Slug took his hat off and began to run his hand back and forth over his flat top. He squinted in the sun. "Hey, kid, stay the night. I want to see you throw tomorrow to make sure I really saw what I just saw."

Standing by Slug with his back to Buhley, Elser gave a low whistle. "I ain't never seen nothin' like that."

Slug shook his head in amazement. "Me neither."

As he started to walk off, he yelled over to Buzzy, "Let this kid stay with you, and don't let him run off!" He stopped and turned to Buhley. "Good job, kid. See you tomorrow."

That night Buhley lay stretched out on the bed in Buzzy Preacher's spare room. Sticking his head in the door, Buzzy said, "I think you raised one of Slug's eyebrows today."

Buhley just smiled. "Get some rest tonight. I think he'll probably give you a good look tomorrow. Good night, Buhley," said Buzzy as he closed the door.

"Good night, Mr. Preacher."

Buzzy's head popped back around the door. "Call me Buzzy."

"Yes, sir, Mr. Preacher."

Buhley lay quietly, thinking of all the day's events. He remembered his dad in the field, Cheryl Dane on the corner, the conversation with the bus driver, and the pitches to Elser in the bullpen. Surprised at how easy he felt being away from home, he felt a lot of gratitude towards Buzzy Preacher for making him feel comfortable. Even so, he missed the humming noise of his oscillating fan by his bed, and it took him longer than usual to go to sleep.

The sunshine made Buhley squint as he got out of Buzzy Preacher's car. Trailing Buzzy through the Atlanta Peaches training complex, they made their way over to Slug. The team manager looked right past Buzzy and said, "Morning, kid."

"Good morning, Mr. Matthews," replied Buhley.

"I got something I gotta do this morning, and then I want to watch you throw again. I'll holler at you when I'm ready. In the meantime, just walk around and drink in some of this baseball. This is the big leagues, kid."

Slug turned and walked away, leaving Buhley to consider where he was. Buhley hardly needed the reminder. He stood in awe, carefully staying out of the way, but getting close enough to appreciate the professionalism with which the players practiced and played the game. He walked down towards a set of pitching mounds -- one occupied by Lefty Pete. Lefty Pete was a right-handed pitcher, thirty years old and in the prime of his career. He was given his name by his father who'd seen a pitcher named Lefty Reaves pitch a perfect game in nineteen thirty-one. So impressed was he with that feat, he swore right then and there to name his first child Lefty. Luckily, his firstborn was a boy. Lefty Pete was not an overpowering pitcher. He was crafty and moved the ball around, changing speeds with every pitch. With one of the lowest ERAs in the league the year before, Lefty was the ace of the pitching staff. He was also their leader and organized all the after-hours shenanigans in which the players participated. Lefty played hard during and after the game. He was good, and he knew it.

Easing up behind him, Buhley watched him throw a couple of pitches. His eyes widened in awe as he looked on. Lefty, noting his audience, turned back and threw a few more pitches. As Buhley moved to get a better view of his wind up, Lefty gave him a sidelong glance and in a slightly sarcastic voice asked, "Something I can help you with?"

"No, sir, I'm just watchin'," replied Buhley.

"Most people have to pay to watch me throw," said Lefty as he threw a hard-breaking curve ball.

Buhley turned to leave. "No, no, you stay right there. You might learn something," said Lefty as he retrieved the ball from the catcher.

Just then Elser Riggs walked up, putting an arm across Buhley's shoulders.

"How you doin', Buhley?" asked Elser.

"Fine, thank you, Elser," replied Buhley.

Turning, Lefty asked Elser, "You know him?"

"Yes, I know him. He's here for a tryout."

"Where you from, kid?" asked Lefty.

```
G J FORD BOOKSHOP
06/05/09 13:27   E   1    29885
   1@ 14.49 9781438950198  $    14.49
          BUHLEY SPARKS TH
[====]
SUBTOTAL                  $    14.49
SALES TAX @ 7.000%        $     1.01
TOTAL                     $    15.50
TENDER Cash               $    20.00
CHANGE                    $     4.50

        (912) 634-6168
    THANK YOU - COME AGAIN SOON
```

'here's that?"

en Waycross and Valdosta

," said Lefty in a voice loud

out, "Hey, see you later,

s Buhley and Elser walked

lser.

......, ...ug.

"He gets his butt kicked once a year. Looks like it's gonna be early this year."

They walked down to the batting cage to watch some batting practice. Moper Mapes was hitting. A solid third baseman, Moper was a two-time all-star. With nine years in the league, he had several gold gloves for his play at third base. When Moper was born, he had a degenerative muscle in his lower lip that caused it to droop. He got the nickname Moper because it always looked like he was moping. That name had been used for so long that most people didn't know his real first name. He even signed his legal documents Moper Mapes. He was one of the nicest players in the league and felt himself fortunate to get paid to play a game he loved. After Moper finished hitting, Elser called him over. "Moper, I want you to meet Buhley Sparks. He's a pitcher, and he's down here for a tryout."

Moper stuck out his hand. "Nice to meet you, Buhley. You're a pitcher, huh?"

Trying not to stare at Moper's lower lip, Buhley stammered, "Y-yes, sir."

"Good luck with your tryout. You never can have enough pitching, kid. Let me know if there's anything I can do for you," offered Moper, putting down his bat and picking up his glove to take some ground balls.

"Thank you."

"Hey, kid!" The voice sounded loudly.

Everybody stopped and looked around. Buhley peered around and saw Slug staring him down. "Hey, kid, you and Elser come over here," he yelled.

Elser and Buhley jogged over to Slug. "Buhley Sparks, meet Bullard Haynes. He's our pitching coach," said Slug.

A former ace pitcher in the major leagues, Bullard Haynes was known for his fierce competitiveness and wouldn't hesitate to throw at a batter when the situation arose and sometimes when it didn't. He got the nickname Bull for his strong outings and his never-give-an-inch approach to pitching. Bull was an imposing figure in his playing days and remained so. He stuck out his hand. "Good to meet you, Buhley."

"Thank you, Mr. Haynes. Nice to meet you, too," replied Buhley.

Bullard Haynes had Slug Matthews' ear and total respect. Whatever he mentioned to Slug usually got done. "Let's go down to the pen, kid, and throw some more. I want Bull to see you throw. Your arm feel okay?"

"Yes, sir."

"Elser, just whistle when he's loose, and we'll come watch," said Slug.

Elser nodded in the affirmative. They began to throw the ball back and forth. "I think you wet Slug's whistle a little bit yesterday. He ain't gonna bother Bull unless he's seen something. You throw like you did yesterday, and you'll have Bull a little light in the shoes. He'll be dancing on air."

They continued to throw for a while. With Buhley's signal that he was ready, Elser turned and whistled. Slug and Bullard made their way to the pen.

"Move it all around, Elser. Give him the full cycle," said Slug.

"All right," replied Elser.

Putting on his mask, he squatted behind the plate. Elser set the target on the right side down on the back part of the plate. Buhley wound up and threw. The ball whizzed through the air and landed perfectly in the motionless catcher's mitt. Moving to the other side with a low setup, Elser snagged another perfect pitch. The noise from the ball popping the mitt resounded around the park. Players stopped, looking over in Buhley's direction. Bull and Slug looked at each other. Neither spoke. As Elser moved in, out, up and down, Buhley pounded every target with precise aim. "Damn, Slug, where'd you find this guy?" asked Bullard.

"We got him directly out of the woods," replied Slug. "Somebody told me he's never pitched an organized baseball game in his life."

"Well, somebody's still laughing at you, or they ain't never seen an organized baseball game."

"What do you think, Bull?"

"I think you oughta get him over to the field house as quickly as possible and get him a uniform. Throw him a scrimmage or two and see how he reacts. If he throws out there like he's doing right here, those balls ain't gonna be feeling much wood."

Slug looked around for Buzzy. "Buzzy, take Buhley to the field house and get him some baseball clothes. He's done for the day," yelled Slug.

Elser walked up to Buhley and shook his hand. "Way to throw. I think you got Bull pretty excited. I seen guys come down here and throw one time, and then all you see is their backside as they're leaving. I ain't a betting man, but if I was, I'd say you got a shot."

Buhley grinned. "What you doing tonight?" asked Elser.

"Nothing," replied Buhley.

"Then let's go get some supper."

"All right."

With a punch to his mitt, Elser turned to leave, calling over his shoulder, "Pick you up at seven."

Buzzy signaled Buhley to follow him to the field house. "Hey, kid, rest that arm!" yelled Slug.

Buhley called back, "Yes, sir."

Slug yelled again. "Hey, kid!"

Buhley turned to look at him. "Great job!"

"Thank you," Buhley politely replied. Outwardly, he tried to project an image of calm assurance, as if this were an everyday occurrence. Inside, he felt he would burst open with joy. He could hardly wait to tell someone about his day.

CHAPTER 11

The phone rang at Hawkins' grocery. "Hello, Hawkins' Grocery, the only grocer in town. We charge whatever we want, and there's nothing nobody can do about it. May I help you?" Parley blurted his lines as fast as he could.

Smothering a laugh, Buhley spoke. "Mr. Parley, this is Buhley."

"Buhley!" yelled Parley into the phone. "How you doing down there? Everybody has been asking about you. Tell me what's going on!"

"I've thrown twice, and they gave me a uniform today, but that doesn't mean anything. Tomorrow I'm supposed to throw to some of the team in a scrimmage. How's Daddy?"

"He's fine. Soon as I hang up from you, I'm gonna ride out there and visit with him. He's real proud of you, Buhley. Everybody is. Is there anything you need? Anything I can do for you?"

"No, sir, I don't think so. Most everybody is nice, and I'm staying with Mr. Preacher."

"Edsel Moon came in today and said if you pitched a game, he was gonna jump a train and come watch you. Hooty Lou asked about you. Everybody wants to know how you're doing."

"Thanks for everything, Mr. Parley, and tell Daddy I miss him."

"I will, son. I will."

With a slight wave of homesickness, Buhley ended the call. "I'll call you again in a day or so, Mr. Parley."

August was rocking on the porch when Parley drove up. Some ladies from the church were in the kitchen arranging a week's worth of suppers for him. Parley sat down in a rocking chair and gave his news. "I just got off the phone with Buhley."

He noticed August perked up when he heard those words. "He said he's thrown twice, and they gave him a uniform, but not to get excited because that don't mean nothing." Parley paused for a moment. "You got a fine boy there, August."

He waited for a response, and none came. Parley looked over at August and saw a tear rolling down the side of his face.

They sat in silence for a short while. When August finally spoke, he said, "I watched that boy throw a ball all his life. That's what he liked to do. Almost knocked down my barn a time or two. I'll be damned if I'm gonna stand in the way of that boy trying to fulfill his dream of chunkin' with the big boys. But, I miss 'im every inch of the day. I miss 'im."

Parley reached over and patted his arm. Not another word was spoken as they enjoyed the cool evening breeze.

Elser turned into the parking lot past the sign that read "Fatty Long's - Come on in." He and Buhley went inside, finding Fatty Long behind the counter cooking cheeseburgers. Long's place was a landmark in Bradenton and his food legendary. Fatty knew how to put just the right amount of butter on everything to make people come back time and time again. With no wife and no family, the restaurant was his life. He lived in a place connected to the back of the eatery. Cooking and visiting with his customers were his specialties and what he enjoyed most in life. Fatty spotted Elser and turned around, spatula in hand. "Elser Riggs, 'bout time you come see me. Y'all gonna do nothing this year?"

"We're gonna try," answered Elser as he and Buhley sat down at a table.

Buhley had a puzzled look on his face. "What's he mean, 'Y'all gonna do nothing'?"

"Fatty talks backwards. You gotta know him a little while to understand what he means. I'll introduce you."

The puzzled look remained on Buhley's face. The waitress brought over two tall glasses of sweet iced tea.

"What's this?" asked Buhley.

"It's sweet iced tea. It's all they serve past eleven o'clock in the morning. I suppose you could ask for milk or somethin', but you wouldn't get it," said Elser.

Buhley took a swig from his glass. "Wow!" he exclaimed. "I ain't tasted tea like that since my mamma made it for Sunday dinner after church."

Within a few seconds, his glass was emptied. The waitress brought a pitcher and refilled his glass. Fatty Long walked over, spun a chair around and sat down by their table. His stomach protruded through the wooden slats in the back of the chair. Sweating from the hot work of cooking over a grill, Fatty picked up a napkin from the table and wiped the perspiration from his face. Fatty pointed to Buhley, looked at Elser and asked, "Who's this young man?"

"This is Buhley Sparks. He's a pitcher down here on a tryout."

Fatty stuck out his stubby hand to shake Buhley's. "You no good?" he asked.

Buhley gave his head a shake and looked at Elser who jumped in answering, "He's good all right, Fatty. He's pretty darn good."

"Y'all want nothin'? I'll fix it myself," offered Fatty.

"How 'bout two cheeseburgers with plenty of grease?" replied Elser.

"You no ask that. It come that way." As Fatty rose to go fix the cheeseburgers, he smiled and added, "Nice to meet you, Buhley Sparks."

Deep in conversation with Buhley, Elser felt a light tap on his shoulder and turned around to see a young boy. "Can I have your autograph, Mr. Riggs?" he asked.

"Of course," replied Elser.

When the little boy got the signature, he looked over at Buhley and said, "Are you anybody, mister?"

Elser laughed. "He ain't yet, but you'll be hearing about him soon."

It didn't take long for Fatty to come back with the burgers, cheese dripping down onto the bottom bun. Buhley looked up and asked, "Can I have some ketchup?"

Fatty quickly replied, "Don't need none. You take a bite. No good burger like this nowhere."

Buhley picked up the cheeseburger and chomped down. Watching Buhley chew and swallow, Fatty asked, "It no good?"

Instead of speaking, Buhley quickly took another large bite. "I think he just answered you, Fatty," stated Elser with an amused grin.

Fatty turned and walked away, muttering under his breath. "Just the right amount of butter, that's what it is. Just the right amount of butter."

Finished with supper, Elser and Buhley got up to leave. "See ya, Fatty," yelled Elser.

Turning with spatula in hand, Fatty called back, "Y'all come everyday. Sundays, too!"

It was a beautiful spring evening, and they decided to put down the top on Elser's white GTO convertible. Buhley studied the sky as they rode back to the spring training complex. The stars were bright -- too many to count. Elser pulled into the parking lot near Buzzy Preacher's place. Stopping the car, he reclined his seat and gazed towards the heavens. After a moment of contented silence, Elser asked, "Buhley, what makes you happy?"

Briefly thinking, Buhley replied, "I like sitting on the porch with my daddy in the late evening. He chews tobacco, and I do most of the talking. It's the only time we really spend together. He don't say much, but I can kind of tell he likes it when I sit there with him. What about you, Elser? Where are you from and how'd you get into baseball?"

"Missouri. Red Bud, Missouri. It's a small farming town south of St. Louis. In high school, I played baseball and the banjo. I worked on that five-string banjo for about three years and finally figured out I could play the radio a lot better than that thing."

Buhley interjected. "How'd you get to the majors?"

"In high school, we had a coach who loved the game. Max Bain was his name. He chewed tobacco and worked our butts off. We practiced every day of the week -- Sundays, too. He taught us the fundamentals, and we were good. My junior year, we won the state championship. We had some really good players, and scouts came to our practices and games. I peaked at the right time and got drafted in the second round. Been here ever since. My days are numbered now. Ain't much call for a thirty-five-year-old catcher who can't run anymore."

Completely relaxed, Buhley asked, "What makes you happy, Elser?"

"What would make me happy? I'll tell you what. It's my dream and every catcher's dream to catch a perfect game. That would be a great way to end my career. We've had some good pitchers come through here, but I've never come close to that. It's like a hole-in-one in golf. Everything has to be perfect for that to happen. The ball has to be struck solid, it has to hit the green in just the right way, and nothing can be on the green in the way of the ball and the hole. In a baseball game, so many things can happen -- a walk, an error, base hit, passed ball on third strike, etc. That's why they call it a perfect game. Everything has to go just right. This is probably my last year, and the odds are way against me, but to catch a perfect game would be my dream."

Buhley, resting comfortably in his reclined seat, struggled to respond. "You never know, Elser. Look at me. I'm sittin' at home just livin' life, and the next thing I know, I'm down here with y'all."

"We better stop dreaming and come back to reality. You gotta pitch in a scrimmage tomorrow, so you better go to bed."

Buhley slowly got out of the car. "Thanks for supper, Elser. See you tomorrow."

"Night, Buhley."

The next morning brought sunshine and warm winds. Buhley walked to the main field, his eyes riveted on a player taking ground balls with his bare hands. Manny Lopez stood as shortstop and yelled for the coach to hit the balls harder. Manny Lopez, a second-year player from the Dominican Republic, was known for his defense. At a young age in his homeland, he started picking tobacco -- labor that toughened and quickened his hands. Manny grew up in poverty and never had enough money for a glove, so he practiced and played without one. Although only in his second year, he was recognized as one of the rising premier shortstops in the game. Joining Buhley, Elser commented, "You ever seen such?"

"How come he ain't got a glove?" Buhley asked.

"Manny figures if he can field those balls with his bare hands, a glove makes it that much easier. Plus, that's the way he grew up, playing barehanded."

"Beats anything I've ever seen."

From a distance, Slug yelled, "Hey, kid."

Everybody stopped and looked. When Buhley turned, he saw the manager's squinty eyes staring directly at him. "Get loose."

"Yes, sir," replied Buhley.

Jogging over to one of the side mounds, Elser and Buhley began throwing. "Remember, I know these guys' tendencies. Just throw what I call and where I frame it, and you'll do fine," Elser instructed.

"I'm a little nervous," confessed Buhley.

"Don't worry about it. All pitching is is fooling the batter. If you have your stuff and throw what and where I call, then you'll get 'em out. If you don't, then your grandfather could hit it. At this level, it's hit your spots and change speed; otherwise, the Bradenton Ladies' Auxiliary Club could hit five hundred off of you."

Buhley nodded as they continued to throw. After a few minutes, Buhley signaled he was loose. They began walking down to the main field where players were taking a round of infield.

Slug yelled from the dugout. "You ready, kid?"

"Yes, sir."

"It's your show. Take the mound!"

Heading across the chalk of the third base line, Buhley went through the grass to the mound. Lefty Pete sat with some players in the first base dugout and yelled, "Well, looka here. Country come to town. Da huh, da huh, da huh!"

The players around him laughed. Elser squatted down behind home plate and turned to the first base dugout. "Hey, Lefty! I got a new sign for you," he yelled. Elser clinched his fist and put it down near his crotch. He slowly moved it to his chest and inched his middle finger straight up. "You understand what that means, Lefty? We can't mess up our signs, Lefty. If you don't understand, I'll be glad to clarify it for you after practice. What ya say, Lefty?"

Lefty said nothing. He knew Elser was serious and would meet him after the workout. Ignoring the voices, Buhley dug a small trench with his cleats between the rubber and the mound. As the umpire yelled, "Batter up," Elser squatted down and gave the first signal. He called for a fastball on the outside part of the plate. Hershal Davis, a triple-A second baseman, dug in the batter's box. Buhley affirmed the signal, kicked and fired. Hershal froze as the ball whizzed into Elser's glove. "Strike one!" yelled the umpire.

Hershal cut his eyes to Elser. "He had some mustard on that one," he said.

Elser called for the same pitch. Buhley let fly, and Hershal tapped it slowly to the second baseman for out number one. Clevis Boyd, the starting center fielder for the Peaches, stepped in the box as the second batter. Clevis dug in, and Elser set up on the outside part of the plate. Buhley let fly, and the ball spanked into Elser's mitt before Clevis could muster a weak swing. "Strike one!" yelled the umpire.

Elser moved to the inside, and Buhley threw another perfect pitch. It handcuffed Clevis, and he hit a weak grounder to Moper Mapes at third, which he handled routinely. The next batter was Harland Bunch. Harland was a power hitting left-handed first baseman. A mainstay in the Peaches' lineup, he was a consistent producer at the plate. Elser knew he always looked at the first pitch, so he called for a fastball down the middle. "Strike one!" yelled the umpire.

On the next pitch, Elser signaled for a change up. Buhley wound and threw. The bottom fell out of the pitch right at the plate, and Harland swung mightily just over the top of the ball. "What the hell was that?" Harland asked in exasperation.

"Strike two," replied Elser without batting an eye.

Elser called for a breaking ball on the inside part of the plate. Buhley stared at his target, kicked and fired. The ball sailed right at Harland's shoulder. He leaned back out of the way only to see the ball dart sharply down and in, catching the corner of the plate for strike three. On the bench in the third base dugout, Slug and Bull looked at each other, and at the same time said, "Damn."

As Buhley walked off the infield, Elser ran over to him and said, "Magical! That's what that was. Magical!"

Throwing down his bat near the third base dugout, Harland Bunch looked at Slug. "You better not trade him or me, 'cause I don't want to have to face him all year long."

Slug took off his hat and rubbed his hand back over his flat top again and again. Buhley sat down on the bench, and one player after another congratulated him on his pitching. After pitching two more innings with the same results, Buhley stepped into the dugout. With a shake of his head, Slug said, "You're done, kid. Go down and run some sprints with the other pitchers."

Buhley turned to leave, and Elser grabbed his arm. "How 'bout supper tonight?"

"That'd be great," replied Buhley.

"Same time!"

"See you then." With one long stride, Buhley took the dugout steps and headed out to run sprints.

With a low whisper, Elser looked at Slug. "You better look at him good and hard. He's the best I ever saw."

Slug sat in silence as he watched Buhley walk away.

Parley walked into Hooty Lou's Barber Shop and sat down in the chair. "What's shakin', Hooty?" he asked.

"Not much. Been a slow day." With a huge yawn making his point, Hooty continued, "You want a haircut?"

"I reckon. It's a necessary evil in this town. I ordered a tonic that was supposed to stop my hair from growing, but all it did was make my neck itch."

"Ha, ha, ha! You better hush. You forgot who holds the razor in here."

Leaning back in the chair, Parley relaxed, a grin on his face. "You want the usual?" asked Hooty.

"If'n that's all that's available," drawled Parley as he closed his eyes. Placing a barber sheet and tissue around Parley's neck, Hooty began to clip his hair.

"You heard from Buhley?"

Trying to rest, Parley responded slowly. "He called me the other day and said they were going to give him a uniform and let him pitch in a scrimmage, but he said it didn't mean nothin'."

Hooty kept cutting and didn't respond. When he was almost finished with the haircut, he cleared his throat and said, "You know Buhley keeps calling me."

"Oh, yeah?" Parley opened his eyes and gave them a disbelieving roll.

"Yep, he said he was having trouble snapping his curve ball, an' I gave him some pointers."

Parley sat up straight in the chair. "Hooty, you know as much about curve balls as you do about giving a good haircut!"

"That stings, Parley. That stings right here." Hooty pointed to his chest and let out a long and loud hyena laugh. He spun the chair around, facing Parley to the mirror. "How's that?" he asked.

Parley noticed one side was higher than the other. Slapping some bills on the counter, he laughed. "You're consistent, Hooty. I'll say that for you. See you next time. If I talk to Buhley, I'll say you asked about him."

At the spring training complex, Slug Matthews leaned back in his desk chair. Reaching into a cooler, he pulled out a cold beer and threw one across to Bullard Haynes. Slug popped one for himself, took a swig and asked, "Bull, what do you think about the Sparks kid?"

"He's a diamond in the rough," answered Bullard, using the cold beer can to cool his face.

"He's rough around the edges. I'm not even sure he knows how to tie his shoes." Said Slug.

"You want him to tie his shoes or pitch?" replied Bullard.

"He doesn't know cutoffs, where to cover, or any of the intricacies of the game," Slug pointed out.

"Hell, Slug, neither did I until I learned them. Put him in rookie ball, and let him learn. You may be looking at a twenty-game winner. You may be looking at a guy that can get us to the series. We've been one pitcher short for three years. I've seen him throw in the pen and in a scrimmage, and I ain't seen him throw a ball yet!"

Slug sat, just for a moment imagining himself being introduced to the World Series. "The World Series, aye?"

"Throw him in another scrimmage in a day or two, and see what happens. If he does good again, give him a contract in the minor leagues. Start him in rookie ball. Let him learn. I tell you what. I see a lot in this boy. Take him with us to Atlanta for opening day and our first home stand, and let him see what big league baseball is all about."

"Good idea, Bull. I'll throw him in day after tomorrow and then make a decision." He paused for a moment. "The World Series, huh?"

"Could be."

They sat in silence drinking their beer, excited about the prospects.

Buhley was glad when Elser pulled into the parking lot of Fatty Long's. A rerun of their last meal sounded great to him. Sweating over the grill, Fatty had his burgers sizzling and buns frying in plenty of butter. Buhley could just about taste the perfectly crisped edges of those buns. Sitting down at a two-top, Buhley and Elser were immediately brought glasses of sweet iced tea. Thirsty, Buhley drained his glass before the waitress could leave. "Ma'am, could you please bring us a pitcher?" he asked.

"Anything for you, cutie," she replied.

Bringing a pitcher of sweet iced tea, she leaned over as she filled Buhley's glass. Buhley noticed her more than ample chest - the upper part of an hour-glass figure. "You just holler if you need anything else, darlin'," she said in a honey-sweet voice, rising from pouring Buhley's tea.

"Yes, ma'am." His eyes still locked on the waitress's bust line. As she walked away, Elser held back from laughing. "I believe she's sweet on you. You good with the ladies, Buhley?"

Buhley looked at him as seriously as he could. "I could never get my fill."

"Well, you sure got an eye full of her."

"I got a girl back home that I'm waiting on. I'm not sure she's waiting on me. I been sweet on her since the first day of school."

"You got it bad, don't you, boy?"

"Some days nothing else rests on my mind except girls. My daddy says you can't live with 'em and you can't live without 'em. He told me he's seen men beat down to nothin', gone from an oak tree to a twig, all because of a woman and then go back for more."

"He's right. Everybody thinks because we play professional league baseball, the women will wait on you. But if you're gone on the road all the time, there's some fella there, and he's taking her flowers and seeing her all the time and tellin' her she looks good whether she does or not, and pretty soon if you ain't there to counter punch, she's gone. What's your girl like?"

"She's prettier than a cloudless spring day."

Turning from the grill, Fatty Long yelled, "You boys want nothin'?"

Elser ordered. "Two big ones!"

Fatty turned and slapped two large beef patties on the grill, the sizzling so loud it could be heard two blocks away. As Elser and Buhley talked, the waitress kept cutting her eyes on Buhley - something both he and Elser noticed. When she finally brought their food, it was obvious to whom she was partial. Elser looked at his plate, counting seven French fries. The pile of fries on Buhley's plate was a little too many to count in one evening.

As she left, the waitress ran her hand across Buhley's back, saying in a soft voice, "Honey, if there's anything else you need, you just holler."

Red as a beet, he answered, "Yes ma'am."

Elser smiled, not able to resist. "Buhley, I believe you got her in heat. You keep this up, and she's gonna give you more than a plate full of French fries."

"Hush, Elser! She's only bein' friendly."

Just then the front door to Fatty Long's burst open and a barrel-chested man bolted in. With a grim look for Buhley, he made his way over to the waitress where the two of them engaged in a heated conversation. The man pointed directly at Buhley and then stomped his way to the table. Standing over Buhley and giving a caveman grunt, he growled, "You messin' with my woman?"

Buhley stared ahead, not saying a word. Choking back a laugh, Elser interrupted the silence, addressing the man. "Hello, friend," he began.

Angry eyes shifted to Elser. "I can't lie to you, big fella. My buddy right here did look at your girlfriend. But that's nothing compared to what the man in the bathroom did."

"Bathroom?" the man asked.

"Yes, sir," said Elser. "I saw that man kiss her square on the jaw with both lips. He walked in the bathroom just before you came in." With that, Elser pointed at the bathroom door.

The man looked at the door, back at Elser, again at the door and back to Elser. "On the jaw, he kissed her?" he asked.

"Yep, flush on the jaw, and he's right in there." Once more Elser pointed to the bathroom door. The man looked back at the door, and without saying a word, he took off in a heavy-booted run towards the bathroom. Not slowing down, he ran into and completely through the door.

Turning to Elser, Buhley stated, "I didn't see no man kiss her."

"Neither did I, Buhley. It's time to get the hell outta here, 'cause there's nobody in the bathroom."

Picking up the uneaten cheeseburgers, they made a hasty departure from the restaurant. "Gotta go, Fatty!" Elser yelled.

Fatty waved with a spatula and didn't say anything.

With a jump into Elser's convertible, they peeled out of the parking lot, back tires throwing rocks.

Walking slowly from the doorless bathroom, the man said to anybody who would listen, "Ain't nobody in there. You reckon that man was foolin' me?"

The waitress walked up, kissed him on the cheek and said, "Just sit down over there, sweetie, and I'll get you somethin' to drink."

Buhley and Elser laughed about their little adventure as they ran sprints at practice the next day. Buzzy Preacher walked up as the two finished their sprints. "Slug wants you to throw about thirty pitches today and then throw in tomorrow's scrimmage game," said Buzzy.

"Yes, sir," answered Buhley.

Elser and he walked over to the bullpen and began throwing. Slipping into the adjoining bullpen, Bullard Haynes stood behind a tarp hanging between the two. He put an eye up to a small tear in the tarp and watched as Buhley threw strike after strike. "Damn," he said in a whisper after each pitch landed in Elser's unmoved glove. Looking to the heavens, he softly said, "If this is a gift from you, I sure appreciate it."

Slug reached down in the cooler, pulled out two beers and threw one to

Bullard. Leaning back in his chair, he propped up his feet on his desk. Bullard opened a beer and held it away from himself long enough for the foam to stop spewing out of the can. "Wha'd you see today, Bull?" asked Slug.

"I watched Buhley throw in the pen. I know he's corn-rowed and fresh out of the garden, but he can flat pitch. I think everybody's anxious to watch him throw in the scrimmage tomorrow."

With a gulp that took down about half his beer, Slug let out a loud burp. "You wanna stick to our plan and move him along slowly? Start him in rookie ball, see how he does and take him up one step at a time?"

Bullard lowered his beer and leaned forward in the chair. "It's like this, Slug. When you hook a big fish and he's fighting you with everything he's got, you just let him fight and wear himself down, and when the time's right, you reel him into the boat. Same thing with Buhley. We keep a close eye on him wherever he's assigned, and we'll know when the time's right. When that time comes, we reel him on up to Atlanta with us."

"I like your thinking," said Slug. "What's say we go get us a steak?"

"You took the thought right outta my head!"

Manny Lopez shook his head as he walked from the batter box back to the dugout. He had just watched Buhley throw a perfect pitch on the outside corner of the plate for strike three. Moper Mapes was the next man up, and on the second pitch, hit a weak grounder to the second baseman for out number three. Slug and Bullard sat on the bench, looking at the scorer's book. Bullard read the statistics to Slug. "Four innings pitched, no hits, no walks, seven strikeouts and forty-three pitches thrown." Bullard raised his eyebrows till they nearly met his hairline. "Now, that's major league pitching!"

Slug didn't respond. Looking around for Buhley, he spotted him and yelled, "Buhley! Buhley, come over here!"

Entering the dugout, Buhley asked, "Yes, sir?"

"Great job, kid. Go get a shower. I want to see you in my office at five o'clock this afternoon," said Slug.

CHAPTER 12

Buhley tentatively walked up to the entrance of Slug Matthew's office. His knock jarred the door slightly open. "Come in on in, kid!" called Slug from behind his desk. "Take a seat right there." He pointed to a three and a half legged chair.

Buhley gave a nod to Bullard Haynes who sat next to Slug behind his desk. Nervous as he walked to the chair, he failed to notice the one short leg. Sitting down and leaning back, Buhley found himself thrown off balance and directly onto the floor like a bronco bull rider. Acting as if nothing had happened, he hopped up and righted the chair, seating himself on the chair's left edge to balance the weight. Bullard plastered a broad smile across his face, successfully suppressing a laugh as Buhley balanced on his perch. Spitting a stream of tobacco juice into a can, Slug shifted his chaw and said, "Watch that chair, kid. I been meaning to get it fixed, but just hadn't cared to."

Not really listening, Buhley's eyes were fixed on the many pictures on the office wall -- pictures of Slug and the great ballplayers he knew. The images solidified in Buhley's mind the fact that this was the big leagues. It made him more in awe of his surroundings.

Noticing Buhley's focus, Slug said in a loud voice, "Kid, them pictures ain't the reason why I called you in here today."

Eyes darting back to Slug, Buhley quickly replied, "Yes, sir."

Slug spun around in his chair with back to Buhley and pulled off his hat. He pointed to a bald spot in the back of his head -- a small area he'd scalded when he was little. The hair in that patch had never grown back. "See this, kid?" He pointed to the bare spot.

Spinning back around to face Buhley, he began. "That's what I got from scratching my head over what to do about you. I can't figure you out, kid. The first time I seen you, I figured you'd be back on the bus that afternoon, but you keep hanging around. You never played a game of baseball in your life, and yet none of our boys has put a good piece of wood on one of your balls. There's more to pitching than just throwing a ball. There's coverages, cutoffs, and things like that. You don't know them now, but you can learn'em."

Buhley sat on the left edge of the chair, listening intently and not knowing whether Slug was praising him or aiming to throw him out. "There's three ways to win in this game," Slug continued. "Pitching, pitching and pitching. That's how you win. Everybody comes to watch the power hitters, but that don't win the game. Pitching does. You can never get enough pitching. Bullard and I have watched you. To us, you're like a nice garden with a mess of weeds. You get them weeds out, and you'll be something to look at. We like you, kid. But more important than that, we think you can pitch." Slug paused to spit his tobacco juice and then continued. "We'd like to sign you to a minor league contract and see what you can do on a day-in-day-out basis. Bullard wants to take you with us to opening day and our first home stand in Atlanta to let you get the feel of what we do and what it's like. Then we'll assign you to a farm league club. And kid, we'll be watching you everyday. You got any questions?"

Blankly, Buhley stared at Slug, wondering if what he had just heard was a dream or reality. An impatient man, Slug raised his voice. "Kid, you got any questions or not?"

"No, sir," Buhley answered, standing up slowly and walking towards the door. He stopped, turning to face Slug. With amazement, he asked, "You mean you're gonna pay me to pitch?"

"That's about the size of it, kid."

"Thank you, Mr. Matthews. Thank you, Mr. Haynes," Buhley said in a grateful voice. Fumbling for the doorknob, he opened the door. He walked down the hallway and outside of the clubhouse, trying to absorb all that had just happened.

Slug looked at Bullard and shook his head. "I still ain't figured him out."

"Yeah, but he can flat pitch," replied Bullard.

Stunned, Buhley walked like a zombie to the bleachers, sitting down on the first row. Moper Mapes and Manny Lopez were taking ground balls from third base and shortstop. Buhley watched as a gloveless Manny Lopez fielded every ground ball and made flawless throws to first base. Moper Mapes turned to Buhley and yelled, "Congratulations, Buhley! I heard you got a contract. Way to go!"

"Thank you," returned Buhley.

Buzzy Preacher walked over and sat down beside Buhley. He stuck out his hand to shake Buhley's. "Congratulations, Buhley, you've done a great job this spring, and I think you have great things ahead of you. Everybody in our organization is pleased you'll be playing with us. Get on over to my office and call home and tell them the good news. Take all the time you need to talk. This is a once in a lifetime experience for you."

"Thank you. I'd like to call. Thank you for everything, Mr. Preacher."

"You're welcome, and please call me Buzzy."

"Yes, sir, Mr. Preacher."

Still on cloud nine, he walked towards Buzzy's office. Hearing someone loudly calling his name, he turned to see Elser running towards him in a sore knee run. "I just heard!" said Elser grabbing Buhley in a quick bear hug. "I knew they'd have to sign you after the way you pitched. Congratulations! I have only one regret. I'm probably done after this year and will probably never get to catch you in the big leagues. I don't have any doubt you'll make it one day, but I likely won't be around to experience it with you."

"Thank you, Elser. Thank you for all your help and for being a friend. You made me feel at home down here and helped me learn more about pitching. I don't know whats gonna happen from here, but I'll always be grateful to you for what you've done."

Elser gave Buhley an appreciative nod. "Let's go celebrate tonight."

"That'd be great!"

"Pick you up around seven-thirty."

With a wave to Elser, Buhley walked into Buzzy Preacher's office. Sitting on the side of the desk, he picked up the phone and began dialing.

Parley Hawkins had just finished counting his receipts for the day and was heading out to make an evening deposit. Walking towards his car, he heard the phone ringing. After a moment's debate over whether to return and answer it, he disgusted himself by doing a 180-degree turn and walked back inside. Grabbing the receiver on the fifth ring, Parley answered, "Hawkins, may I help you?"

"Mr. Parley," Buhley began.

"Buhley, is that you?" Parley asked quickly before anything else could be said.

"Yes, sir."

"Well, tell me what's goin' on, how you're doin' and all that!" Parley's eagerness vibrated through the phone.

"Mr. Parley, they're givin' me a contract to play in their minor league system!"

Holding his breath, Parley had to be sure. "They're signin' you to play?"

"Yes, sir."

"Hot dang, hot dang, hot dang!" Parley yelled, putting the receiver down on the counter and dancing a jig. Picking up the phone again, he hooted. "Well, I'll be a monkey's uncle! I'm gonna ride over and tell your daddy right now. You wait 'til word gets around. Folks won't believe it. Buhley Sparks playing baseball. Congratulations, son. I'm so proud I can't quit!"

Out of breath with excitement, Parley sat down on the checkout counter. "What happens now?" he asked.

"They've asked me to go to Atlanta with the team for opening day and the first home stand, so I can see what its like. Then they'll assign me to a farm team. I think I'll be able to come home for a few days before I have to report. I'll call and let you know as soon as I find out for sure."

"Man, oh, man, I can't believe it. They signed you. You're playing baseball!"

They talked for a while, and Parley got as many details as he could. When Parley hung up the phone, he headed straight for the Sparks' farm. August was in the kitchen eating supper when Parley walked up the back porch steps. Seeing him coming, August called out, "Come on in, Parley."

The screen door creaked in welcome as Parley opened it, entering the kitchen. Waiting for the familiar door slap, August nodded and put a slice of fresh tomato on his plate, covering it with mayonnaise. "What brings you here?"

Taking a seat across the table, Parley casually said, "Well, I thought you might be interested. I just heard from Buhley."

August perked up. "What did he say?" he asked excitedly.

"Well, not much. Same old stuff, August." With a nonchalant attitude, Parley looked around as if he were bored and then couldn't hold it any longer. He slammed his hand down on the corner of the table and yelled, "They signed him, August! They signed him! Buhley's got a contract!" Jumping up from the table, Parley danced around the small kitchen.

"They signed him?"

"Yesiree!"

Parley pulled August out of his chair and gave him a hug. August sat back down looking stunned. "Your boy's in the minor leagues. They're paying him to throw a baseball. What do you think about that?"

"Well, I'll be damned," said August as tears welled up in his eyes. He looked at a picture of Ranna next to him on the kitchen table and said, "They signed him, sweetie. They signed him."

Parley sat down to catch his breath. After explaining all that Buhley had told him, he reassured August he would let him know any further information he received. August pushed away his half-eaten plate of food, looked at the floor and began to speak. "Ranna and I tried for years to have children and never could. Then one day here come Buhley. From the time I can remember, he liked to throw. Just a little thing, he would pick up a rock, a stone or something and say, 'Daddy, watch this! I'm gonna hit that pole with this rock,' and damned if he wouldn't."

Parley didn't say a word. He sat listening as August continued to talk

"I never paid much attention to it. I'd be in the field working, and I'd look up and see him throwing a ball against the side of the barn. One day I walked in from the field to get a drink of water, and I watched him for a time. I watched him throw ten or eleven pitches at this knot in one of the boards on the wall of the barn. He hit that knot every single time. I just scratched my head and thought to myself, 'That boy's got a gift of some sort.' He never had no pitching lesson or nothin'. Never played organized ball or nothin' like that. He just could always throw. I still thought nothin' would ever come of it. I mean here in Homerville, there ain't much call for a boy who can throw. And how you gonna get out of Homerville so people can see what you can do? We ain't got organized baseball or anything like that. Then that traveling all-star team came to town, and you got him to pitch." Pausing for a moment, August glanced at Parley and added, "You know I didn't even go watch him play!"

Parley held his silence as August looked away and continued talking. "I thought if I wasn't working, I was cheating myself and my family. I've done some things in my life that I ain't very proud of. Gambling and some other bad decisions are a few, but not going to watch Buhley pitch against that all-star team is the one I regret the most. My son, my own flesh and blood, doing what he loves the most, and I ain't there to watch. And another thing, Parley, in the seventeen years he's been alive, I'm not sure I've ever looked him in the eye and told him I love him." August shook his head in disgust. "I tell you this. If Buhley were here right now, I'd wrap these tired old arms around him, and I'd hold him as hard and as long as it took to make him understand that I love him with every ounce of my being."

Parley sat there long enough to let him finish talking and then said, "August, you'll have plenty of time to mend any fences you think need mendin'. But whatever you think you did or didn't do, you raised one of the finest young men I know. You can't say a sore thing about Buhley and be telling the truth, and you can be proud about that."

August nodded his agreement at Parley. Parley got up to leave and shook August's hand. He grabbed August's arm to hold him steady. "You should be able to talk to Buhley in a week or so. He's supposed to go with the team for their opening home stand in Atlanta and then come home for a few days before he gets assigned to a minor league team."

Energized, August stood up as fast as his body would allow, grabbed Parley and hugged him. "Thank you for takin' care of Buhley when I didn't, and thank you for all your help. Please let me know when you hear anything else."

With a smile and a confirming nod, Parley let himself out, savoring the slapping sound of the old screen door behind him.

The phone rang at Clip's, and 56 Johnson picked it up on the first ring. "Clips," said 56 into the receiver. "Hello, Parley," 56 replied. As he listened, his facial expressions went from normal to excited. "He what? They what? You're kiddin! Is that a fact? Great goodness! Hold on a second!"

He put the receiver away from his mouth and yelled over to Benny Armstrong who was playing a game of pool. "Hey, Benny, Atlanta signed Buhley to a minor league contract!"

Benny threw down his pool cue and grabbed the beer from the corner of the pool table. Hiking the can high over his head, he let out a high-pitched exclamation of celebration. Benny gulped down the remaining beer, let out a loud burp and walked quickly over to 56.

"Tell me more," said 56 as he and Benny listened through the receiver together. Parley gave them all the details he knew, explaining that Buhley would be with the team for the home opener and then home for a few days before leaving for his assignment. 56 thanked Parley for calling as he hung up the phone. There were only a handful of people in Clips this evening, but they were all excited when 56 yelled, "Buhley Sparks signed with Atlanta! Drinks are on the house!"

Sitting at the bar next to 56, Benny opened another Pabst Blue Ribbon. "I can't believe it," he said. "Buhley signed with Atlanta. I'll tell you this. I've caught a lot of pitchers in my day, but I ain't never caught one like Buhley who can throw it where he wants, how he wants and when he wants every time. He's got a gift or somethin'. When he threw that way against Satch Moak's team, I says to myself -- I says maybe that was a fluke or somethin'. But, hell, if Atlanta signed him, then he must be for real!"

56 nodded in agreement. "I remember hearing a time or two that he could throw," said 56. "Then he did that at the Fourth of July celebration and against Satch Moak. I think you're right. Some people are born with looks. Buhley was just born with throwing."

Buhley got into the convertible with Elser. He was still floating between reality and a dream. It hadn't sunk in that the Atlanta Peaches were offering him a contract to play baseball. Remembering what it was like when he first signed, Elser knew what Buhley probably was thinking and also what he needed to hear. "So, where do you want to eat?" he asked.

"Don't matter to me," came the answer. Buhley stared straight ahead.

"What you thinkin' about, Buhley?"

"It's strange, Elser. Sometimes I think, 'Is this really happening?' Am I dreaming or am I really about to play baseball all the time? Not less than three weeks ago, I was pulpwooding back home, and now I am going with the Atlanta Peaches to their first home stand. Don't you see why I'm a little stumped?"

"I understand completely. I know when I signed right out of high school, it happened so fast I didn't have much time to think about it. At least I was playing baseball at the time and in the flow of being recruited and drafted and everything. But you -- you came right out of the woods into the game. I can see how it will take some adjustment."

Buhley continued. "And then there's Daddy. He ain't young no more. His step has slowed quite a bit. I know folks is looking in on him and everything, but he's all alone since Mamma died and I left. I think about that all the time. 'Should I even be doing this?' I ask myself. I know this is a once in a lifetime dream that will never come again, but at what cost? You understand, Elser?"

Elser nodded in affirmation. "Hey, why don't we just forget all that right now and go celebrate?"

With no response from Buhley as they backed out of the parking lot and onto the highway, Elser repeated his question from earlier. "Where would you like to go tonight?"

"Homerville," he said softly.

"What'd you say?"

"I don't care," Buhley replied. "Anywhere's fine."

"How about a steak?"

"Okay."

The waitress brought out two t-bones still sizzling on the plates. "I hope you boys enjoy these," she said in a soft southern accent.

Buhley watched her walk away. "Okay, Buhley, don't make me have to get you out of another jam with a jealous boyfriend again," said Elser.

Cutting into his steak, Buhley said, "She 's just so nice lookin'."

"So are all the ripe apples in the supermarket, but you don't go in there and take a bite out of each one of them, do you?"

"No, but I sure like to glance at them pretty hard."

"Oh, eat your steak and hush."

Both of them continued to eat, and then Elser said, "I'm betting you've never flown in an airplane."

"That's right."

"Well, that's about to change."

"What do you mean?"

"How do you think we're getting all of us and the equipment to Atlanta? By stagecoach?"

"I hadn't thought about it."

"You better start thinking about a few things now. We'll be leaving day after tomorrow. You got enough clothes and stuff until you get back home?"

"Just barely. I've been washing what little clothes I brought every other day."

"You better start thinking about stuff like that. You're a professional baseball player now, and you gotta start acting like one, not some no-account who's just fallen off a tree stump."

Just then the waitress came over and in her soft southern voice said, "Can I offer you boys some dessert?"

Buhley stared at her, enjoying every syllable of her question. Her voice floated softly into his ear and relaxed his whole body. Noticing what was happening, Elser said, "Ma'am, could you please tell us what's available for dessert, so my friend here can enjoy your voice a little longer? I believe you have him under a spell."

Buhley was so relaxed he didn't respond to Elser's picking.

"Why, of course," the waitress's soft voice replied. "We have apple pie, ice cream -- either vanilla or chocolate, chocolate cake, pecan pie, lemon meringue pie and a brownie sundae."

"I'll have hot apple pie with vanilla ice cream on top. What about you, Buhley?" asked Elser.

Buhley sat heavy-eyed and relaxed, not saying a word. Amused at his young friend's behavior, Elser explained, "Just bring us two of those, please, ma'am. He'll be all right in a minute, soon as you get out of earshot of him. He's a little homesick, and I'm sure you've just reminded him of his sweetheart back home's all."

As soon as the waitress left, Elser said, "Boy, you do have it bad, don't you?"

"I could sit and listen to her for days," said Buhley still in a half-trance.

With the apple pies a la mode safely delivered, Buhley and Elser dug in, and soon the sound of forks hitting empty plates could be heard. As they got up to leave, the waitress said, "Y'all have a good evening and come back to see us real soon."

The soft voice words wafted through the air and into Buhley's ears. Once again, her voice put him in a transcendental state. He stared back at her as he was leaving. Not looking where he was going, he ran into the corner of an empty table, causing his leg to charley horse. He fell directly to the floor. The waitress began to laugh as Elser helped Buhley to his feet and out the door. Limping to the car, Buhley asked, "Can we eat here tomorrow night?"

"Hell, no," replied Elser. "She probably has a boyfriend or something. Buhley Sparks, women are going to be the death of you yet."

The next day after a light workout the Peaches gathered together with Slug for a team meeting. "Look around you, fellas. What you see is this year's team. We got pitching, we got defense, and we got hitting. We got it all, and there ain't no reason why we can't take it to the house this year and win it all. Some of the people who are supposed to know these things are saying just that." Slug gave a nod in Buhley's direction and continued. "All of you know Buhley Sparks. We're gonna take Buhley with us for the opening home stand and let him see what the big show is all about. Buhley has all the talent in the world, but he's a little green and needs to learn more about the game. He'll be assigned to one of our farm teams, and we hope that one day soon he'll join us permanently in Atlanta. In the meantime, I want you to make him feel like he's part of the team, because he is. I don't believe he's ever been to the big city. Have you, kid?"

"No, sir," answered Buhley.

"Elser's been nice and showed him the ropes down here, and I want y'all to do the same for him in Atlanta."

Sitting in the back of the group, Lefty Pete couldn't resist making a loud mooing sound when Slug was talking about Buhley. "Is that you making that noise, Pete?" asked Slug.

Although Lefty didn't respond, Slug knew the answer. "You should've made the sound of a jackass, Pete. That would have been way more authentic," he pointed out.

Everybody laughed aloud while Lefty slumped down behind two players. Slug continued. "You boys know we play day after tomorrow. You also know this is my thirteenth year here, and I ain't never lost an opening game, and I don't intend to start now. Y'all need to start getting your heads right and thinking about that first game." Looking over at Lefty, he said, "Lefty, if you can stop making animal noises, you get the ball opening night."

Lefty nodded in approval. "Bullard and I will let the rest of the pitching staff know the rotation tomorrow. I want y'all to get a good night's sleep and be on the bus to go to the airport at eleven o'clock in the morning. Any questions?" he asked. "Good," he said before giving anyone a chance to ask one. "Hit the showers, and be careful tonight."

As Slug turned and walked away, Lefty Pete gathered all the pitchers together and reminded them of their pre-first game ritual. Lefty always took the pitchers out for a night on the town the day before the first game and paid for everything. No pitcher dared turn him down. "Everybody in?" he asked.

All the pitchers answered in the affirmative. "The car leaves from the stadium at seven o'clock sharp," Lefty said as he patted them all on the shoulders.

Calling Buhley off to the side, Buzzy Preacher put his arm around him. "I'm proud of you, Buhley. All of the throwing you did when you were growing up has paid off. There are a lot of boys who'd sell their souls to sign a contract to play baseball. When you got off the bus, I thought maybe you were in over your head. Slug thought the same thing. He told me to keep the car running, so I could get you the hell back to the bus station. You proved him wrong. I don't think he and Bullard have decided where to send you, but they are excited and probably consider you on the fast track to Atlanta. Are you okay with everything you need until you go home?" asked Buzzy.

"Yes, sir," replied Buhley.

They began walking to the clubhouse. "Mr. Preacher," said Buhley, "I sure do want to thank you for all of your help. I appreciate the opportunity to come down here for this experience. The folks back home won't believe it when they find out what I've been doing."

"You're welcome. I'm going to call Satch Moak and tell him we signed you. He'll be thrilled to hear the news. I do need to remind you that this is a business, and you will be paid to help us win ball games just as every other player is. Sometimes we have to let players go who are no longer able to perform their job at the necessary level. It's unfortunate, but it's part of the game. I have no idea what will happen to you in our organization, but you'll see it happen to other people if you stay around long enough. I don't want you to have the wrong idea about why we are here. We are here to win baseball games, and if we don't, all of our jobs are in jeopardy. Do you understand?"

"Yes, sir."

CHAPTER 13

Word spread fast in Homerville about Buhley signing with the Atlanta Peaches. Cheryl Dane picked up the paper and for the first time turned to the sports page to see when the Peaches were playing their first game. "Daddy, will Buhley play in the Peaches' first game?" she asked.

"I don't think so, sugar," he replied. "From what Parley Hawkins told me, Buhley is going to be at the game, but he isn't on the major league roster and will be assigned to a farm team somewhere else."

"Oh." Cheryl pretended she understood what her father had just said.

Elbert File pulled up to Hooty Lou's house and honked the horn. He came out and hopped in the car to ride over to Matty Lee's for the regular weekly night poker game. Pulling a jar of moonshine from under the seat, Elbert took a large gulp and offered some to Hooty. "How 'bout a shot?" he asked.

"No, thanks," answered Hooty. "If I get to tasting too much of that, I'll look at my cards and think I have three of everything and start bettin' the house when I ain't even got a pair." Always appreciative of his own humor, he let out a loud hyena laugh.

"I don't mind a taste now and then," stated Elbert as he took another shot before screwing on the lid and putting the jar back under the seat.

Half joking, Hooty raised his voice in question. "Now and then? How about now and again and again and again? You're in a tight race with Early Moon for the title of town drunk. It's anybody's contest right now."

"Don't get on your old fishin' buddy like that, Hooty," said Elbert with a slight slur in a word or two.

"Fishin' buddy? The last time we went fishing, you fell out of the boat and floated down the river until you got hung up on a stump sticking out of the water. I had to tow you back to the boat ramp to get you in the boat. Do you remember that?"

"I don't believe I do," said Elbert in a slow and puzzled voice. "But I was wondering how them twigs and branch pieces got in my overalls."

"You're just this side of certifiable. You know that Elbert?" said Hooty forcefully.

"I guess I am," Elbert replied in an uncaring manner.

They pulled into the front drive of Matty Lee's house and got out of the car. Hooty walked up to the front door and jarred it open just a touch. "Matty, you in there?" he yelled.

"Yeah, come on in," came the reply.

Parley was already sitting at the poker table when Hooty and Elbert walked in. Entering from the kitchen, Matty said, "Parley brought some ice cold Coca-Colas. Anybody want one?"

"Yeah, I'll have one," said Parley and Hooty in unison.

"How 'bout you, Elbert?" asked Matty.

"No, thanks."

Hooty couldn't resist butting in. "He better not drink a Coca-Cola. He's already had some of Early Moon's Kool-Aid, and if he puts any carbonation on top of that, he's liable to explode."

"You still taking a snort every now and then?" asked Parley.

Elbert sat in silence, and Hooty, never short for words, jumped in. "Every now and then? How about more now than then? He could tell you about it 'cept he can't remember it."

Matty brought in the drinks and opened up a brand new deck of cards. "Before we deal, Parley, tell us about Buhley," he requested.

"Y'all probably heard that rascal signed with the Atlanta Peaches. They're going to assign him somewhere in their organization. He's going with them to their home opener and the first home stand. Then he'll come home for a few days before he goes to his team. Makes you want to cut that radio on extra early for the game Friday night, don't it? Maybe they'll mention his name or something."

Jumping into the conversation, Hooty announced, "Buhley called me a couple of days ago and asked me how much to ask for in his contract. You know that boy never makes a move without asking me."

Matty Lee played along and asked, "Wha'd you tell him?"

"I told him to ask for the moon and settle for a crater." Hooty reared back his head and started laughing. Seeing that nobody else was amused, he brought his laughter to a slow, almost embarrassing, stop.

Seeing an opening to pick on Hooty a little, Parley jumped. "Hold on! Wait a minute, Matty. Turn your head to the left. Now turn your head back to the right. Just as I suspected. Your hair's uneven. One side's higher than the other. Can you believe that? We pay good money for our haircuts around here, and what do we get? Unevens! That's what we get. Unevens. What do you think we oughtta do about it, Matty?"

Matty saw where he was going and played right along. "I think a lynchin' is in order. There's nothin' worse to me than an uneven haircut. I pay good money for a haircut, and what do I get? Uneven."

Hooty sat and took as much as he could. "Now, just wait a minute, boys. There's no law that says I have to give y'all even haircuts. Besides, remember the sign - 'Don't worry. It'll grow back.'"

Sobered up to a degree, Elbert Files said, "Are we gonna talk about barbering or play cards? Deal 'em up, Matty. I'm feelin' lucky tonight."

Matty shuffled the deck a few times, licked his fingers and began dealing.

Laying a pillow on the floor next to his bed, August slowly knelt down and rested his elbows on the edge of the mattress. He bowed his head and began to pray. "Lord, I ain't done good." He paused to let the lump in his throat clear. "You've given me such a bounty, and I squandered it. This land that you gave to me has been good. It's fed me and my family all these years. I'm not sure, Lord, that I have properly thanked you for that, but I do now. And another thing, Lord, you gave me many years with a woman I never deserved. I miss her, Lord, but I know she is in Your loving arms. I thank you for that, Lord. And lastly, Lord, You gave me my boy, Buhley. He turned out to be a fine young man, Lord, despite me. I know I haven't gone to the house of worship like I should have all these years. I'm not much of a social person. I prefer to commence with You by myself. I hope You can forgive me for that. And I promise to do more commencing with You more often from now on. But, Lord, I'd be grateful if You could grant me just one mercy. Buhley is supposed to come home in a few days, and could You bring him to me safely? Can You let me see him just one more time, so I can tell him face to face that I love him? Please have mercy on me, Lord, 'cause I ain't done so good. For Christ's sake, Amen."

August wiped his eyes and slowly climbed into bed. He fell asleep quickly and slept the best he had in many nights.

Buhley walked up the steps and into the jetliner. Halfway down the aisle, he took a seat next to Elser. Buhley sat and stared straight ahead. "You okay?" asked Elser.

"Just a touch nervous."

At that moment, a beautiful stewardess walked down the aisle. Elser got her attention and called her over. He pointed at Buhley and said, "This is my friend's first trip on a plane."

The stewardess knelt down to talk to Buhley eye to eye. Putting her hand on his shoulder, she said, "You just let me know if there is anything I can do for you. We want your first flight to be a wonderful experience. Is there anything you need right now?"

"No, ma'am." Buhley still looked straight ahead.

The stewardess rose to leave and gently removed her hand from Buhley's shoulder. "Don't you hesitate to call me," she said as she left.

"Man, Buhley, did you see how gorgeous she is?" asked Elser.

"I ain't got time for that," replied Buhley still with his eyes locked straight ahead.

"I guess there's a first time for everything," said Elser as he shook his head and looked out the window.

Slug walked to the back of the plane where the players were and got everyone's attention. "When we get to Atlanta, there will be a bus waiting to take us to the stadium. I want every one of you to go to the clubhouse, head straight to your locker and make sure your uniform and equipment are all there. We'll have a meeting at five o'clock, and after that, you're free to go. Our game is at seven o'clock tomorrow afternoon. Anybody have any questions?"

"Good," he said before anyone had time to raise a hand.

As the plane taxied down the runway, the captain spoke over the intercom. "Good morning, I'm David Lassiter. I'll be your captain for this flight. We have a beautiful day for flying. Our estimated time of arrival is one forty-five. Atlanta skies are clear, and the temperature is seventy-eight degrees. Thank you for flying with us, and good luck on your new season. I hope you get off to a good start and go all the way this year. Please let us know if there is anything you need. Thank you, and please fasten your seat belts for take off."

Elser made sure Buhley was settled. "Here we go, Buhley," he said.

As the pilot throttled the engines, the plane raced forward. Buhley felt his head jerk back against the headrest. Glancing over, Elser noticed Buhley's eyes were as big as saucers. The nose of the plane eased upward, and soon they were off the ground. A routine flight for Elser, he was three minutes into a nap after five minutes in the air. Keeping his eyes glued to the seatback in front of him, Buhley hoped it would be over soon. He didn't dare look out the window of the plane to see the blue sky, the clouds or the land below. Buhley held tightly to the armrest of his chair. His grip was so strong that his knuckles soon turned stark white. After what seemed like an eternity, the captain's voice came through the intercom. "Please fasten your seat belts. We will be landing in approximately ten minutes."

Buhley was somewhat relieved that his first flight was about to be over. He continued to hold on tightly just in case. Waking from his nap, Elser noticed Buhley's hands. "Damn, Buhley, I believe you've strangled those armrests to death. You choked the life clean out of them."

"How much longer, Elser?" asked Buhley.

"We're almost ready to touch down. It'll only be a couple more minutes."

"Don't bother me 'til then," Buhley curtly replied.

Elser looked out the window and saw the Atlanta skyline. He looked back to the right and saw Atlanta Stadium where the Peaches played. Elser thought to himself, "This may be my last season. I better savor every moment."

Just then the plane bumped. Buhley stiffened. "What was that?" he asked in a concerned voice.

"We just landed. You can relax now," Elser assured him.

As the plane slowed and began taxiing to the terminal, Buhley loosened his grip on the armrests and began to massage his knuckles to get the color to return. Buhley had squeezed the foam in the armrests so hard and for so long, they remained indented with his finger formation. Elser noticed the armrests. "You did kill those armrests. Look at 'em. You strangled them and left your fingerprints as evidence."

Buhley didn't respond. He let out a sigh of relief. "I'm glad that's over."

"How'd you like it?" asked Elser.

"My heart was beating the whole time, Elser," replied Buhley.

"Well, I'm glad of that, or you would have been dead a while back."

"You know what I mean," said Buhley in a serious tone.

Buhley unfastened his seatbelt, stood up and stretched. He grabbed his bag and walked towards the exit. The team boarded the bus and headed for the stadium. Buhley sat next to the window and gazed at sights he had never seen before. Skyscrapers dotted the skyline of Atlanta as they neared the city. "I ain't never seen buildings that tall," Buhley told Elser. "They sure got a lot of pavement up here -- not much grass. Back home, it's just the other way around. We got mostly grass and not much paving."

Buhley made a quick turn towards Elser. "Hey, did you see that lady on the airplane with us? She was nice looking. Did you notice her?"

"You mean the stewardess?"

"Yeah, I think that's what they called her."

"No, I didn't see her, Buhley," Elser said with eyes rolling. To himself, he thought, "Well, he's back to normal."

He watched with amusement as Buhley continued to look out the window, taking in all the sights of Atlanta. "You're like a kid in a candy store, ain't you, boy?"

"I wish my friend Crawdad was here to see all this, 'cause he won't believe it when I tell him what I saw."

The bus pulled into the stadium and took them to the players' entrance. "This place is big," said Buhley. "It's a lot bigger than that stadium I went to in Jacksonville when I was a kid."

As the bus stopped near the clubhouse door, Slug stood up and said, "Check your lockers real good. Make sure your uniform and all your equipment are in order. Meeting at five o'clock. Don't be late."

First to exit the bus, Slug took Bullard and went straight to his office. "Just follow me, and I'll show you everything," Elser directed Buhley. Leading the way inside, he said, "This is the clubhouse, Buhley."

Buhley's eyes slowly went all around the room. He noticed the large oak lockers engraved with each player's name. "These lockers are nicer than any furniture we got in our house," he marveled, still taking in the surroundings.

Neatly pressed uniforms hung in the lockers. He took note that each piece of equipment was laid precisely in place where every player could take inventory of what he had. Buhley gazed at the end of the room to see a table full of sandwiches, fruit and candy bars. At the side of the table was a large ice-filled tub loaded with cold beer and Coca-Colas. "Man, this is really something," said Buhley.

Elser patted him on the back and did his best Slug Matthews' imitation. "This is the big leagues, kid!"

Just then a loud voice came from across the room. "Elser Riggs, you old rascal, how you been?"

Elser looked around and responded, "Argie Tuttle, you old possum, get over here!"

Argie Tuttle was the man in charge of the clubhouse for the Atlanta Peaches and had been with the club ever since they came to Atlanta. Known as the best clubhouse manager in the business, Argie took pride in the way he laid out everyone's locker. The uniforms and the equipment had to be just so. Argie was in his mid-fifties, and during the off season, he worked odd jobs to make ends meet until the season rolled around. He always went above and beyond what was asked of him. Argie Tuttle lived for Atlanta Peaches baseball.

Making his way across the clubhouse room, Argie embraced Elser. "Did you have a good off season?" inquired Elser.

"We did all right," replied Argie. "The season opener couldn't get here quick enough for me."

"Me neither," agreed Elser. "When we flew over the stadium, I looked down and thought to myself that I don't know how many more games I have left. I better savor every moment."

"Oh, you got lots of years left. If you play like you did last year, you'll make all-stars again," said Argie in an effort to lift Elser's spirits.

Elser shrugged. "We'll see. Argie, I want you to meet a good friend of mine -- Buhley Sparks. Buhley, this is Argie Tuttle. He's the glue that holds this team together. If you ever need anything, anything at all, he's the man to see. Argie, Buhley is a pitcher like you ain't never seen. He's come out of the woods and impressed Slug and Bull, and they signed him to a contract. He'll be assigned to one of our farm leagues. They brought him to our first home stand for him to see what the big leagues are all about."

"Nice to meet you, Buhley," said Argie as he stuck out his hand.

"Nice to meet you, Mr. Tuttle," said Buhley, returning the firm grip.

"Call me Argie."

"Yes, sir, Mr. Tuttle."

"I'll bet you're a lefty."

"Yes, sir, how'd you know?"

"Look at your arms. Your left arm is twice the size of your right one. I'll bet you threw a lot growing up. You don't build up an arm like that overnight; it takes time and a lot of throwing."

"Yes, sir, I did."

"They must think a lot of you if they brought you here for the first home stand. I ain't never seen them do that before."

Buhley sheepishly did not respond to the compliment.

"Where's Footrace?" asked Elser.

"He's in my office. He's always a little shy at first. He'll come out in a minute or two," said Argie.

"Who's Footrace?" Buhley inquired.

Argie explained. "That's my son, Amos. They call him Footrace because he loves to race everybody. He's thirteen years old. When he was born, the umbilical cord was wrapped around his neck and cut off the oxygen to his brain, and he is a little slow mentally. But God gifted him with speed, and he loves to show it off. He can beat everybody on this team except for Manny Lopez. Nice to meet you, Buhley, and good luck this season wherever you end up."

"Thank you, Mr. Tuttle."

"Call me Argie," he requested as he walked away.

"Yes, sir, Mr. Tuttle."

Buhley walked around the clubhouse admiring the surroundings. He walked by Lefty Pete's locker. Lefty was sitting on his locker and noticed Buhley. "Hey, Sparks!" he said.

Buhley stopped and looked at Lefty who pointed to his jersey and his engraved nameplate on the locker. "This is what it's all about right here, Sparks. You better enjoy this time in a major league clubhouse, because it may be the only time you ever see one. Right now, I'm here, and you're not. You understand, Sparks?" stated Lefty in a demeaning tone.

"I guess so," replied Buhley, not really understanding what Lefty meant.

Buhley didn't understand that Lefty felt threatened by him. Lefty had never seen anybody come in and pitch like Buhley had done. He was king of the hill as far as pitching went for the Peaches. Lefty was in his prime and didn't want a rookie upstaging him while he was still in his glory. He tried to shake Buhley's confidence whenever he could. Lefty couldn't battle Buhley Sparks on the mound, so he resorted to the mind.

After thoroughly exploring the clubhouse, Buhley walked over to Moper Mapes and sat down. "This is pretty neat, Moper," he said shaking his head in amazement.

"I never take this for granted, Buhley. I feel fortunate to play in the majors, especially for the Peaches. They're one of the best organizations in the league. Look at this clubhouse. Can it get any better than this?" said Moper.

Buhley tried not to stare at Moper's lower turned down lip. He liked Moper a lot and appreciated his kindness. "You have all of this to look forward to in your future, and when you get here, remember to appreciate it," said Moper as he patted Buhley on the back.

"I hope so, Moper," Buhley replied as he got up to walk away.

"Buhley, come over here," a voice said.

Buhley looked around and saw Elser standing by the food table and made his way over to him. "Buhley, I want you to meet a good friend of mine. Buhley, this is Amos Tuttle, better known as Footrace. Footrace is the fastest hombre east of the Pecos," said Elser.

Amos tapped Elser on the shoulder and asked, "Elser, what are the Pecos?"

"I don't know, Footrace, but I saw 'em on a western one time."

"Oh," sighed Footrace.

"Footrace, this is Buhley Sparks. He's in our minor league organization and a real good pitcher," said Elser.

"Nice to meet you, Amos," said Buhley.

"Nice to meet you, Buhley Sparks." Footrace slowly accented every word. Pointing to his head, Footrace added, "I'm a little slow up here, but down here, I'm fast." He pointed to his legs.

"You wanna footrace, Buhley Sparks?" he asked slowly.

Buhley looked at Elser with a slightly puzzled look on his face. Elser nodded in the affirmative. "Sure, I would," answered Buhley.

Elser looked at Amos. "Go on to the field, and we'll be there in a minute," he said.

Amos smiled, turned and walked away.

"Should I let him win?" asked Buhley.

Elser laughed. "You don't understand, Buhley. I've seen you run, and I've seen him run. You have average speed like a mule. He has real fast speed like a thoroughbred. That's what the race will be like, a mule and a thoroughbred, and you're the mule. You ready?"

"I guess so."

"Let me go check my locker, and then we'll go to the field," said Elser.

Buhley followed Elser to his locker. Elser thoroughly checked everything to make sure he was ready for the first game the next day. "Let's go," he said.

They walked out of the clubhouse and down the tunnel into the dugout. Buhley followed as Elser walked up the steps of the dugout and onto the field. Looking around, Buhley marveled at the beauty of the stadium and the seemingly infinite number of seats. The grass on the field had been freshly mown, and Buhley paused as the smell of the grass took him back to Homerville and his childhood. He remembered that smell when his dad would mow the yard or mow the field with his tractor. Buhley thought about his mom and saw how she always met his every need. He was lost deep in thought about his wonderful childhood when a voice broke his trance. "Buhley Sparks, you ready for a whipping?"

Buhley looked up to see Amos standing sixty yards out on the right field foul line. He walked over to Amos. Elser yelled back to Buhley, "First one to touch my hand wins. I'll yell, 'On your mark, get set, go.'"

Elser held his hands all the way out to the side with his palms facing Buhley and Amos. Amos looked at Buhley and said slowly, "You fixin' to get a mess of beat, Buhley Sparks."

They stepped up to the line and got in racing stance. Elser yelled, "On your mark, get set, go!"

Buhley took off as fast as he could. He got a few yards off the foul line, and out of the corner of his right eye, he caught sight of a blur. The blur passed him and pieces of grass flew up in his face and into his mouth. When Buhley reached Elser, he already had put his arm down. Amos stood beside Elser barely breathing hard. Buhley bent over and caught his breath.

"Wha'd you think of that, Buhley?" asked Elser.

"He's a thoroughbred, all right," replied Buhley, still out of breath.

"Yep, and you're a mule," said Elser.

Buhley looked at Amos and said, "I ain't never seen nobody run that fast."

Amos smiled. "I'm slow from the neck up, but fast from the waist down. You got you a mess of beat, didn't you, Buhley Sparks?"

"I sure did, Amos," agreed Buhley.

"My friends call me Footrace. You call me Footrace, Buhley Sparks."

"Okay," replied Buhley.

He put his arm around Footrace as they walked back to the dugout. Buhley thought how fun it would be to watch Footrace and Edsel Moon race each other. Standing on the top step of the dugout with Elser, Buhley looked all around the stadium. "You could put everybody from back home in this place and not even notice them. They got a mess of chairs in this place."

"Tomorrow night there won't be an empty one in the house," said Elser.

Buhley looked at the field. "I know some farmers back home that would kill for a garden this green."

"You wait until tomorrow night when the field is lined, the clay is drug, and the grass is painted. When they play the 'Star Spangled Banner,' you'll think you're in God's country."

Buhley paused for a moment and looked at Elser. "I already do," he replied.

Elser patted him on the shoulder and walked down into the dugout towards the tunnel. "Let's go. We have a meeting at five," he said.

Slug walked into the clubhouse and got everyone's attention. "Let me start by saying what a great job Argie once again has done getting our equipment in order and preparing us to play. He makes my job and your job that much easier, and we should appreciate his efforts." Slug looked back at Argie who was standing in the corner of the clubhouse. "Thank you, Argie!"

Argie acknowledged Slug with a nod of his head. Slug shifted his attention back to his team. "You players know there will be fifty thousand people here tomorrow night. These good people are paying their hard-earned money to come watch you play baseball. They expect you to play hard, and I expect you to play hard. That means you will hustle on and off the field. You will keep your mind on the game. If you are in the field, you better be thinking where the ball is going to go and what you are gonna do. We're gonna make the people proud who come watch us play. They are gonna be proud to be fans of the Atlanta Peaches. They are gonna be proud and excited to come watch the type of hard-nosed baseball we are gonna play. And let me make myself perfectly clear. Anyone, and I mean anyone, who does not apply these standards to the way he plays the game won't be playing on this team very long. I don't care who you are, what you've done in the past, what kind of contract you have or any of that other crap. If you ain't playing hard, you ain't playing. I'll go one step further and say if you ain't playing hard, you're gonna come to your locker one day, and there ain't gonna be nothin' in it but a one-way bus ticket back home. That ain't just me talking either. I got that from the top. We got a lot of talent on this team, and if we play hard and up to our potential, there is no reason we can't get to and win the World Series. That's what we're here for and nothing less. I'm proud of the way you worked hard in spring, and now is the time to reap your harvest. So, come tomorrow night and every night after that, we take no prisoners. I want every team in the league to know when you play the Peaches, you better bring it all."

He slowly looked at every player in the room. "You boys understand what I just said?" he asked.

Nobody said a word. "Good. I want you to get plenty of rest tonight. Early batting practice is at two, and required is at four. See you tomorrow."

Chapter 14

Lefty Pete and the other seven pitchers climbed into Lefty's red El Dorado Cadillac convertible. The Cadillac was one of the largest cars on the road. Everyone in Atlanta knew it was Lefty's car even without the personalized license plate that read "LEFTY." He took pride in his car and had someone keep it in immaculate condition. Driving slowly out of the stadium parking lot, he pulled onto the highway into downtown Atlanta. At every stoplight, people recognized Lefty and shouted words of encouragement to him and the other pitchers. Lefty acknowledged their words with a thumbs-up. He drove slowly through the city, hoping to be noticed and draw attention to himself. As he drove, Lefty hung his arm out over the large door of the car in order to let everyone know he was in charge. He was in his element. Atlanta was his town. These were his fans. They paid money to come watch him pitch. He was one of the best pitchers in baseball, and he wanted to make sure everyone else knew the same.

Lefty drove down a couple of side streets, pulling up in front of Mr. Woo's Fish House. He got out of the car and walked into the front door of the restaurant like he owned the place. Lefty removed his sunglasses and looked around. Mr. Woo immediately greeted him. "Ah, Mr. Pete, good see you again," said Mr. Woo.

Mr. Woo was a Chinese immigrant who had come to America twenty years ago, and through hard work, he'd built one of the finest seafood restaurants in

Atlanta. Lefty motioned for the other pitchers to follow. "Mr. Woo, I've got seven of my friends with me tonight like I told you. Are you ready for us?"

"Back room ready for you. I fly special fish in just for you. I fix myself. You gonna like. I promise."

Lefty handed Mr. Wood a wad of cash and said, "Keep the food and drinks coming."

"Of course, Mr. Pete. Anything for you, Mr. Pete. This way please," said Mr. Woo as he led them to a back private dining area.

All of the customers recognized Lefty as he walked through the restaurant. He enjoyed the notoriety as they stopped to watch him make his way to the back room. Lefty sat at the head of the table and presided over it like a father at a Thanksgiving dinner. He signaled for a waitress, and one appeared immediately and opened a large beer-filled cooler on the floor. She opened a bottle of beer for each of the players, setting it before them. Lefty picked up his beer and said, "A toast to the best damn pitching staff in the major leagues."

"Here, here," the players chanted as they raised their beers high and then gulped them down like water.

"Another toast," said Lefty, "to a pennant, then the World Series and all new fat contracts next year."

The players raised their drinks, then put them down and gave themselves a rousing round of applause. The waitress came out of the kitchen with a big platter of hors d'oeuvres and served each player individually. She set down the empty tray, went to the cooler and pulled out another beer for each. As she walked by Lefty, he reached out and patted her on the behind. "Oh, Mr. Pete, you naughty man," she said with a smile.

"You don't know the half of it, darling," said Lefty as the whole table broke into laughter.

When the waitress went back into the kitchen, Lefty said, "Hey, I sure would like to bait her hook. You know what I mean?"

He started to laugh and slapped the corner of the table with his hand. They drank more beer, and then Mr. Woo came into the room with the main entree. He announced, "Mr. Pete and friends, I fly this fish in just for you. I fix myself. Special recipe just for you. Enjoy, enjoy, enjoy!" Mr. Woo held his hands above his head in exclamation. Lefty and the group applauded as Mr. Wood took a bow and exited to the kitchen.

Billy Hawks was one of the pitchers in the group. He was a hard-throwing left-hander who was a bit stumpy. With one hundred and ninety-five pounds on his five foot nine frame, Billy sweat profusely, and his sweat had a certain unenviable odor. Everybody called him "Stinky." Billy was a middle relief pitcher who had been raised in the South and wasn't used to fine dining. When he lifted the cover off his entree, the eye of the fish was staring at him. "This thing's lookin' at me!" he said with a southern drawl as he pushed back from the table.

Lefty jumped in. "Stinky, it ain't looking at you."

"Its eye follows me like a picture. Everywhere I move, the eye moves with me," said Stinky as he moved his head from side to side. "Back home, we have respect for the fish we eat. We cut their heads off before we eat 'em. That way they don't see us picking the meat off their bones and eatin' it."

"Well, that's down right neighborly of you, Stinky," Lefty said in a mock Southern accent. Lefty looked around the table and said, "Fellas, you can take some people out of the country, but you can't take the country out of some people."

He looked back at Stinky. "Ain't that right, Stinky?" said Lefty.

"I reckon," said Stinky still staring at the fish. "I got it!" he said excitedly.

He picked up his knife and cut the head off of the fish. Then he stabbed it with his fork and lowered it under the table, knocking the fish head off the fork and onto the floor.

Lefty couldn't resist picking a little more. "Stinky, you're a problem solver; that's what you are -- a real problem solver. And I'm proud to know you."

Stinky didn't respond. He was busy eating fish. More drinks filled the evening, and pretty soon, Lefty and the boys were seeing two of everything. Lefty stood up and said, "I've got an impression. Guess who it is."

Lefty ran his hand back over the top of his hair three or four times and then said, "Okay, kid, I've seen enough kid. Hit the showers, kid."

In unison, the pitchers yelled, "Slug!"

By this time, the waitress had stopped serving them. Mr. Woo entered the dining area and announced, "Mr. Pete and friends, I hope you enjoyed everything. We close now. Thank you very much. Please come back soon and tell friends. Thank you, thank you, thank you."

He bowed and backed out of the room into the kitchen. Lefty, Stinky and the other pitchers staggered through the empty restaurant and out to Lefty's Cadillac convertible. He cranked it up and weaved his way back to the stadium where the other pitchers' cars were parked.

"Buhley, better get to bed now. I'm going in early tomorrow for extra batting practice," said Elser.

"All right, Elser," said Buhley. "I appreciate your letting me stay with you."

"I wouldn't have it any other way," said Elser.

"How many games you reckon you've caught?"

"Oh, I don't know - thirteen hundred or so."

"How about your batting average? What's your lifetime?"

"Two eighty-nine," Elser said without hesitation.

"What about home runs?"

"Three ninety-six," Elser said, again without hesitation.

"Man, that's pretty good."

"It ain't bad for an old boy from Rosebud, Missouri."

"Thanks for everything, Elser."

"You bet. See you in the morning."

Wadeus Wadkins stuck his head into the door of the kitchen and addressed his wife, Sweetiepie. "Darlin,' it's late. You better come to bed."

"I will," she replied. "It's a strange thing, Wadeus. I've had Buhley Sparks on my heart all day long. I woke up thinking about him, and I ain't stopped since. I think I'll pray just a minute, and then I'll be on in."

Wadeus walked over to the kitchen table where Sweetiepie was sitting and sat down beside her. "You reckon the Lord is trying to tell you something?" he asked.

"Maybe, Wadeus. I've had these feelings before, and then you find out later on that the person was going through a misery when you was thinkin' about them. Maybe the Lord is asking me to pray for Buhley. I ain't seen nor thought of him for a time. He left to play baseball is what I was told. I think I'll pray for him before I come back to bed. Maybe it'll do some good for him. I know it'll ease my mind."

"You want me to pray with you?" asked Wadeus.

"No, sugar, I feel led to pray by myself."

Wadeus got up from the table and leaned down, kissing Sweetiepie on the cheek. "Good night, darlin'. I love you."

"I love you, too, sugar," replied Sweetiepie.

Wadeus walked back down the hall into the bedroom. Sweetiepie sat in deep thought at the kitchen table. After minute or so passed, she slowly bowed her head and in a soft voice began to pray. "Gracious Lord, I have been burdened all day long thinking about Buhley Sparks. I don't know where he is or what he is doing. I don't know if he is doing well or suffering a misery, but I humbly ask You to lay Your hand upon him at this very hour. I pray that Your guidance and strength would be given to him so that whatever misery lay before him, You would see him through. I also pray for August and his walk with You. I pray he would submit to and rely on You more. Keep him safe and peaceful as he is alone. Thank you for this house and our blessings, and keep us safe. For Christ's sake, Amen."

She slowly lifted up her head and breathed a sigh of relief.

Lefty Pete hung off the side of his bed and looked at the clock, which read 3:13 a.m. His stomach had never ached this badly. Lefty eased to his feet, and clutching his stomach, gingerly walked into the bathroom. He leaned over to the toilet, violently vomiting into the urinal. After finishing in the bathroom, Lefty had just enough strength to put on some clothes and drive himself to Grady Memorial Hospital. He walked into the emergency room holding his stomach and struggling for every breath. Lefty reached the admissions desk and collapsed to the floor. "Oh, my goodness!" a nurse screamed as she ran over to attend to him.

She leaned over him. "What's the matter, sir?" she asked.

Lefty didn't answer immediately. He struggled to get the words out. "My stomach's killing me. It hasn't ever hurt this bad before," he said with a grimace.

Another nurse reached over, and they helped him up and guided him to the back of the emergency room where the doctor was working. "We've got another one for you, doctor," one nurse said as they helped Lefty onto a bed.

The doctor walked over to Lefty's bed. "You're Lefty Pete, aren't you?" asked the doctor. Lefty nodded. "You must have eaten at Mr. Woo's Fish House tonight."

"How did you know?" Lefty strained to ask.

"We've got seven other patients with the same symptoms as you, and they all ate at Mr. Woos."

"Damn you, Mr. Woo," hissed Lefty under his breath.

"You've got food poisoning, Mr. Pete," continued the doctor. "You're gonna feel like you're gonna die for another couple of hours or so, and then the pain will subside. You'll be weak for a couple of days, and then gradually, your strength will return."

Lefty named all the pitchers he had eaten with that night. "Yep, they're all here," replied the doctor.

"That's every pitcher we have on our roster. Somebody needs to call Slug Matthews as soon as possible, and let him know what's happened," Lefty struggled to say.

"I'll call him in a couple of hours and let him know. There's nothing that can be done at this hour. You need to rest and let the medicine do its job," replied the doctor.

Lefty grimaced as he tried to sit up in bed. "Doc, I'm supposed to pitch tomorrow!"

"I don't know much about pitching, but I know about food poisoning, and neither you nor the others will be pitching tomorrow. That I can guarantee," said the doctor as he patted Lefty on the shoulder and exited the room.

As the phone rang, Slug Matthews leaned over the bed and looked at the clock, which read 6:11 a.m. He picked up the phone. "Hello," he answered in a groggy voice. "This is who? Doctor who? You've got who in the emergency room?" Slug's voice grew stronger. "What is this, a joke? Is this Lefty Pete's joke? You tell him I'll have his ass," Slug said sternly as he slammed down the phone.

He rolled back over in bed, and the phone immediately rang again. "What?" Slug answered in exasperation.

"Mr. Matthews, please listen to me," the voice said. "I'm Doctor Ralph Hurley at Grady Memorial Hospital. We've got eight of your players here who are very sick with food poisoning."

Slug sat up, and with concern in his voice, said, "Name them, doctor."

The doctor read the names. "That's all of my pitchers!" Slug exclaimed. "Will any of them be able to pitch tonight?"

"No way. They're all very sick. We've treated them, but they'll be weak for a couple of days."

"How in the hell did every one of my pitchers get food poisoning?" asked Slug.

"Apparently, they all ate at the same restaurant and had the same dish which was contaminated," replied Dr. Hurley. "You see the food they ate had a bacteria which reacted with their system and got into their stomach lining causing severe pain. The body reacts...."

"Doc! Doc! Doc!" interrupted Slug. "I ain't got time for med school here. I got to get a pitcher for tonight. I don't mean to be rude, but I gotta go."

Slug hung the phone up before the doctor could respond. He sat on the edge of his bed and stared straight ahead. "Damn it," he muttered under his breath.

Slug picked up the phone and quickly dialed. "Hello," the voice said wearily.

"Bull, we got a problem," said Slug.

"What's the matter?" asked Bull.

"It's a long story. Bottom line is we ain't got a pitcher for tonight."

"No pitcher? What the hell happened?"

"I'll explain it later. Call Buzzy and tell him to meet us in my office in an hour."

Sweetiepie Wadkins walked down the sidewalk in front of Matty Lee's hardware store. Pastor Jones came out of the store and saw Sweetiepie. "Sweetiepie, how are you today?" he asked.

"I'm fine, Pastor Jones. How are you?" she replied.

"Fine, thank you."

"Can I ask you something, Pastor?"

"Of course."

"Yesterday, all day long, I thought about Buhley Sparks. I couldn't get him off my mind. I ain't seen him since he left to play ball. I don't even know where he is. But yesterday I was burdened with him all day. Last night before I went to bed, I prayed for him, and it was as if a weight had been lifted off my shoulders. I prayed for him again this morning. You ever heard of such?"

"Oh, yes," replied Pastor Jones. "It's happened to me quite a bit. I believe it's the Holy Spirit petitioning you to pray for Buhley. I don't know where he is right now or what he is doing, but God does. And your prayers will help him in whatever his situation is. I'll ride out and see August today and make sure everything is okay. I'll also remember him in my morning prayer time."

"Thank you, Pastor. I'll see you Sunday. Tell Wilma hello!"

"You're welcome. I'll tell Wilma hello. See you soon," said Pastor Jones as he got in his car.

Slug Matthews paced back and forth in his office. He rubbed his hand through his hair again and again. He looked at Bullard and Buzzy. "You got any suggestions?" he asked.

"The doctor said none of our guys could go today?" asked Buzzy.

"That's right. He started talking all this medical crap to me, and I wasn't listening to him. Hell, I hung up on him and called Bull immediately."

"What about our guys in the minors? Can we get one of them here in time for tonight?" asked Bullard.

Slug looked at his watch. "It's already 10:30. That's only eight and a half hours before the first pitch. Buzzy, go to your office and make some calls. Maybe we'll get lucky and have one of our farm pitchers close enough to get here. I know we can get them here for tomorrow's game. It's tonight I'm worried about."

Buzzy got up immediately. "Anybody you want me to try first?" he asked.

"Try Pendergrass in Richmond. Then call Owens. Hell, call any of them. We gotta have a pitcher," said Slug.

Buzzy left without responding. Slug continued to pace back and forth in his office.

"Bull, we got anybody on the roster we can throw?" he asked.

"I've been thinking about that, and I haven't come up with anyone. All the guys left are position players who've thrown a little batting practice, but they're not pitchers."

Slug finally sat down in his desk chair. Still running his hand through his flat top, he began laughing. "Can you believe this, Bull? Pete takes every pitcher we got and gets them sick. Can you believe this? Opening night. Here comes St. Louis, and they're going to beat us eighty to nothing. Eighty to nothing, Bull, because Pete took every one of our pitchers. You know when the President does the State of the Union and all the big wigs are there? You know what I'm talkin' about, Bull?"

Bull nodded as Slug continued. "Well, they always leave one big wig behind just in case the building collapses or something crazy like that happens, so there will be a big wig to run things. But not Pete! He took all of them with him, and the building collapsed. Good ol' Pete! Leave it to him to screw us up." Slug shook his head in disbelief. "Bull, does the league have a run rule?"

"What do you mean?"

"You know. If St. Louis is beating us thirty-three to three in the third inning, will they call the game?"

"I see what you're talking about. I don't think there's any kind of rule like that."

"Well, I bet after tonight, the league will have to adopt one. When it's eighty-three to three in the top of the sixth and we've been playing nine hours, I'll bet something will give," Slug said sarcastically.

"Come on, Slug. Something will work out. People will understand what happened. It won't be as bad as you think," reassured Bullard.

Buhley walked into Elser's kitchen to the smell of sausage and eggs. He glanced at the stove and noticed a pot of grits and a pan of biscuits. "This is just like I was raised. You eat breakfast like this every day?" asked Buhley.

"Only on game days when I'm home. I like to eat a big breakfast and then a late light lunch before the game. It's always worked for me. You like all this stuff?" asked Elser.

"I sure do. The only thing missing is some snorts from a hog or two and maybe a cow's moo. That and I'd think I was home."

They sat down to eat, and Buhley mixed his eggs and grits together the way August had always done. "You always mix your eggs and grits?" asked Elser.

"Yeah, that's the way my dad always eats them."

Buhley put a forkful of eggs and grits up to his mouth and then slowly lowered it back to his plate. Overcome with sentiment, his eyes filled with tears. "I wonder what daddy's doing right now," said Buhley staring straight ahead.

Seeing Buhley was homesick, Elser quickly changed the subject. "Hey, buddy, when we go to the ballpark today, bring your glove and cleats because they might let you throw batting practice."

Buhley did not respond at first and then said, "Yeah, okay, that'd be great."

Buzzy Preacher walked back into Slug's office. "I got Pendergrass, Owens, Tate and Lockhart. They're all on their way. The only problem is none of them can be here in time for tonight's game. There's just no way."

"Damn it!" steamed Slug.

Buzzy sat down. "What about Sparks?" he asked.

Slug looked at him. "Wha'd you say?"

"I said, 'What about Buhley Sparks?'"

"Are you crazy or something? He would last one-third of an inning. I'd be the laughing stock of the league. They'd question my sanity starting someone who never played organized baseball on opening day in the major leagues!"

"Think about this, Slug. He's familiar with Elser, and none of our boys hit him in the scrimmages he threw against them. Now either he's a good pitcher, or we're lousy hitters, and you know we can hit."

"Pitching a scrimmage in spring training and pitching on opening night in front of fifty thousand people are two entirely different things."

"You're right. You're right, but what are our choices at this hour?" replied Buzzy.

Slug hung his head down on his desk and shook it back and forth. "Why me? Why me?" he muttered in a feel-sorry-for-himself sort of tone.

"Buzzy's got a point," said Bullard.

Slug immediately lifted his head off the desk. "You say something, Bull?" he asked.

"Buzzy's got a point," Bullard repeated.

"What do you mean?" Slug inquired.

"Look at the facts. Buhley threw in a couple of our scrimmages and didn't give up a single hit. Our guys know he can pitch. They'll have confidence in him. St. Louis comes in. They hear the story about our pitchers, and they'll be licking their chops. We throw Buhley out there and let everybody know he ain't never played baseball, and they'll think they've died and gone to heaven. If he throws like he did in spring training, their heaven will be turned to hell, and you'll look like a genius. If he gets bombed, well, you didn't have a choice under the circumstances, and everybody gives you a pass. For you, it's a no-lose situation," stated Bullard.

Slug started to respond, but was interrupted when the phone rang on his desk. "Hello," answered Slug with slight impatience in his voice.

"Slug, this is Dick Kramer," said a voice on the other end. Dick Kramer was the baseball writer for *The Atlanta Constitution* newspaper. He and Slug had a professional relationship, but it stopped right there. Dick always thought the Peaches had enough talent to reach the World Series and questioned why they never did. This didn't sit well with Slug, and he had let Dick know it a time or two.

"Hey, Dick, what can I do for you?" asked Slug in a businesslike voice.

"I just got a call that said Lefty Pete, Bill Hawks and the rest of your pitchers are in the hospital with food poisoning. Is that true?" asked Dick.

"That's right."

"That's too bad," said Dick in a condescending tone. "What happened to them?"

"They went to a restaurant, and all of them ate the same dish and got sick."

"Don't you have curfews and rules the night before games?"

"I'm a baseball manager, not a babysitter. These are grown men for heaven's sake. When they're not in uniform, they make their own choices," replied Slug with definite irritation growing.

"How long are they gonna be out, and who are you gonna throw tonight?" asked Dick.

"I don't know, and I don't know."

"The press secretary for the Reds called and asked if it was true."

"Well, I guess you can call him and tell him it is."

"I'll see you in a few hours, Slug. Good luck finding a pitcher for tonight."

"Goodbye, Dick."

Hanging up the phone, Slug looked at Bullard. "That son of a bitch almost sounded happy we ain't got a pitcher for tonight."

"You want me to whip his ass?" asked Bullard in a serious tone.

"Don't waste your time. Where were we? Oh, yeah, I remember. You're right, Bull, it's a no-lose for me, but hell, we ain't lost an opening night game since we been here."

"We gotta play with the cards we're dealt," said Bullard.

"Are we all in agreement here?" asked Slug.

He looked at Buzzy. "Buzzy?"

Buzzy nodded. "Bull?" asked Slug.

Bull gave a thumbs-up. Slug took a deep breath. "Okay, then Sparks it is. Buzzy, go call the league office and get him on the roster and tell Argie to come in here."

Pastor Jones closed the door to his office. He looked on the wall and saw a picture of his son, Crawford, and Buhley with their arms around one another. Pastor Jones bowed his head and began to pray. "Lord, I bring before You, Buhley Sparks. If he is burdened, ease him. If he is sick, heal him. Whatever his situation is, Lord, show Yourself to him, and bring him comfort. I also pray for August Sparks. I pray that whatever hurt he is carrying will be lifted from him. I pray that You will magnify Yourself before him and show Your mercy to him. Lord, Your will be done this day and always in the precious name of Christ, I pray. Amen."

He lifted his head, looked at the picture of Buhley and said, "May God be with you, Buhley Sparks."

Argie Tuttle stuck his head in Slug's office. "You wanted to see me, boss?"

"Argie, did you meet Buhley Sparks yesterday?" asked Slug.

"Yes, sir, I did. Seemed like a nice young man."

"Get him a uniform. Just guess at the size if you have to, or suit him up when he comes. Get him a locker, also."

"Whose locker you want me to use? We ain't got any spares."

Slug looked at Bullard and back at Argie. "Use Pete's locker. Get all his stuff out of it, and put Sparks in there. Pete ain't gonna be around for a few days."

"Yes, sir. Anything else, boss?"

"Nope, that's it."

Argie immediately left the office and in walked Buzzy. "It's done, Slug. Buhley's on the roster and can go tonight."

Slug looked at Bullard. "What do you think, Bull?"

Bullard placed his hands behind his head and leaned back in his chair. "At the very least, it's going to be interesting, real interesting."

CHAPTER 15

Cheryl Dane lay on her bed and stared at the ceiling. At seventeen, she had blossomed into a beautiful young woman who caught the eye of every available male in Homerville. Her mamma walked in the room to put up some freshly washed clothes. "What are you thinking about, Cheryl?" she asked.

"Oh, nothing," came the reply.

"That nothing must be pretty important. You've been in here all morning long," said Mrs. Dane as she left the room.

"Mamma!" called Cheryl.

Walking back in her daughter's room, Mrs. Dane answered, "Yes, dear?"

"Can I ask you something?"

Her mother sat on the side of the bed. "Of course."

"How do you let someone know you like them, you know, without being too forward? How did you let Daddy know you liked him?"

Her mother thought for a few seconds and then looked down at Cheryl. "Usually, it's a natural progression that starts out with some innocent get togethers. As females, we can't be pushy because the man is supposed to do the asking. In your father's and my case, he asked me out, and I had fun and wanted him to call me again. He did, and it went from there to where it is now. Does that help you at all, sweetie?"

"I guess so," said Cheryl half-heartedly.

Her mom could see she was still troubled. "Who is this person you're interested in?"

Cheryl was quiet for a moment. "It's Buhley Sparks, Mamma."

"Oh, I see what you're up against. He's a fine young man, but he's not here, is he?"

"No, ma'am, but he's supposed to be coming home for a few days before he goes to his assigned team. I've been talking to Mr. Hawkins about him, and he's been keeping me up to date with the information he has."

"Does he know you have feelings for him?"

"I'm not sure. When he left to go to spring training, I stood on the corner until the bus got out of sight. I've been living on that hope ever since."

"I see. I see."

"Do you think it would be forward if I went over to his house while he was home and visited with him and maybe even cooked supper for him and his dad?"

"Not at all. Let me think about it for a day or two, and I'll give you some other ideas on how to get his attention." Getting up to leave the room, she turned around. "Don't you worry about it, sweetheart. If he's not interested in you, it will be his loss."

Studying her ceiling again, Cheryl murmured, "Thank you, Mamma."

Buhley stared at the skyscrapers of Atlanta as he and Elser drove to the stadium. "I can't get used to these big buildings and all the people," said Buhley.

Elser grinned. "I've been here thirteen years, and neither can I. I'm just a country boy same as you. I'd rather be in a field hunting or on a lake fishing than fighting all these people and traffic. But I love baseball, and they don't pay to see it in the small towns we grew up in."

They drove into the stadium and parked in the special section for players. "Elser, would it be all right if I walked out onto the field?"

"Sure, you can go anywhere you want. You're a part of this organization. I'm going on in the clubhouse. Just come on in when you're ready."

"Thanks."

Buhley walked towards the field. The grounds crew was just finishing their work for the game, and the field looked immaculate. The grass was stark green and mown in a distinct pattern. The infield clay was brown and as smooth as a baby's behind. The white chalk lines running from home plate to the outfield corners were perfectly straight and contrasted sharply with the green grass and brown clay. The pitcher's mound was perfectly rounded and manicured for the awaited battle. In strategic locations on the grassy field, the Peaches' logo was painted to let everyone know this was their home park. Red, white and blue banners hung from the left and right field stands as well as from the upper decks, signaling that baseball season had arrived. Buhley stood on the front base side near the Peaches dugout and slowly eyed the field. He drank in all the beauty the ballpark offered. One of the grounds crew walked past. Without looking at him, Buhley asked, "Is this heaven?"

"No, but it's as close as it gets down here," replied the worker.

Elser walked into the clubhouse. Argie Tuttle was in the corner separating everyones' bats. "Hey, Argie, am I the first one here?" asked Elser.

"Yep. Elser, Slug wants to see you in his office right away. He needs to talk to you."

"What about?"

"Didn't tell me. Just said, 'As soon as you see Elser, ask him to come to my office.'"

"Thanks, Argie."

Elser threw his stuff in his locker and walked down the hall to Slug's office. He knocked on the closed door. "Come in," came the muffled voice.

Elser opened the door and walked in. "You wanted to see me, Slug?"

"Yeah, sit down. I need to talk to you."

Sitting down, Elser acknowledged Bullard who was near Slug.

"What's up, Coach?"

"Elser, we got a problem. We ain't got a pitcher for tonight's game. Lefty and all the others went out last night and ate some damn fish and got food poisoning."

"Everyone of them?"

"Everyone of them. We've got Pendergrass, Owens, Tate and Lockhart coming in tomorrow, but for tonight, we're naked. We ain't got a pitcher."

"When will our boys be ready?"

"I don't know. It could be a couple of days or a week or two. I haven't quite had time to find that out yet. We've been scrambling pretty good this morning just trying to get us through the weekend."

"Damn!"

"Elser, Bull and Buzzy and I decided to throw Buhley tonight. What do you think?"

There was silence in the office. Elser sat in his chair unable to absorb all he had just heard.

"This is inconceivable. Am I dreaming or is this really happening?"

"It's happening, all right. What do you think?"

Elser sat up. "He's got all the ability in the world. I just don't know how he will react to the pressure, the crowd and everything else."

Slug stood up from behind his desk. "Listen to me real good. You're closer to him than anyone on this team. I want you to tell him. I want you to get him ready. I want you to keep him away from everyone else and especially from any asshole reporter that may pester him. The first time I want anyone to see him is when he walks out to the mound to throw his first warm up tosses. You understand?"

"I do."

"The word is already out about our pitching situation. Nobody knows about Buhley, and let's keep it that way for his sake."

"Does anybody else know Buhley's pitching?"

"Just us four and Argie. Argie's got a uniform for him."

Elser got up to leave. "I'll tell you this," he said. "If we can keep him calm and keep the pressure off of him, I think he can surprise some people."

"Let's hope so."

Elser walked out of the office and back to the clubhouse where Argie was still arranging equipment. "You seen Buhley?" he asked.

"Nope, he ain't been in here. I got his uniform in Lefty's locker. Does he know he's playing yet?"

"Not yet. I've got to figure out a way of telling him that won't scare him to death. Somehow I'm going to try to ease him into the situation. You better tell the players to see Slug right when they come in to let them know about the situation. Some of them probably already know from the news. Slug told me to keep Buhley away from everybody until just before game time."

"That's probably the best thing."

Buhley walked through the first base dugout and into the tunnel leading to the clubhouse. He strode by Argie's office. Just as he went past, Footrace stuck his head out and said, "I beat you good, Buhley Sparks. You had grass in your mouth."

Buhley turned and looked at him. "You sure did!"

As Buhley turned to walk away, Footrace added, "You're pitching tonight, Buhley Sparks."

Buhley stopped quickly. Footrace had disappeared back into the office out of sight. "Huh? What did you say?"

Buhley slowly walked away from the office door and back towards the clubhouse.

On his bed, Macy Reid laid out his clothes, none of which matched. He dressed quickly, combed his hair, looked in the mirror with a smile and walked into the kitchen. Macy kissed his wife goodbye. "Your outfit looks terrible," she commented.

Heading out the door, Macy reminded her, "It's my signature, darling. I love you. I'll be home late."

Macy Reid was the Atlanta Peaches' radio play-by-play announcer. He was colorful and color blind. Macy's clothes never matched, but his voice brought the game of baseball to thousands around the southeast. He was a died-in-the-wool Peaches fan. Everybody in the organization liked Macy. Best friends, Slug and he hunted and fished together in the off-season. Macy was famous around the South for his silky smooth voice and for the mismatched clothes he wore. He had already been inducted into the broadcasters' hall of fame and had nothing more to accomplish in the business. Macy worked for the love of the Peaches and the love of the game. Parking in his assigned stadium spot, he headed for Slug's office. "Come in," said Slug to Macy's knock on the door.

"How you doing Slug? Bull? Opening day of baseball! This is the day the Lord hath made!"

He got no response from either Slug or Bullard. They sat stone-faced, deep in thought. "Somebody die or something?" asked Macy referring to the greeting he'd just received.

"Sit down, Macy, and let me tell you what's going on," answered Slug.

Macy's face went from happy to disbelief as he heard Slug recount the story of the pitchers and all that had happened in one short morning.

"So, who we throwing tonight?" he asked

"Don't know yet, Macy. I've got someone in mind, but he's raw, real raw. It would probably benefit everyone involved, including the pitcher, if I let both of you know right before game time. You understand?"

"Sure I do. You know the personnel a lot better than I do. I'll put the best face on this for the radio that I possibly can. Look on the bright side.

At least I don't have to interview Lefty and listen to him tell me what a great pitcher he is."

"This kid may surprise us all," said Bullard out of the blue.

Macy got up to leave. "I hope so, Bull. Wouldn't that be a great story?" With a look at his watch and then at Slug, he added, "Only four hours until broadcast. I'd better go up in the booth and go over my notes. As soon as you get your lineup, get me a copy. If there's anything I can do for y'all, I'll be around. You want me to mention anything about the pitching in our pre-game interview?"

"No, let's make it a standard; we're excited to get started and all that stuff. I'll send you a note with a small bio on the pitcher right before game time, and you can announce it then," replied Slug.

"Sure thing," confirmed Macy as he left the office.

Benny Armstrong walked out the gate at the saw mill in Homerville. "Hey, Benny," yelled Pinky Stubbs.

Pinky Stubbs worked at the saw mill. A slight man with large forearms, he loved to give his money away to Benny playing pool. Pinky got his name because he lost both of his little fingers in a sawmill accident. With only eight fingers, he managed himself well enough to give Benny a good pool game every now and then. "You gonna be at Clip's tonight?" he hollered.

"Yep."

"Bring some money," yelled Pinky.

"I'll bring some of yours," Benny shouted back.

"What time?"

"Six thirty! The game starts at seven, and I want to hear it."

"56 got a good radio?"

"Yep!"

Pinky got in his car with one more shout. "I'll see you there!"

Buhley walked back in the clubhouse. Elser motioned him over to his locker. With players starting to come in for batting practice, the clubhouse was getting busy. "You wanted me, Elser?" asked Buhley.

"Yeah, Buhley, get your cleats and glove. Come throw with me in the bullpen, so I can get these old knees loosened up."

"All right. Hey, I thought you were going to take early batting practice."

"I took a few swings in the indoor cage while you looked at the field." Elser hated to lie to Buhley, but felt he had no choice. They walked to the bullpen and sat while Buhley put on his cleats. They could hear the crack of the ball off the bat as players took batting practice. "This may be my last opening game," said Elser, cutting his eyes sideways to Buhley.

Buhley was bent down tying his cleats. Elser continued. "I'd hoped I'd be able to catch you up here in the big leagues, Buhley. I've never seen anyone throw like you do at such a young age. As raw as you are, there's no way you should be pitching like you do. It's got to be a gift from above. There's no other explanation."

Buhley straightened up from tying his shoes. "It's all I've ever wanted to do. I ain't never had another passion like this except maybe for girls," he said.

Elser looked at Buhley. "I love nothing more than to set up for a pitch and have the pitcher throw a perfect ball when I don't even move my glove, and you do that better than anyone I ever caught. Ever."

"Thank you. You ready to throw now?"

Elser got up and went behind the bullpen plate. They got loose, and Buhley began to pitch. Macy Reid walked around the batting cage greeting players and getting answers to questions he could use on the radio during the game. Elser called for a series of fastballs, which Buhley delivered perfectly into his catcher's mitt. "That's what I'm talking about, Buhley. I get up in the morning wanting to catch a ball thrown like that. Hell, I believe you could pitch tonight if you had to."

"My arm feels strong today."

"Let this next pitch go, and let me see what you got."

Buhley wound up and threw a four-seam fastball that hissed all the way into Elser's mitt. It made a popping sound that cracked all through the stadium. Macy Reid's head jerked up when he heard the ball hit the glove. "What was that?" he asked.

"I think it's Elser getting loose down in the bullpen," replied Moper Mapes.

Without a response, Macy walked hurriedly in that direction. Buhley threw a few more hard ones, and the loud noise that followed each pitch quickened Macy's pace. He approached the wall that separated the bullpen from the field and stuck his head over to see Elser.

"Hello, Elser," said Macy.

Elser looked quickly at Macy. "What do you say, Macy?"

"Not much. I heard a racket down here, and I wanted to come see what it was all about. What do we got going on down here?"

"I'm trying to get these knees ready for tonight and the season, and Buhley was kind enough to throw me a few pitches."

"Who's your pitcher there?" asked Macy as he looked at Buhley.

"Macy, this is Buhley Sparks. Buhley, this is Macy Reid, our radio announcer."

"Nice to meet you, Buhley."

"I know you, Mr. Reid. When I was a youngun', you put me to sleep many a night," said Buhley.

"Was I that bad?" cracked Macy.

"No, sir, what I meant was I listened to the game on the radio by my bed, and usually I fell asleep by the fifth inning or so. If I hadn't, my mamma would have come in and cut the radio off anyway."

"Well, I'm glad to have been of service. You popping his mitt with that ball, Buhley?"

"Ye, sir." replied Buhley.

Realizing Macy probably knew about the pitching situation, Elser quickly interjected. "Buhley is one of our future prospects. He's just here observing the home stand before he goes to his assignment in the minors."

"Is Buhley on the roster?" asked Macy.

"No, he's being assigned after the home stand."

"Mind if I watch him throw a few?"

"Not at all, but we're almost done," said Elser as he knelt down behind the plate.

He signaled Buhley for a fastball and set up on the outside corner of the plate. Buhley wound up and threw. The ball sizzled through the air and slammed into Elser's glove before Macy's eyes could see it.

"Woo, let me see that again," exclaimed Macy.

Elser threw the ball back to Buhley and set up on the opposite corner of the plate. Again, Buhley threw a perfect pitch. The ball landed in Elser's unmoved glove. "Where did you learn to do that, son?" asked Macy.

"Throwing against the barn," replied Buhley.

"The barn?"

"Yes, sir. I'd go out and pick out a knot on a board and throw at that knot over and over again."

"Must've worked."

"Yes, sir."

Macy looked at Elser. "We need more barn throwers," he said as he walked away.

Elser nodded in agreement.

"Sit down for a minute, Buhley. I need to talk to you," said Elser.

Buhley watched Macy walk away. "Mr. Reid is a nice man," commented Buhley.

"One of the finest I know. We're lucky to have him in our organization. Every other broadcaster in the business stands in his shadow."

Elser took a seat beside Buhley on the bench.

Slug gathered all the players in the clubhouse. "This is not the usual pre-first game talk I'm fixing to give you. Some of you may have noticed or already know we ain't got any pitchers in this meeting. They ain't here. All of them are in the hospital sick with food poisoning. It's a long story, and we got a ballgame to win, so here's what we're doing. We've called up Pendergrass, Tate, Lockhart and Owens. They'll be here tomorrow. For tonight, we had to make a decision based on how we thought the best chance to win was. Bull and I think our best chance to win the game is to throw Buhley Sparks."

Slug paused to see the response. Most of the players looked at each other and nodded in approval. Slug continued. "The majority of you know Buhley's story. He's never pitched in a real game of baseball in his life. Buhley comes from a town where everybody in it could fit comfortably in our dugout. You all remember how nervous and scared you were the first time you played in a major league game in front of fifty thousand people? Just imagine how Buhley's gonna feel tonight. I have confidence in him, and if he throws like he can, we'll have a chance to win the game. Hell, raise your hand right now if you got a hit off of him during a scrimmage."

Slug looked around. No hands went up. "I thought so. Then, you oughta feel as confident in him as Bull and I do. I told Elser to take Buhley somewhere and keep him out of sight until game time. They've been throwing in the bullpen. I don't want any of you to say anything to Buhley before the game. I don't even know if Elser's told him yet. As soon as we take the field, that's when Buhley will take the mound from the bullpen. The story is all out in the press, and I'm sure you're gonna get asked about it, and here's the answer to give to any reporter who asks. Look him straight in the eye and say, 'I have no idea who's pitching tonight.' If they keep pressing you, answer them just like a prisoner of war with the same answer over and over, 'I have no idea who's pitching tonight.' Anybody not understand what I just said?"

Nobody moved. Slug looked at his watch. "Good. We've got an hour and a half before game time. Let's relax, get our minds right, have a good round of infield and go kick some butt."

Elser sat on the bullpen bench and rubbed his knees. "These knees take longer and longer to limber up every year. I wish I had an oilcan so that I could just squirt oil in them like the tin man in *The Wizard of Oz*. Get 'em real loose and lubed up. He may not have had a heart, but he had that oilcan."

"I seen that movie once, and that witch scared me," said Buhley.

"Me, too," replied Elser.

Elser slid down the bench towards Buhley and put his arm around him. "Life's funny sometimes, Buhley. Sometimes you're just in the right place at the right time, and then others work hard all their lives and never get the opportunity they want. Someone said everybody gets fifteen minutes of fame once in his life. You ever heard that, Buhley?"

"What are you talking about, Elser? You ain't makin' no sense."

"I'm talking about opportunity. I'm talking about what made this country great. I'm talking about your pitching tonight."

Elser continued to look forward while cutting his eyes on Buhley to catch his response.

"Huh?" replied Buhley as his head snapped quickly towards Elser. "What did you say?"

"I said this is your night. You got the ball. You're pitching."

Buhley got up off the bench and started pacing. "Is this a joke or somethin'?"

"Nope."

"Where's Lefty or somebody else?"

"Come sit down, and I'll tell you."

Buhley fidgeted on the bench as Elser explained to him what had happened to Lefty and the other pitchers. "Slug and Bullard figured you are our best chance to win the game tonight. They put you on the roster and everything."

Buhley looked around at the seats that were visible from the bullpen. "People gonna be in those seats tonight?" he asked pointing to a section of the stadium.

"Every one of them. They'll be coming in here in about thirty minutes, and by seven o'clock, it will be full. We better go on to the clubhouse and get dressed."

"Get dressed?!"

"Yeah, they got a locker and a uniform for you. The league wouldn't take kindly to you pitching in those street clothes."

They walked out of the bullpen to the dugout and back up the tunnel to the clubhouse. As they walked by Argie Tuttle's office, Footrace stuck his head out of the door. "What do you know, Footrace?" asked Elser.

Footrace smiled and said slowly, "I know Buhley Sparks is pitching tonight, 'cause my daddy told me."

"That's right," replied Elser as he patted him on the head.

The clubhouse was busy as Elser and Buhley made their way to their lockers. Buhley watched as Elser put on his uniform. He followed everything Elser did to make sure he dressed properly. Everything fit nicely except for the pants, which were extremely baggy. Elser noticed, and though he held back a laugh, he couldn't help saying something. "Looks like you're wearing a pair of sails there, Buhley. Are they baggy enough, or do we need to let them out some more? I hope it's not windy tonight. The wind might catch one of those sails when you're in your windup and blow you right outta here."

"That ain't funny, Elser. My stomach is turning in knots, and you're makin' fun," said Buhley seriously.

Elser put his arm around Buhley. "I'm sorry. You'll do fine tonight. Let's go back to the bullpen and start getting loose and working on your pitches. Slug doesn't want anybody seeing you or talking to you before the game. You're gonna take the mound from the bullpen, not the dugout. Let's go."

Buhley tried not to notice the people starting to fill the stadium as they walked back to the bullpen. The players in the clubhouse hadn't said a word to him per Slug's instructions. Buhley and Elser sat down on the bullpen bench while Elser went over some rules of the game and the ballpark to make sure Buhley understood. He looked at the bullpen clock, which read six thirty. "Let's just sit here and relax, and we'll start throwing in about fifteen minutes."

"Relax?" exclaimed Buhley. "That's easy for you to say."

Buhley looked around the stadium and noticed the crowd was pouring in. His stomach knotted up a little more.

Chapter 16

Benny Armstrong busted through the door of Clips. 56 Johnson was behind the bar in his usual spot. "What's shakin', 56?" asked Benny.

"My gut when I walk. What about you? You know anything good?" asked 56.

"Hell, yeah. I got Pinky Stubbs on the pool table, the Peaches are playing on the radio, and I'll bet you got six or eight ice cold Pabst Blue Ribbons waiting for me."

"That'll do," said 56 as he popped an icy cold beer and slid it down the bar to Benny. "Try that one. It's just this side of frozen."

Benny took a big swig. "Wow, I been waiting on that all day long."

"Well, it's been here," said 56 sarcastically.

"You better get ready to get me another cold one," said Benny as he walked over to the pool table.

Pinky Stubbs, eight fingers and all, had already racked the balls and chalked his cue stick. Benny got his cue stick chalked, and they lagged for the break. Both of them slapped a twenty-dollar bill on the side of the pool table. Pinky won the lag and got ready to break. He looked at Benny. "Good luck to you and yours," said Pinky.

"I ain't got no yours." replied Benny.

Pinky busted the rack, and the game was on.

178

Macy Reid sat in the broadcast booth just minutes before airtime. All of his prep for the first game was complete. Beside him sat Gibbs Powell. Gibbs Powell was the color man for the Atlanta Peaches and was in line to replace Macy if he ever retired. Everyone, including Gibbs, hoped that day would never come. Gibbs was talented, but was not in the same league as Macy. He made appropriate comments during the radio broadcast, but mostly he sat and listened to the master beautifully describe the game. A stadium usher walked into the broadcast booth and handed Macy a white envelope. Macy slowly opened the envelope and smiled as he read its contents. The note read, "Macy, sorry I had to be coy about our situation this morning. We are going to throw a left-hander named Buhley Sparks. He was an invitee to camp this spring and impressed us with his stuff. He's from Homerville, Georgia and is only seventeen years old. He's never pitched in high school or any organized game. We think a lot of him and invited him to our home opener before assigning him in our minor league organization. I have no idea how he'll handle the pressure, but Bull and I think he's our best chance to win. Thanks for your understanding. Slug."

Macy handed the note to Gibbs. "This boy may be something special. I saw him throw a few in the bullpen earlier this afternoon."

"Can you imagine what that boy's going through right this minute?" mused Gibbs.

"Terror, shear terror, I would guess."

The producer walked into the booth. "One minute before air time," he said.

Macy looked at Gibbs. "This oughta be interesting," said Macy as he cleared his throat. Looking at the beautiful field and the capacity crowd, he added, "God must have created this game. Man could not produce something this spectacular."

"Amen, brother," replied Gibbs.

Harold Dane sat in his chair and opened his paper to the sports section. He scanned it quickly and put the paper in his lap long enough to reach over the table beside his seat and turn on the radio. Harold brought out a pipe and carefully stuffed it with tobacco. Lighting his pipe, he turned in the paper to the crossword puzzle. Harold settled comfortably in his chair and began completing the puzzle while he waited for the Atlanta Peaches baseball game on the radio.

Just across town, Wadeus Wadkins sat down at the kitchen table to a larger than normal bowl of vanilla ice cream. He put a heaping spoonful in his mouth and moved it around to take off some of the cold chill. With his free hand, he reached over and turned on his radio to the station that carried the Peaches game. Sweetiepie Wadkins moved around in the kitchen as quickly as her extra weight would allow, making dry, stale-tasting pound cakes for those in need.

At Clips, Benny Armstrong stroked the cue ball, sending it slamming into the eight ball, which flew directly into the corner pocket. "Game," he said picking up his beer and gulping down the last half. He grabbed the two twenty-dollar bills on the table and crammed them into his pocket. Benny yelled from across the room. "56, get me another beer and turn on the radio. The game's fixin' to start. You want somethin', Pink?"

Pinky threw another twenty-dollar bill on the table and answered. "Yeah, I want another game."

"You got it!"

Benny walked towards the bar. 56 eased himself off his stool and reached in his cooler. Pulling out another ice cold Pabst Blue Ribbon, he laid it on the bar and slid it down to Benny at the other end. 56 ambled his way to the radio and turned it on. "It should be coming on any minute," he called out.

"Thanks," yelled Benny.

Pinky had racked up the balls. "Bust 'em up, Champ," he said to Benny.

Benny laid his twenty-dollar bill on the table next to Pinky's and chalked up his cue stick.

Sporty Schuster caught the ball thrown by his son, Butch. "Nice throw. It's getting a little dark. Can you still see?"

"Yes, sir," answered Butch.

"Okay, I'm gonna throw you a few high pops, and then we'll go in and listen to the Peaches game on the radio."

"Yes, sir."

Butch was seven years old and loved the game of baseball. He and his dad threw everyday. Butch was an advanced player for his age and was fundamentally sound. Sporty threw the ball over a tree so that Butch could only pick it up well after its descent. The ball went high into the air. "Here it comes," yelled Sporty.

Butch waited and quickly located the ball as it cleared the tree. He patted his glove with his fist and stuck both the glove and his other hand above his head and never let the ball out of his sight. The ball landed perfectly in his glove as it always did. The tree was a large oak tree, and Sporty couldn't see Butch. "Did you catch it?" yelled Sporty.

"Yes, sir!"

"Atta boy," said Sporty as he ran around the tree, scooped up Butch and gave him a hug. "You're a ballplayer. That's what you are."

"Can we throw again tomorrow?"

"You bet. You know Buhley's in Atlanta at the Peaches game. Did you know that?"

"No, sir. He's at the game? How'd he get to do that?"

"All his life he worked hard at pitching, and they thought he was good enough to give him a job with them. One day, maybe we'll get to listen to Buhley pitch a game."

"Wow!" exclaimed Butch as he climbed up on his daddy's shoulders for a ride into the house.

Elser knelt down behind the plate in the bullpen. "Okay, Buhley, nice and easy. Just give me a good rhythm. Throw the pitch I call and where I locate it, and we'll be fine. Block everything out. It's just you and me. Nothing else matters."

Out of the corner of his eye, Buhley could see the stadium was full. He was shaking, and his wind up lost its fluidity. Elser caught a few errant throws and took off his mask. He trotted over to Buhley. "We've got fifteen minutes to get ready. After 'The Star Spangled Banner' is played, we take the field. Are you loose?"

"Yeah, but I'm shaking so bad, I can barely hold the ball."

"Sit down for a minute," said Elser. "You've been pitching all your life. Be it by yourself or whatever, you've been throwing all your life. Am I right?"

"Yep."

"And what did you hope to accomplish with all that pitching?"

"To be able to throw in the major leagues."

"Well, good golly, Miss Molly, here you are. This is the major leagues. Buhley, I love you. I would never let you go out there if I didn't think you have the stuff to win. If you pitch tonight like you did in spring training, the Reds won't know what hit 'em. You can do it. Just relax and play catch with me, and everything else will take care of itself."

Buhley half-heartedly nodded in the affirmative.

The producer stuck his head into the broadcast booth. "Ten seconds, Macy!"

He counted down the seconds out loud and pointed at Macy. Macy settled himself in his chair and took his usual pose over the microphone. "Good evening, ladies and gentlemen, and welcome to another year of Atlanta Peaches baseball. It's a beautiful night for a game. The grass is green, the clay is brown and the hopes are high that this will be the year the Peaches take it all the way to the World Championship. My name is Macy Reid, and along with me is Gibbs Powell. We'll be bringing you play-by-play action of every pitch this season. When I grew up in Shellman, Georgia, all of our family lived close together. Whenever there was something that happened out of the ordinary, my grandmother would say, 'We got us a situation here.' That's what she'd say. Well, folks, something out of the ordinary has happened to this baseball team on opening day, and we got ourselves a situation here. Some of you may already know that our entire pitching staff is in Grady Memorial Hospital as we broadcast. That's right, every last pitcher on the Peaches roster is in the hospital tonight with food poisoning. I talked with Slug Matthews, and he seems to think they'll all be ready in a week or so. In the meantime, he's called up some minor league pitchers in our organization. The situation we have is the minor league pitchers will not be here until tomorrow. That leaves us without a bonafide hurler for tonight. Let me now take this opportunity to introduce you to tonight's pitcher. It's quite an interesting story. He's a southpaw from down in South Georgia -- Homerville to be exact. He's a mere seventeen years old, just a pup by my standards. Slug Matthews related to me that this young pitcher has no organized baseball experience at all. Slug said he grew up throwing against a barn. He's a barn thrower, ladies and gentlemen, and I must admit I have never met a barn thrower I didn't like. It's odd how life presents opportunities now and then, and this young man has just been presented with a once in a lifetime. It seems that he was an invitee to spring training and so impressed Slug Matthews and Bullard Haynes that he was asked to sign a minor league contract. Slug thought it would be a good idea to bring this prodigy to the home opener to see how things are done at the top.

Circumstances being what they are, Slug Matthews felt this lefthander is the best chance we have to win tonight. I'll not hold you in suspense any longer and deny you the name of our starter for tonight's game. The barn thrower from Homerville's name is Buhley Sparks."

Wadeus Wadkins spit a large mouthful of ice cream all over the kitchen table. Sweetiepie turned around from the stove. "Wadeus, what in the world?"

Wadeus coughed a time or two. "Baby, I swear I heard that radio announcer say Buhley Spark's name. I swear it," he said. He quickly turned up the radio and leaned over the table to where his ear was almost touching the speaker. "There! He did it again. I knew he said it!"

Sweetiepie lumbered over to the kitchen table with a wet rag to mop up the ice cream. "Oh, my goodness, baby, Buhley Sparks is pitching tonight. He's pitching for the Peaches! Can you believe it? He's pitching!" yelled Wadeus excitedly.

"Yes, I can," answered Sweetiepie calmly. "Now I know why the Lord laid him on my heart."

"That's right. I remember you telling me that."

Sweetiepie wiped up the ice cream and pushed herself away from the table. She waddled towards the telephone. "I've got to call Pastor Jones and tell him Buhley's pitching."

Wadeus was locked into the radio and did not respond.

Crawford Jones ran into the living room of his house. "Daddy! Daddy! Daddy! Turn on the radio. Hurry! Turn it on quick!"

"What's the matter, Crawdad?" asked Pastor Jones.

"Hurry! Just turn it on, and listen. Put it on the Peaches station quick!"

Pastor Jones found the station and leaned forward in his chair to hear the broadcast better. He sat back in disbelief. "Buhley Sparks is pitching tonight for the Peaches. Our Buhley Sparks! Your best friend, Buhley Sparks. August's boy, Buhley Sparks," said Pastor Jones in bewilderment.

"Yes, sir! Ain't that something, Daddy?"

"It sure is, son. Call your Mamma in here, and let's all listen."

He relaxed in his chair for a moment and then remembered the conversation he'd had with Sweetiepie Wadkins a couple of days before about how the Lord had laid Buhley on her heart. Just then the phone rang, and Pastor Jones picked it up. "Hello," he answered. "Oh, hello, Sweetiepie. I was just thinking of you." He paused to listen and then replied. "That's a great idea. Why don't we call some of our prayer warriors in the church and get them praying for Buhley right this minute and throughout the game? Okay, then I'll speak with you later." He hung up the phone and bowed his head to pray.

Jubel Odom sucked the last piece of chicken off the bone and laid it, clean-picked, on his plate. He looked at his wife. "Woman, you make the best fried chicken I ever ate. Sure do. Sure nuff. I couldn't wait to put Buckswamp up in the barn when I smelled yous cookin' some fried chicken."

His wife, Mabel, brought over a bowl of freshly baked peach cobbler and laid it down at Jubel's plate. "Lean over and give me some sugar," said Jubel.

Mabel leaned over, and Jubel gently kissed her on the cheek. "I love you, darlin'. I love you more than Buckswamp loves a day off, and you know that can't be measured," he said with a chuckle. "Please turn that radio on so's I can listen to the ball game."

Walking over to the counter, Mabel turned it on. She paused to listen for a moment to make sure it was on the correct station. "Oh, my goodness! Oh, my goodness!" she breathed. Her legs got weak, and she held onto the counter for support.

Jubel jumped up from his chair and helped her to the table. "What it is, darlin'? What's wrong?"

Mabel was speechless and just pointed to the radio. Jubel listened and then exclaimed, "Lord, have mercy! Lord, have mercy! Buhley Boy is chunkin' that ball! What's Mister August gonna do when he finds out! He can chunk that ball, Mabel. He can chunk it good. I knowed he had a gift. A gift from the Lord!" He sat next to Mabel and grabbed her hand. "Darlin', we best go to the Lord and ask blessings on Buhley Boy. I imagine he's carryin' a big burden 'bout now." They bowed their heads and began to pray.

56 Johnson walked down the bar and stopped dead in his tracks. He stood frozen for a moment and then let out a loud whistle. "Hush!" he yelled at the top of his lungs.

56 placed his ear next to the radio and listened intently. All eyes in the place were on him. 56 quickly pulled his head away from the radio. "Benny, get over here quick! Hurry! Listen to the radio, and tell me what you hear."

Benny rushed behind the bar and held tight to the radio. Everyone else sat in silence. He stood there and listened for a minute or so. "Yee Haw!" he yelled at the top of his lungs. He turned to the crowd. "Buhley Sparks is pitching for the Peaches! He's pitching tonight in a few minutes!" Without thinking, he hollered, "Drinks are on me!"

Everyone crowded up to the bar and ordered another round. Benny turned the radio up full blast. "I can't hear it," someone said.

"I'll fix that!" said Benny.

He ran out the front door and left it open. Jumping in his car, he backed it up just inches from the front door. Then he turned on his radio and opened the trunk. Macy Reid's voice reverberated through Clip's as if he was broadcasting right there on the spot. "There! Now we're set," said Benny as he let out another loud, "Yee Haw!"

Benny walked over to his pool game. "Your shot, Benny," said Pinky.

Benny shot the cue ball directly into the side pocket. "Oops, I scratched. You win," said Benny as he put his cue stick back in the rack.

"Wha'd you do that for?" asked Pinky.

"My boy Buhley's pitching. There ain't no way I'm gonna miss one syllable of this!" Walking over to the bar, Benny grabbed a stool by 56.

"You believe this? It beats anything I ever heard of," said 56.

"I bet he does proud tonight. He's the best I ever caught!" Benny replied.

Harold Danes' eyes were heavy. The pencil he held in his right hand landed on the half-completed crossword puzzle. His head cocked back and forth, slowly doing the bob and weave as he tried to rest his eyes and steady his head at the same time. He was in an almost asleep mode when in one motion his whole body jerked awake. "Did somebody say Buhley Sparks?" he asked to no one. Harold rubbed his eyes. "Did you say something dear?" he yelled to his wife, June, in the kitchen.

"No, Harold," came the reply.

He leaned down to pick up the pencil and newspaper. Harold straightened back up hastily and stared at the radio. "June! Cheryl! Get in here fast!" he yelled. "I just heard Buhley Sparks' name on the radio!"

Cheryl came in first. "You heard Buhley's name mentioned on the radio?" she asked excitedly.

"Yes, I thought they said he was pitching tonight, but that couldn't be right, could it?"

"I do know he's in Atlanta with the team."

"Quiet, quiet, quiet! Let's listen," said Harold as he leaned in close to the radio. They all remained perfectly still as Macy Reid announced Buhley as the starter for the night's game. "He is pitching! This is the most exciting thing to happen in Homerville since the mayor of Atlanta's car broke down here on his way to Florida ten or twelve years ago."

"Daddy, please get quiet. I'm tryin' to listen," begged Cheryl, focusing her full attention on the radio.

"Sorry," mouthed Harold without saying the word.

CHAPTER 17

Slug Matthews walked from the dugout to home plate. He shook hands with the St. Louis Reds' manager, Alston Hunt. Alston and Slug went back a long way. They played minor league baseball together and had a deep admiration for one another. Alston's Reds had won the World Series two years ago and were picked to be one of the few teams contending again this year. Like Slug, he was a no-nonsense manager for whom the players played hard.

"Sorry to hear about your pitching problems. Our boys were looking forward to getting a crack at Pete," said Alston.

"I wouldn't wish this on my worst enemy. You gonna take it easy on us?" Slug asked, half joking and half serious.

"These boys are tired of beating up on each other. They're ready to jump on somebody."

Slug looked at Alston and said, "This boy I got pitching tonight - he ain't never...."

Alston interrupted. "I know. I know. If it gets ugly, we'll back off. I don't want to embarrass anyone."

Slug and Alston exchanged lineup cards, shook hands and went to their respective dugouts.

In Homerville, phones rang off the hook with the news of Buhley Sparks pitching for the Atlanta Peaches. Women and men, husbands and wives

gathered around radios to listen to the game. The prayer groups of the
Homerville Baptist Church and other churches were in full force.

The stadium announcer spoke over the PA system. "Would everyone please
rise for the playing of our national anthem?"

With hats removed and placed over their hearts, all of the players from
both teams lined the respective infield baselines. Elser and Buhley remained
in the bullpen. Buhley's hand shook as he placed it over his heart. His whole
body was numb, and his stomach was tied in knots. The flag was raised to
the top of the pole just as "The Star Spangled Banner" ended. Thunderous
applause erupted from the capacity crowd as both teams retreated to their
dugouts. Buhley sat beside Elser on the bullpen bench. "Okay, this is us,"
said Elser. "You ready?"

Buhley nodded his head, not uttering a sound. "Remember, just throw
what I call, where I set up, and we'll do fine. These guys are real good, so don't
get upset if they knock you around a little. They hit everybody. Lefty don't
like to pitch to these guys." Buhley just sat and stared straight ahead. "You
hear me?" asked Elser in a firm voice.

Buhley nodded again without making a sound. Suddenly over the PA
system came, "Ladies and gentlemen, the Atlanta Peaches!"

The players darted out of the dugout and over to their positions on the
field. "Here we go," said Elser as he grabbed Buhley's arm and led him to the
gate of the bullpen and out onto the field. Both Elser and Buhley made a
slow jog to the infield area. The noise from the stadium crowd was deafening.
Buhley and Crawdad always had laid down near the train tracks as the trains
passed. The noise was as loud as he could remember. Out on the ball field, he
had never heard a noise so loud, and he thought to himself, "This must be a
thousand trains."

As Buhley jogged to the mound, Gibbs Powell noticed his pants. "Look
at Buhley's pants. Have you ever seen baggier britches?" he asked.

Looking at the trousers, Macy Reid replied, "Here comes the baggy pants barn thrower from Homerville -- Buhley Sparks!"

Buhley took the mound, his whole body trembling. Elser reached home plate, and with his cleats, marked his spot. "How you been, Elser?" asked Dallas Branch.

Dallas Branch was the home plate umpire. He had been an umpire in the major leagues for the last fifteen years. Before that, he was a high school football and baseball coach. Dallas had massive oak tree arms and had to cut the sleeves of his shirt up the hem in order to give his arms enough room. Very few managers dared to argue his calls. One coach brought Dallas' mamma into an argument once, and Dallas hit him with a quick punch to the nose with his iron-like arm, knocking the coach out cold. He was well respected for his fairness and ability to call balls and strikes. Under the circumstances, Elser was glad he was behind the plate.

"Been fine, Dallas. How 'bout you?" replied Elser.

"Good, good! Ready for the season to start," replied Dallas.

"Me, too," said Elser as he squatted down behind the plate.

Dallas picked out a ball from his pouch and threw it to Buhley on the mound. "You got a rookie out there tonight."

"I'm not sure he could be classified as a rookie," answered Elser.

Buhley began to throw his warm up tosses. The balls were going everywhere except where Elser put his target. "I heard about your pitching problems," said Dallas as he slipped on his mask and knelt down behind Elser to look at Buhley's pitches. Buhley continued to throw the ball all over the plate. Dallas watched about five throws -- all of them balls. "Is he going to throw a strike?"

Elser threw the ball back to Buhley. "I'm not sure," he answered.

"Two more, then throw it down," said Dallas.

Elser motioned for Buhley to calm down. He threw two more pitches, and Elser yelled, "Coming down."

The last pitch was as close as he had come to a strike. Elser caught it and threw a perfect strike to second base. The infielders threw the ball around, and third baseman Moper Mapes handed the ball to Buhley. "Let's get 'em," said Moper smacking him on the butt.

Elser was out at the mound. "Just relax, and throw to the target. Just me and you playin' catch."

He could see that Buhley was visibly shaken. He looked at the ball in Buhley's hand, and both were trembling. Elser patted him on the shoulder and jogged back to the plate.

"Batter up!" yelled Dallas.

Roddrick Brown kicked the weighted donut off his bat from the on-deck circle and began walking towards the batter's box. Roddrick Brown, in many baseball people's estimate, was the game's best lead-off hitter. During the previous year, he had batted .317 and led the league in stolen bases. He also had won a gold glove for his defensive prowess in centerfield. Roddrick reached the lefthander's batter's box, and with his back foot, dug in.

Buhley was on the mound, and Dallas pointed at him and yelled, "Play ball!"

The emotions and nervousness overcame Buhley. He turned with his back to home plate and vomited on the grass. What little breakfast he had eaten was now on the field. "Did he just throw up?" asked Dallas.

"Yep," said Elser as he hurried to the mound.

Standing on the dugout's second step, Slug turned to Bullard who was on the bench. "He throws all his warm-up tosses for balls and then tosses his breakfast on the field. Can this get any worse?" asked Slug.

"Yep. It could be raining," replied Bullard.

"Raining," said Slug. "I prayed for rain. Rain would be an improvement. We need two weeks of hard, steady rain so we can buy some time and get some pitching for this team." He turned and looked out to the field and kept on talking. "I've had some real bad nightmares before, but I always woke up and thought, 'Wow! I'm glad that's over.' I don't think I'm gonna wake up from this one. This one I'm gonna have to live with for the rest of my life."

"You all right?" asked Elser as he reached the mound.

"I'll be fine. I feel better now," responded Buhley.

All of the players for Atlanta and St. Louis stood in a line on the dugout steps. "Come on. Let's go!" said Elser as he jogged back to the plate.

Buhley turned towards home plate. Elser called for a fastball away from the outer half of the plate. Buhley had thrown a baseball a million times and always felt natural and comfortable. He had never felt as uncoordinated as he did now. It was as if he were throwing with his opposite hand. Buhley set, wound up, and let go. The ball headed directly for Roddrick Brown in the left-handed batter's box. It was a low pitch, and Roddrick jumped up as the ball hit, skipped under his feet and went all the way to the backstop. "Whoa! Brown had to do a skip-to-my-Lou to avoid being hit with that pitch," said Macy.

Dallas threw Buhley another ball. Elser called for another pitch away and outside. Buhley kicked and fired. The ball sailed wildly outside, and Elser barely reached it before it went all the way to the backstop. Elser thought a breaking ball possibly would help Buhley grab his focus. He called for a curve ball and set up again on the outer half of the plate. Buhley snapped his release, and the ball spun sharply as it raced towards the plate. The pitch broke quickly downward and caught the front of home plate, sending the ball bounding up over Elser's glove and directly into the unprotected part of Dallas Branch's right shoulder.

"Dadgumit! That hurts," yelled Dallas as he threw down his mask and began rubbing his shoulder.

"You all right?" asked Elser.

"Yeah, I'll be fine. Go out and talk to that boy before he kills somebody."

Elser trotted out to the mound as did Moper Mapes. Macy Reid shook his head. "Folks, I'm like Winston Churchill. If we're losing the war, I'm gonna tell you, and right now, we're losing the war. The baggy pants barn thrower from Homerville has thrown three pitches, none of which were close to being strikes. He almost killed the umpire with his last pitch. Elser and Moper have gone to the mound to talk to him to try and calm him down. I can imagine what's going on in Slug Matthew's mind right now," said Macy.

Slug quickly turned away from the field and threw his hat against the dugout wall. He looked at Buzzy Preacher. "What the hell did you get me into?" he screamed.

Buzzy sat on the bench and stared straight ahead. "Come on, kid! Throw strikes!" yelled a hatless Slug.

"What's the matter, Buhley?" asked Elser.

Buhley looked at the crowd. "They're all staring at me," he answered.

"Of course they are. You're pitching," replied Elser.

"I ain't never seen this many people. I didn't know there was this many people in the world!"

Moper grabbed Buhley's shoulder. "See these players behind you? We believe in you, Buhley. You can do it!" he said as he patted Buhley on the shoulder and went back to third base.

"Where were you most comfortable throwing when you grew up?" asked Elser.

"The side of the barn. A knot in the wood on the side of the barn," replied Buhley.

Elser held up his catcher's mitt to Buhley. "This is the knot. Take yourself back to the barn, and throw to the knot. This is the knot." Elser again showed his glove to Buhley.

Dallas had walked halfway to the mound to break up the meeting. Buhley stepped off the mound and took a deep breath. He looked to the heavens in a cloudless, starry sky. Suddenly, a calm came over him -- a peace that he had felt only in the arms of his mother. He remembered how she told him she loved him as she stroked his hair when he lay in bed. He remembered how, through the kitchen window, she watched him throw pitch after pitch against the side of the barn. To Buhley, it felt as if Ranna was with him now. He stepped back on the mound and looked down at his hand, which held the ball. His hand was still. Buhley took another deep breath and got the signal from Elser. Elser called for a fastball right down the middle. Buhley's wind up felt natural for the first time in the game. He let go, and the ball sizzled into Elser's unmoved glove. "Ste-rike!" yelled Dallas as he gave his famous strike signal.

The stadium erupted into the loudest ovation of the night. Elser nodded and pointed at Buhley as he returned the ball to him. He called for another fastball, this time a little to the outside of the plate. Buhley kicked off and fired, and again the ball riveted into Elser's unmoved mitt. "Ste-rike!" signaled Dallas.

Roddrick had taken both pitches at the orders of the third base coach. He dug in for the full count pitch. Elser moved inside, and Buhley threw a perfect inside fastball that sawed off Roddrick who hit a slow roller to second base, which was scooped up and thrown to first base for out number one. The infielders threw the ball around. "Way to come back!" said Moper as he gave the ball to Buhley.

Macy looked at Gibbs. "Those last three pitches were as good as the first three were bad," he said. "But the important thing is that we got out number one, and Roddrick Brown is in the dugout and not on first base."

"Amen, brother! Amen!" chimed in Gibbs.

"Well, that's a start," said Slug as he picked up his hat, placed it back on his head and returned to his perch on the dugout steps. "Come on, kid! Keep it up!" he yelled.

Benny Armstrong slammed his fist on the bar at Clip's. "Way to battle back, Buhley! Way to battle back! That's my boy," he said. He shook hands with 56 Johnson who opened another beer and set it next to him on the bar.

Sweetiepie Wadkins was in her living room in her favorite rocking chair. She hung out of every side as she rocked back and forth in prayer. Wadeus was in the kitchen eating his second larger than average bowl of vanilla ice cream.

Cory Beckham stepped into the right-hander batter's box. He was the St. Louis Reds shortstop. Cory was in his third year in the majors and was a rising star. Buhley felt calm and confident as Elser called for a curve ball on the outside corner. He nodded his approval as he began his wind up. The ball started off the plate and darted down and in as it crossed the back of the outside corner. "Ste-rike!" yelled Dallas.

Cory stepped out of the box and shook his head. He looked down to the third base coach for a signal and returned to the batter's box. Buhley threw a perfect pitch on the outside part of the plate, which Cory weakly grounded to the second baseman for out number two.

The number three batter for the Reds was Oliver Davis. He was a strong right fielder who intimidated opposing pitchers with his tape measure home runs. Oliver was so strong he handled the bat like it was plastic. Stepping into the batter's box, he took a first pitch strike on the inside. Elser called for the same pitch, and Oliver slapped a hard line drive over the third base dugout into the stands. Buhley readied for the change up he was about to throw. Oliver dug in the batter's box, swinging the bat back and forth over his head like it was a toothpick. Buhley threw the change up over the middle of the plate. Oliver's eyes grew large as he swung at the ball that, to him, looked like a beach ball. Buhley had taken about fifteen miles off the change up, and Oliver swung well before the ball ever reached the plate. His swing was massive and almost corkscrewed him into the ground. "Ste-rike three!" yelled Dallas.

Elser rolled the ball back to the mound as he started for the dugout. "Hey, Elser," said Dallas.

Elser turned around. "Yeah?" he replied.

"That boy's Dr. Jekyll and Mr. Hyde, ain't he?" asked Dallas.

"Yep." Elser turned back towards the dugout.

Up in the booth, Macy shook his head. "The baggy pants barn thrower dug quite a hole in that first inning but filled it in nicely." he said.

"Buhley seemed to gain confidence after the first batter," interjected Gibbs as they went to a commercial.

Buhley jogged off the field into the dugout. "Atta boy, kid," said Slug as Buhley passed by him and sat down. Players came up and patted Buhley, congratulating and encouraging him. Elser took off his catching gear and sat next to Buhley. "Any questions?" he asked.

"Nope," replied Buhley.

"Let's keep it simple, just you and me," said Elser as he patted Buhley on the knee.

"Okay."

"Look at Big Foot," said Elser. "Now that can be intimidating."

Big Cat Hughes walked out to the mound. He was an imposing six foot six inches and weighed around two hundred and fifty pounds. Big Cat sported a full mustache and beard and came out of the Ozark Mountains. All the opposing teams called him Big Foot. He threw extremely hard and had the attitude of "Here it is. Hit it." Not many teams did. Big Cat was coming off an eighteen-game winning season against only five losses. He threw his warm up tosses and stared at Manny Lopez as he watched him walk to the batter's box. Strike one was the call on a pitch Lopez barely saw. He squared to bunt on the second pitch and fanned at a ball. The count was two strikes, no balls when Big Cat reared back and threw a blazing fastball that Manny swung at weakly and missed. He walked back to the dugout and sat down on the bench, muttering in Spanish, "Big Foot can pitch."

Danny Harris stepped to the plate. Danny was the Peaches' second baseman. He was a hardnosed player who made good contact at the plate and solid plays in the field. Danny always sported a big chew of tobacco on the right side of his mouth. He had already made two plays in the field as he stepped into the batter's box. Danny spit a wad of tobacco juice. "Hello, Mr. Branch," he said, glancing at Dallas as he dug his right foot in the right side of the batter's box.

"Young man," replied Dallas as he pointed to Big Cat.

Danny watched the first pitch, a fastball, for strike number one. He was a student of the game and had watched and read the scouting report on Big Cat Hughes. He knew to watch for a slider. A slider is what he got, and he hit a hard line drive directly to the center fielder who moved two steps to his right, making the catch.

Harland Bunch, the left-handed first baseman, took a blazing fastball for strike one. "Is he allowed to throw that hard?" he asked as he looked at Dallas.

"Yep, they took the governors off this year," replied Dallas.

"Well, it ain't fair," said Harland as he dug back into the batter's box. He took two balls to run the count to two balls and one strike. Harland recognized a slider and hit it sharply to the second baseman for out number three.

"Big Cat looks like he's right where he left off," said Gibbs as the players changed sides.

"Yes, we'll be lucky to scratch a run or two off him tonight," replied Macy. "Usually a good pitcher has the advantage over a hitter at the beginning of the year and that seems to be the case tonight, at least in the early going."

Buhley picked up his glove from the bench and started a brisk run out of the dugout to the mound. "Kid, kid, kid, slow down! You just walk out there. You need to conserve your energy!" said Slug as Buhley slowed himself and walked to the field.

Elser met him at the mound. "Same as before. Just you and me. This is the knot," reminded Elser, showing Buhley his catcher's mitt.

Buhley's warm up tosses were sharp and crisp. He no longer heard or was affected by the crowd. The clean up batter to St. Louis was their left fielder, Chip Foley. Year in and year out, Chip was right up at the top of the league in runs batted in. He led the league in doubles the year before. He was in the lineup for his bat, not his glove. From left field, Chip's arm was average at best. In the batter's box, however, he had few peers. Chip stepped to the plate. "Elser, that pitcher looks like he oughtta be in math class," said Chip, referring to Buhley's youthful appearance.

"No, actually English would probably be better. His grammar ain't so good," replied Elser as he gave Buhley the sign.

"Ste-rike!" bellowed Dallas as the ball whizzed perfectly into Elser's unmoved glove.

The popping sound of ball against leather was heard all through the stadium. "Big Cat has nothing on baggy pants barn thrower in the velocity department," said Macy as he admired the pitch.

"You want to see another one of those?" asked Elser.

"Hell, I didn't see the first one. Who is that kid?" asked Chip.

"Oh, he's just a spare tire we brought along for an emergency."

"Damn," said Chip as he stepped back in the box.

Buhley threw a curve ball that froze the batter for strike two. The next pitch was a ball. Elser called for an outside corner fastball, which Buhley delivered perfectly. "That got the black. Ste-rike three!" yelled Dallas.

Chip walked back to the dugout, shaking his head. Art Drury, the catcher for the Reds, was a grizzled veteran who, like Elser, was on the downside of a solid career. He stepped into the box. Buhley threw an outside pitch that broke back over the black on the plate. "Ste-rike," yelled Dallas.

Elser called for the exact same pitch, which Buhley delivered perfectly for strike two. Buhley threw the third pitch, a curve ball. The pitch started well away which relaxed Art's bat. As the ball neared the plate, it darted down and in for strike three. "That boy's a surgeon," growled Art as he walked back to the dugout.

Mike Thrower, the third baseman, knocked the doughnut off of his bat and made his way to the plate. He touched the pine tar on his bat with both hands and dug in on the right side. Buhley threw him a first pitch curve ball for a strike. The next pitch was off the corner for ball one. Then Elser called for a fastball inside. Buhley threw the ball exactly at the target. The pitch handcuffed Mike, and he hit the ball on the handle of the bat, which broke in two. The ball was popped weakly to Harland Bunch at first base. "Masterful is what that was. Three outs of masterful pitching," said Macy.

"His pants don't look so baggy anymore," quipped Gibbs.

"I don't think anyone has noticed his pants since the fourth pitch of the game. I realize it's only the bottom of the second inning, and there's a lot of baseball yet to play, but this young man, Buhley Sparks, has mowed down the herd of St. Louis Reds in a pretty tight fashion. Let me remind you that they led nearly every offensive category in the league last year. Up to this point, this young man is pitching like a thirty-year-old veteran," said Macy.

Lefty Pete lay in bed at Grady Memorial Hospital. "Is there anything I can get you?" asked the nurse.

"Yeah, the hell outta here. That country boy pitcher is trying to take my job," grumbled Lefty as he listened to Macy's praises of Buhley over the radio.

Sweetiepie continued to rock and pray in her living room. She paused from praying for just a moment. "How's Buhley doing?" she hollered into the kitchen.

Wadeus put the spoon down in his bowl of ice cream. "He's doin' good, baby. He's doin' real good," Wadeus yelled back.

"Thank you, Lord," said Sweetiepie as she once again started to pray.

Macy Reid's voice continued to fill every nook and cranny at Clips. Benny sat on the bar directly in front of 56 who remained behind the workstation. All customers hung onto every pitch Buhley threw. "He's doin' proud. Ain't he, Benny?" said 56.

"I ain't gonna say nothin' that'll jinx him now. It's too early to tell," replied Benny. "He's gotta see the heart of that order another two times at least, and there ain't a pitcher in the majors that can fool them boys three times in a row."

Buhley walked into the dugout, sitting in the same spot as before. The players congratulated him again. "Atta boy, kid! Stay focused," said Slug from across the way.

"Yes, sir," replied Buhley.

Elser walked by and patted him on the shoulder. "Just you and me, Buhley," he said as he prepared to bat.

Big Cat Hughes got Moper Mapes to ground out to the shortstop. Elser struck out on five pitches, and Clevis Boyd, the center fielder, got under a pitch and flew out to the shortstop for out number three. "Well, through two innings, we've got ourselves a pitching duel. But there's seven innings yet to play, and the night is young. Coming into this contest, you would have thought it would be twenty to nothing right now. That's what makes this game great. It's unpredictable," said Macy.

"On paper, that's what it should be. But the game's not played on paper. It's played on the field," interjected Gibbs.

"Well said, partner! Well said!" replied Macy.

Buhley walked to the mound and waited for Elser to emerge from the dugout. Slug walked onto the field and caught the eye of Dallas. Dallas motioned for Slug to come over. "Where'd you get this pitcher?" he asked.

"You wouldn't believe it if I told you," replied Slug.

"If he keeps this up, you better hog tie him and not let him get away."

"Don't worry, Dallas. We're already looking for some rope."

Dallas walked back over to home plate. "Batter up!" he yelled.

Keith Parsons was an all-star first baseman. The fact that he batted seventh in the Reds' lineup showed what a potent hitting team they were. Keith was in his fifth season and had batted a cool .315 the previous year. Stepping in the box, he prepared for the first pitch. Buhley delivered a fastball on the inside corner which was fouled down the left field line. The next pitch was a fastball on the outside corner, which Keith hit on the ground to second base. Danny Harris scooped up the grounder and threw to first for out number one. Second baseman Bill Shavers was next to bat. Although not the best hitting second baseman in the league, he had made only three errors throughout the last season. Buhley quickly got him two strikes, no balls. Elser called for a breaking ball, which made the second baseman look silly as he swung and missed by a foot.

As Big Cat Hughes walked to the plate, Elser called time out and went to the mound. "Buhley, we need to keep the ball away from Big Foot. He takes it personally when a pitch gets too close. Since you're up next inning, protect yourself, and keep the ball away from him. Show him some respect. He ain't a very good hitter, but he's a hell of a bean ball thrower. You understand?"

"Heck, yeah, I understand. I already thought of that. Set him up outside, and I'll hit the target," said Buhley.

"Three fast ones, and let's go sit down." Elser turned to jog back to home plate.

Buhley threw three perfect pitches on the outside corner, the last of which brought a weak swing from Big Cat Hughes for strike three. Back in the dugout, Buhley took a seat and again was congratulated by the players. "Hey, kid," yelled Slug.

Everyone looked over. Slug's eye was on Buhley. "Come here, kid."

Buhley got up off the bench and jogged over to Slug. "Yes, sir," said Buhley.

"Grab a bat, kid. You're up third this inning. Listen, kid, just go in the batter's box and stand away from the plate and don't let the ball hit you. Don't swing the bat. Just take the pitches, and come back to the dugout."

"I can hit, Coach," Buhley said optimistically.

"Listen, kid. That's Big Cat Hughes out there. If you get hit by one of his pitches, they'll hear you scream all the way back in that one horse town you're from."

"Homerville, Coach," interrupted Buhley.

"Yeah, Homerville. You understand?" asked Slug.

"Yes, sir."

Big Cat Hughes retired the first two batters in order. Buhley stood in the on-deck circle and sheepishly swung the bat. He walked to the plate and stood midway in the batter's box. Big Cat let fire with a fastball that whizzed into

Art Drury's glove. Buhley had never seen anything that fast and was glad to back further away from the plate. He took two more pitches for strikes and walked back to the dugout.

"You're right, Coach. I can't hit his ball, and I for sure would not want to be hit by his pitch. That thing's scary," Buhley said, putting up his bat and getting his glove to head out to the mound.

In the top of the fourth, Buhley faced the top of the order again. Elser remembered how they had pitched to the players the first time, mixing the pitches on them. Buhley continued to maintain pinpoint control. He got Roddrick Brown to pop up to Manny Lopez at shortstop. Cory Beckham was fooled on a change up and hit a weak ground ball to third for out number two. Oliver Davis literally fell down swinging at another change up to end the top half of the fourth inning.

Dick Kramer of *The Atlanta Constitution* stuck his head into the broadcast booth and looked at Macy Reid. "Can you believe this pitcher?" he asked.

Macy shook his head 'no' in mid-sentence and continued to broadcast. "Ladies and gentlemen, through three and one-half innings, we've got a beautiful ballgame brewing. The good Lord made April nights for such as this. A young boy from Homerville, Georgia so far has been able to tame the mighty Goliath. If this pattern continues, we could well be witnessing something very special," he said as the two teams changed sides.

CHAPTER 18

Jubel Odom still sat in his kitchen. "Jubel, it's past your bed time. You comin'?" asked Mabel.

Jubel pondered whether or not to answer her. He didn't want to disturb the flow of the game. He sat in silence. Mabel entered the kitchen. "What's going on?" she asked.

"Somethin' special, darlin'. Somethin' real special. I can't say no more. If it happens, I'll tell you. Right now, here I sits until I know," replied Jubel.

Mabel kissed Jubel on the forehead and left the kitchen. "Turn out the light, baby," said Jubel.

Mabel cut off the light as she left the kitchen. Jubel sat in darkness with only the radio and the light of the moon to keep him company. "Come on, Buhley Boy. Come on. You can do it," he softly repeated over and over.

Big Cat Hughes gave up a hit to Manny Lopez and then got Danny Harris to hit a sharp one-hop grounder to the shortstop to force a double play. Harland Bunch hit a double into right center field. Big Cat made Elser look silly on four pitches for a strike out to end the inning.

"Daddy, Buhley's doing good, isn't he?" asked Cheryl.

Harold Dane knew his daughter didn't fully understand how well Buhley was pitching. Harold also knew that he could get knocked out of the game anytime. "Yes, Cheryl, he's doing fine," answered Harold, trying to downplay the significance of what was happening.

"Anybody want popcorn?" asked June.

Harold answered half-heartedly. "Yeah, that would be fine."

He was locked into the game. June was not a baseball fan, and the novelty of Buhley pitching was wearing off. Harold, an avid fan, comprehended the possibility of what could happen. He didn't want to be rude to his family, but he would have preferred to be listening to the game alone.

Butch Schuster lay on the sofa next to his daddy. His eyes were heavy, and he was going in and out of a state of awareness. Sitting next to him on the sofa, Sporty ran his hand through his son's hair. He tried to remain still as he listened to the game. It became harder as the innings and the outs passed. Sporty's wife, Sheila, walked into the room. She offered to take Butch and put him in bed. "Thank you, honey," whispered Sporty as he picked up Butch and gave him to Sheila.

Sporty hurried into the kitchen to get a cold Coca-Cola between innings. Running back to the sofa, he settled in for the rest of the game. Sporty pumped his fist in the air as Macy Reid continued to extol the virtues of the baggy pants barn thrower from Homerville.

The game went by quickly. Big Cat Hughes had scattered a few hits here and there, but had gotten out of the innings unscathed. Buhley remained sharp and continued to have three up, three down innings. "The air is sweet with the smell of freshly popped popcorn as we go to the bottom of the seventh inning. Buhley Sparks has just retired the side, and the score remains zero to zero," reported Macy as they went to a station break.

Off the air, Gibbs asked, "You think it will hold?"

"I don't know, but I've crossed every finger, toe and appendage that I possibly can," replied Macy.

Buhley entered the dugout and sat by himself. For several innings, no one had spoken a word to him. Elser sat nearby but didn't utter a syllable. In the bottom of the eighth, Buhley led off with a strike out. Manny Lopez followed with a single. Danny Harris hit a sharp grounder in the hole at shortstop, and the ball ricocheted off Cory Beckham's glove and into left field. "Man on first and second, and one out here in the bottom of the eighth. The crowd is on the edge of their seats as the heart of our order is about to bat," said Macy with controlled excitement.

Harland Bunch stepped to the plate and watched two balls go by. "Harland's got a hitter's pitch coming here. No way Big Cat wants to load the bases up with one out," said Macy.

Big Cat got the signal. He kicked and fired. Harland recognized the fastball and timed it perfectly. He drove the ball deep into left center field. Roddrick Brown turned and in a full run made a spectacular reaching catch just short of the warning track. Both Shorty Cortez and Danny Harris moved up on the long line drive to third and second base. Moper Mapes was next to bat. He had hit the ball hard every time at bat and had a double his last time. Art Drury looked in the dugout and got the intentional walk signal from Alston Hunt. Moper stood in the batter's box and watched four balls thrown. He trotted down to first base.

"Well, that was probably a smart move by Alston Hunt to pitch around Moper Mapes to get to Elser Riggs. Elser hasn't touched the ball tonight. But he's in a redemptive situation here, and knowing him as I do, he's welcoming the challenge. Two down, bases loaded, bottom of the eighth," said Macy as Elser dug into the batter's box.

Big Cat knew he had to bear down. He got the sign and blew a fastball right by Elser's late swung bat. "Ste-rike," yelled Dallas.

Another outside corner fastball froze Elser for strike number two. With the count two strikes and no balls, Big Cat threw two pitches off the plate, hoping to get Elser to chase them. The count drew even at two balls and two strikes. Art set up on the outside part of the plate and called for a fastball. Elser made a mistake and looked for a curve ball. Big Cat let go with a sizzling fastball that slammed perfectly into the catcher's glove. Elser froze, and the pitch was by him before he could react. Art held the glove and waited for the call of strike three. There was silence, and Art, still in a crouch, slowly turned his head back towards Dallas. "Just missed. Ball three," said Dallas sharply.

Art returned the ball to Big Cat who caught it and shook his head in disbelief. "We've got a full count, bases loaded, two outs, and they'll be running on the pitch. This is no way for my heart to start this season. Gibbs, you couldn't write this any better if you were in Hollywood," commented Macy.

"You got that right," replied Gibbs.

Big Cat wound up, and the runners took off running from their bases. Just as the pitcher let go of the ball, a drop of sweat fell off Elser's eyebrow into his right eye. The stinging sweat made his eye close automatically. Elser tried to locate the ball, and in a split second, determined to swing. He swung mainly out of desperation. The pitch was slightly low, and Elser felt the ball meet his bat. It was a feeling he had experienced many times - that of a solidly hit baseball. Like a missile, the ball shot off the bat and bounded in the gap in left center field before any of the Reds' outfielders could respond. It careened off the wall away from the fielders scoring both Manny Lopez and Danny Harris. Harold Bunch, slightly slow footed, staggered into third base standing. Elser ran with his eye closed and grand illusions of a triple. He failed to notice Harland stopped at third, and he rounded second base like a bat out of hell. Halfway to third, Elser noticed Harland and the third base coach yelling at him to go back to second base. He was caught in a rundown, which was pathetic for a thirty-five-year-old catcher with bad knees. Cory Beckham tagged Elser for out number three.

"A wonderful at bat for the veteran catcher Elser Riggs. He made the Reds pay, and pay they did with a two-run double to give the Atlanta Peaches a two to nothing advantage going into the bottom of the ninth," said an excited Macy Reid.

Doris Pritchett sat down beside Ihley on their living room couch. "Can I get you another lemonade, Ihley?" asked Doris.

Ihley puffed out his chest. "No, Doris, I just want you to sit down and listen to the rest of the game with me," he replied.

"Yes, dear." She snuggled beside him.

Putting his arm around her, Ihley pulled her close. "What's the score, dear?" asked Doris.

"Atlanta just went up two to nothing and it's the top of the ninth."

"How is Buhley doing?"

Ihley knew Doris wouldn't understand even if he explained it to her. "He's doing fine, Doris. The game is fixing to come back on, so please be quiet so I can hear it."

"Yes, dear." Doris cuddled close to him.

Benny Armstrong stood up off his stool at Clip's and let out a loud whistle. "Don't nobody say nothing until this next inning is over," he yelled as he sat back down. Everyone understood and remained quiet.

Elser jogged back to the dugout and tried to catch his breath as he put the catching gear on. "Nice hit, Elser," said Slug. "Next time, watch where you're going."

"I had sweat in my eye," replied Elser.

"Yeah, right," came the skeptical response.

The cheers had just died down from the two-run double when Buhley walked out of the dugout and made his way to the mound.

"Well, folks, here we are," said Macy, standing up in the booth for the first time during the game. "Twenty-four have come up, and twenty-four have gone down. Three more consecutive outs, and we all know what we will have witnessed -- dare I say it. Buhley will face Keith Parsons, Bill Shavers and almost certainly a pinch hitter here in the bottom of the ninth. He will also face history and his place with baseball's immortals. Here he comes now out to the battlefield to draw blood one last time."

In the dark, Jubel Odom sat in his kitchen and continued to whisper, "Come on, Buhley Boy. You can do it, Buhley Boy. Only three more, Buhley Boy."

"Come on, Buhley!" said Sporty Schuster from his sofa as he pumped his fist in the air.

Across town, Sweetiepie Wadkins rocked and prayed as Wadeus sat in the kitchen and didn't make a sound.

All of the players for Atlanta and St. Louis stood in a line on the dugout steps. Buhley waited for Elser to get behind the plate. He began to throw his warm up tosses.

"Coming down," yelled Elser.

"Batter up!" yelled Dallas.

Moper Mapes handed Buhley the ball. "Remember, we're out here to help you," he said, patting him on the shoulder and returning to third base. Buhley took a deep breath as he tried to collect himself for the last inning. He was growing a little tired, and the rush of adrenaline helped give him strength.

"The whole stadium is standing as Keith Parsons digs in," said Macy.

"The noise is almost deafening," interjected Gibbs.

"This feels liked the seventh game of the World Series," said Macy. "Buhley takes the sign from Elser. He kicks and fires. Ball one a little outside," said Macy in his thick southern drawl.

Elser moved inside, and Buhley missed low with a fastball.

"My goodness, do you realize that's the first time in the game since the very first batter that Buhley has thrown two consecutive balls?" asked Macy.

"Time!" yelled Elser. He ran out to the mound. "You okay, Buhley?" he asked.

"I'm about give out," replied Buhley.

"I figure you need about nine more strong pitches, and that oughta do it. Just nine more. You got it in you?"

"I reckon."

Elser jogged back to the plate.

"Wouldn't you have liked to have heard that conversation?" mused Gibbs.

"I imagine Elser extolled the virtues of throwing strikes this last inning," replied Macy.

Elser called for the next pitch on the outside part of the plate. Buhley dug down deep and mustered a perfect pitch for strike one. Keith Parsons stepped out of the box and realized he still had the advantage in the count at two balls one strike. Elser moved to the inside part of the plate and called for a fastball. Buhley let go, and the ball rode back over the middle of the plate. Keith timed the pitch perfectly and hit a scorching ground ball in the hole at shortstop. Manny Lopez had noticed Buhley's velocity had slowed and had moved over in the hole a couple of steps. The ball was heading on a rope towards left field. Out of pure reaction, Manny took one step and dove to his right. The thousands of grounders he had taken barehanded growing up came back to him in an instant. The ball stopped perfectly in his outstretched, gloveless right hand. Manny slid a couple of feet on the clay and grass and quickly shot up to his feet. He threw a perfect laser across the infield to an outstretched

Harland Bunch at first base for out number one. The crowd, already on its feet, broke into deafening applause.

"Have you ever seen anything like that?" asked Gibbs into his microphone.

"Folks, I could describe to you a thousand times what Manny Lopez just did, and you'd never understand the brilliance of that play," said Macy.

Moper Mapes and Danny Harris ran over and congratulated Manny. He brushed himself off and settled back into his position as if nothing had happened. As Bill Shavers made his way from the batter's box, the excitement in the stadium continued to grow.

"Tommy Henshaw is walking to the batter's box. He was Alston Hunt's best pinch hitter last year with a .289 average off the bench. A right handed hitter, he also hit nine pinch hit home runs," said Macy.

Bill Shavers dug in and took ball one. Getting the sign from third, he watched a breaking ball catch the corner for strike one. Buhley fired a fastball that missed for ball two. Then Elser called for a change up. Unable to hold up in time, the batter hit a weak grounder back to the mound, which Buhley fielded and softly threw to first base for out number two.

Scared to say anything, Macy let the crowd noise sift through his microphone and into the airways. As he dug in, Tommy Henshaw spit a wad of tobacco juice just outside the batter's box. The crowd now was yelling nonstop. Buhley looked at Slug and saw his mouth moving, but couldn't hear a word he was saying. Looking back at Elser, he got the signal. The pitch was low for ball one. The next pitch was outside for ball two. To keep the ball in the infield, the infielders backed up a step or two. Elser motioned for Buhley to calm down as he threw the ball back to him. Tommy Henshaw knew he would get a pitch to hit and spit another wad of tobacco juice as he dug in even harder. Buhley threw a curve ball, which caught Tommy off guard, and he froze on the pitch for strike one. Elser called for another curve ball.

The noise in the stadium reached a fevered pitch. Buhley kicked and fired. This time Tommy Henshaw recognized the spin on the ball and waited for the pitch to break. The ball darted down and in on the inside part of the plate. Tommy swung and caught the ball on the fat part of the bat. The hit, a sharply stung one-hopper, bounced directly over third base.

Macy looked at the umpire as he signaled a fair ball. Everything seemed to move in slow motion as Tommy dropped his bat and began to run to first. Moper Mapes dove into the air, his body parallel with the ground. With his eyes never leaving the ball, Moper felt it hit his glove. The ball snow coned out of the top webbing of the mitt. His glove and body hit the ground at the same time. The ball shot straight up out of his glove. Like a jackrabbit, he jumped to his feet and barehanded the ball in mid air. Moper squared himself to first base and cocked his arm to throw. Tommy Henshaw was fast and in a dead run to first base. With everything he had, Moper Mapes let fly, and the ball was projected on a line about four feet off the ground.

Buhley knelt down to the ground and heard the ball whiz about a foot over his head. Harland Bunch stretched with every inch of his body while maintaining contact with the bag. Tommy Henshaw had almost reached first when the ball one-hopped in front of Harland. With the reaction of a veteran, Harland kept his body outstretched and his eyes on the ball. Tommy's foot came down on the bag a millisecond after Harland felt the ball hit his glove. He secured the ball and held it up for the umpire to see. All eyes riveted on the umpire who stood on the infield in fair territory. The umpire began to run towards the bag, pointing at Harland's glove, which he still displayed and then pointing to the bag. At the top of his lungs, he yelled, "The ball got there before the runner. He's outta there!" He gave the out signal in a very descriptive manner.

"Ball game!" yelled Dallas Branch.

CHAPTER 19

The stadium literally was rocking. Elser threw his mask off behind him and jumped as high in the air as he could. As soon as his feet hit the ground, he ran towards the mound as did everyone on the team. "He did it! He did it! He did it! Buhley Sparks! Buhley Sparks! Buhley Sparks! A perfect game! The first time out. Never been done before!" yelled Macy.

There was a pause on the air as Macy choked up. He wiped tears from his cheeks as they rolled down. "Ladies and gentlemen, please forgive me for the silence. Ladies and gentlemen, in the storied history of the greatest game ever, there have been many monumental moments. What we have witnessed tonight may go down as one of the, if not the most, monumental of them all. I don't think it will sink in for me, and certainly not for the baggy pants barn thrower from Homerville, for some time to come what has just occurred. All of the St. Louis Reds have come out of their dugout and are applauding the feat that has just been exacted upon them," said Macy in a voice filled with awe and excitement.

Elser reached the mound and hoisted Buhley up by his legs and squeezed him tightly. All of the Atlanta players mobbed Buhley with hugs and congratulations. Slug pulled Bullard off to the side. "You were right, Bull. This kid's the real deal. We're gonna ride this stallion all the way to the World Series," said Slug over the noise of the crowd as he waited for his chance to congratulate Buhley.

Lefty Pete lay in his hospital bed, cursing at the ceiling. He didn't know what hurt more -- his stomach or Buhley's perfect game. In his estimation, Lefty had been knocked off his perch by a dumb ol' plowboy.

Wadeus Wadkins rushed into the living room where Sweetiepie was still rocking. "Buhley pitched a perfect game, Sweetiepie!" he said excitedly.

"Is that good?" she asked.

"Baby, that's the best you can do!"

Sweetiepie looked to the heavens. "Thank you, Lord," she said.

At Clip's the excitement was overflowing. Benny looked at 56. "Buhley done better than proud. He done history, 56! History! Can you believe that?" asked Benny.

56 looked away at nothing particular. "Imagine that. One of our own doing history," replied 56, taking his usual lean against the bar.

Jubel Odom got up from the kitchen table. He walked slowly through the dark room and made his way to the bedroom. "Thank you, Lord, for Buhley's mercy, and thank you, Lord, for all of ours. Amen," he said softly, lying down quietly by Mabel.

The media room in Atlanta stadium was overflowing as Buhley and Slug made their way to the table. Buhley was wearing his sweat-soaked uniform. Sitting down at the table, he was amazed at all the microphones in front of him. Slug sat down right beside him. He was wearing his hat pushed back on his head with the front of his flat top visible. Slug had a confident look on his face as if he'd just found buried treasure. He made a few opening remarks and then put his arm around Buhley.

"Are there any questions?" asked Slug.

"Where did you learn to pitch, Buhley?" one reporter asked.

"Where are you from?" asked another.

He soon found himself fielding a barrage of questions hurled at him by one reporter after another. "How did you get hooked up with the Atlanta ball club? Is it true you've never played organized ball? What did you think when you found out you were pitching today?"

He answered all of them as best he could. Every now and then Slug would interject with a comment or two. Buhley didn't know any of the reporters. As he scanned the room to get a good look at all of them, his eyes suddenly stopped, and he craned his neck, looking to the back of the room. The multiple flash bulbs temporarily blinded Buhley. He rubbed his eyes and stood up from the table. Staring again at the back of the room, he rubbed his eyes and shook his head to clear his vision. Without a word, he walked around the table and began to make his way towards the back. Reporters parted way and made a clear path. Thanks to the flash bulbs, his eyes still had dots flashing in them as he stopped. He rubbed his eyes once more and then opened them to see two men standing at the back wall.

"Daddy, you're here!" Buhley said in complete surprise. "Did you see the game?"

"It's the most beautiful sight these eyes have ever seen," replied August, emotion in his voice.

"Hello, Mr. Parley," said Buhley as he walked quickly to his dad.

Buhley grabbed August and hugged him tight. He trembled as emotions overcame him. Buhley wanted to speak, but couldn't. August put his head next to Buhley's ear and whispered, "I'm so proud of you, son. So proud. I love you, Buhley. I've always loved you."

"I love you, too, Daddy," Buhley said between the trembling. He finally composed himself and stepped away from August. Buhley looked and saw both of his daddy's hands shaking and noticed that he was slightly bent over. Buhley realized that August was getting older. He hadn't seen him in this condition before. For the first time in Buhley's eyes, August looked feeble and alone. Buhley shook Parley's hand and asked them to wait right there. He walked back to the table and leaned over the microphones.

"Could I say a few words, please?" asked Buhley. Everyone in the room was quiet and gave him full attention.

"I ain't never wanted to do anything but pitch. That's it. Pitching was the most important thing in my life. Ever since I was a youngun', my dream was to pitch in the major leagues. Tonight, I got to fulfill my dream. I want to thank Mr. Satch Moak who told Atlanta about me. I want to thank Mr. Slug Matthews, Mr. Bullard Haynes, and Mr. Buzzy Preacher for believing in me enough to give me a contract, and thank you to all the players on this team who made me feel at home. And a special thanks goes to Elser Riggs who took me under his wing and taught me a lot about pitching rather than throwing and showed me as much kindness as can be shown to one person from another. Just a few minutes ago, the most important thing to me was throwing a baseball. Now I found something more important. I'm announcing, effective this moment, that I am quitting baseball. Thank you very much."

The room filled with silence. Slug sank down in his chair and pulled his hat over his face. Making his way to the back of the room, Buhley put his arms around August and Parley. "Let's go home," he said.

As they walked down the tunnel to the clubhouse, Buhley heard his name called out. He turned around to see Elser running towards him. "I just heard you're leaving," said Elser.

"Yeah," said Buhley, looking at August.

Elser hugged Buhley. "Thank you for fulfilling my dream."

"What dream?" asked Buhley.

"Remember when we sat in my car at spring training?" asked Elser.

"Oh, yeah," interrupted Buhley. "The perfect game. Heck, that never would've happened without you. You were more a part of that than I was."

"I can't believe you're leaving," said Elser.

"Yeah, Daddy needs me."

"You got a gift, Buhley. Not just throwing a baseball. I'm talking about doing the right thing at the right time to benefit others. Most folks just think of themselves, but I've noticed everyone you're around for any time seems to be better off. You understand?"

"Nope, Elser, you've twisted me up again with your fancy talk."

"Listen, Buhley, you ain't seen the last of me. I'll stay in touch, and after the season, we'll do some hunting and fishing."

"Sounds great!" replied Buhley.

"Take care of yourself, Buhley Sparks, you ol' rascal."

"Okay, Elser, see you later," said Buhley as he headed for the parking lot with Parley and August.

The next afternoon as Parley pulled his brand new Cadillac into the Sparks' driveway, Buhley noticed a pretty girl sitting on the porch.

"Is that Cheryl Dane?" asked Buhley.

"I hope you don't mind. She asked if she could wait for you at the house," replied Parley.

Buhley didn't take his eyes off her. "No, I don't mind at all," he answered.

Cheryl met him halfway in the yard and gave him a great big hug. "Everybody's so proud of you, Buhley -- the whole town, everyone," she said.

Buhley had been waiting practically all of his life for this moment. She stayed in his arms and continued. "I hope it's all right. I bought some groceries and brought them over to cook supper for you and your dad tonight. And one more thing," she added as she leaned up to Buhley's ear. "I love you, Buhley."

Stunned, Buhley stood there as she turned to walk into the house. He quickly gathered himself together and said, "Wait. Cheryl, wait!"

Buhley ran to her, grabbed her and kissed her hard. When he pulled away, he looked into her teared up eyes and said, "I love you, too."

Parley had gotten August up on the porch and into his favorite rocker. "Buhley, I'm gonna leave now and let you all get back to normal." He stuck out his hand to shake Buhley's.

Buhley pushed it away and hugged him. "Mr. Parley, how can I ever thank you for all you've done for me and Daddy? Thank you for bringing him to the game. Thank you for helping me all my life. Thank you for helping me fulfill my dream of playing baseball."

"Watching you pitch that game, seeing you there with your daddy and watching you grow from a little boy into a man -- that's more payment than I deserve," replied Parley. Patting Buhley on the shoulder, he got in his car and drove away.

Buhley walked up the porch steps. He could hear Cheryl in the kitchen fixing supper. He pulled a rocking chair beside August as he had done a thousand times before. Silence held for a long time, and then August stirred. "Buhley, I'll never forget that ball game you pitched. It's the greatest thing I've ever seen. You worked hard, and I'm proud of you."

"Thank you, Daddy." He gently reached over and grabbed August's shaking hand. "I love you, Daddy."

"I love you, too, son."

In the quiet, they sat and began a slow rock in unison just as a cool evening breeze started to blow. Soon they were both asleep.

Printed in the United States
146571LV00011B/155/P